*Also*
*by Ellie Alexander*

Meet Your Baker

A Batter of Life and Death

On Thin Icing

Caught Bread Handed

Fudge and Jury

A Crime of Passion Fruit

Another One Bites the Crust

Till Death Do Us Tart

Live and Let Pie

A Cup of Holiday Fear

Nothing Bundt Trouble

Chilled to the Cone

Mocha, She Wrote

Bake, Borrow, and Steal

Donut Disturb

Muffin But the Truth

Catch Me If You Candy

# A Smoking Bun

## Ellie Alexander

St. Martin's Paperbacks

First published in the United States by St. Martin's Paperbacks, an imprint of St. Martin's Publishing Group.

A SMOKING BUN

Copyright © 2024 by Katherine Dyer-Seeley.
Excerpt from *Sticks and Scones* copyright © 2024 by Katherine Dyer-Seeley.

Town map by Rhys Davies.

For information, address St. Martin's Publishing Group, 120 Broadway, New York, NY 10271.

www.stmartins.com

ISBN: 978-1-250-85442-1

Our books may be purchased in bulk for promotional, educational, or business use. Please contact your local bookseller or the Macmillan Corporate and Premium Sales Department at 1-800-221-7945, ext. 5442, or by email at MacmillanSpecialMarkets@macmillan.com.

Printed in the United States of America

St. Martin's Paperbacks edition / March 2024

10  9  8  7  6  5  4  3  2  1

*To Courtny Bradley and Lily Gill—*
*Your unwavering support has breathed life into*
*these pages.*
*I dedicate this story to you!*

to Emigrant Lake

Oregon Shakespeare Festival

The Merry Windsor

Lithia Park

Ashland Police

Sorte

A Rose By Any
Other Name

Puck's Pub

THE GREEN GOBLIN

The Green Goblin

Ashland

to Crater Lake

# Chapter One

They say you should embrace the seasons of life. It wasn't hard to do amidst the ever-changing landscapes of the lush Rogue Valley. Mother Nature had a way of reminding me to pause at the sight of the pinkish sun rising over the Siskiyou Mountains or delight in the sweet bundles of birdseed that someone left along the fenceposts in Lithia Park to feed the dark-eyed juncos.

Beauty was literally all around me. My problem was more about centering on the moment. Being fully present and not spiraling into imagined worries and plans for my future. As we leaned deeper into winter, I had been somewhat successful at embracing my new quest. It helped that my husband, Carlos, was here to stay. He had opted to make my hometown of Ashland, Oregon, his, too. Having him in our little hamlet in the southern Oregon mountains filled me with a level of joy I hadn't known was possible. Plus, Ramiro, his son from Spain, had been living with us for the last six months.

We enjoyed a leisurely holiday break, cozying up in front of the crackling fireplace as snow drifted down from a dark December sky, dusting Grizzly Peak and blanket-ing Ashland in a soft coat of white. There were family meals, sledding afternoons, game nights, baking copious amounts of Christmas cookies, and weaving in Spanish traditions, like making Ramiro's favorite treats, roscos de vino. The festive donut-shaped biscuits were flavored with a touch of sweet wine and nuts. Their icing sugar coat-ing made them look like they had been dipped in snow. I had made a batch for our family bakeshop, Torte, and cus-tomers had raved about the cookies. They also wanted to know what gave the "wine rolls" their unique flavor and consistency. A baker should never reveal her secrets, but in this case, I explained that the cookies used a base of ground sesame seeds and a splash of anisette liqueur to achieve their flavor. Thanks to Ramiro, roscos de vino had a permanent place on Torte's winter menu.

Ashland's Elizabethan charm was heightened in De-cember and January, when snow covered the Tudor-style rooflines in the plaza. There was a sleepy vibe in town, with the Oregon Shakespeare Festival dark until early spring and only a handful of tourists who came seek-ing snowy adventures. That was one of the things I en-joyed most about living in the Rogue Valley: the shifting rhythm of each season.

With the holidays behind us, we were shifting gears to get ready to ring in the new year and welcome house guests in the form of Ramiro's mom, stepfather, and little sister. They had graciously agreed to share Ramiro with us for a year so that he could do an exchange program in Ashland. I'd been nervous at first about connecting with Sophia, Ramiro's mom, but after weekly FaceTime chats with her and Luis and Marta, I couldn't wait for them to arrive. We had spent the two days before Christmas preparing the house and packing the pantry with everything we might need to entertain our international visitors.

The Torres family was arriving in time to celebrate the new year with us before they continued south to California for more adventures. Sophia and I had been emailing almost daily. I sent her updates on Ramiro's soccer scores, pictures of him baking at Torte, and check-ins about how her only son was doing halfway around the world. Our friendship had blossomed over the miles. It was almost like having a pen pal, and Sophia's genuine gratitude for something as easy as texting her a quick pic of Ramiro in his homecoming tux gave me new appreciation and insight into how hard it must have been for Mom to let me take off on my own global travels.

The morning their flight was due in, Ramiro bounded down the stairs and poured himself an espresso. It had taken me a little while to adjust to his Spanish habits, like breakfast espresso. Not that I was ever one to turn down a strong cup of coffee.

"Today is the day, Jules." He beamed as he added a glug of heavy cream to his mug. "I cannot believe they are finally coming." He sounded more excited than he had been Christmas morning.

"I know. It's going to be so much fun to have them here and show them Ashland. Are you sure about the snowshoe tour? It won't be too late for Marta?"

"She's twelve. She's going to love getting to stay up past her bedtime."

"As long as you're sure." I had booked a midnight snowshoe on Mount Ashland or, as locals called our ski hill, Mount A. The trip would take us from the lodge around the rim of the mountain to a warming hut where we would enjoy hot drinks and a late-night feast under a full moon and a starry sky. I had wanted to make the trek for years, and Ramiro's family visit seemed like the perfect opportunity. The brochure had sold me with its description: "experience the serenity of winter while an expert guides you on a snow-packed trail under a romantic starry sky."

The snowshoe trip sounded like the perfect way to kick off the Torres family's visit. Sophia had told me they loved the outdoors, and aside from spending time with Ramiro and us, they wanted to see Oregon's rugged landscapes.

This was where my tendency to overthink and overplan might have gotten the best of me. I had arranged for another snow outing for the next day. It was Mount A's annual downhill dummy competition—an event I had wanted to participate in for a few years but hadn't made the time for. Last summer, after Carlos and I had taken a vacation to travel through Europe with Ramiro, I promised to do more things for myself. Running a bakeshop, winery, and pop-up summer ice cream stand had been fulfilling, but in the process of growing my little Ashland empire, I might have focused too much of my attention on work. My intention for the new year was to find a better balance between work and play.

Ramiro living with us had given me the perfect excuse to change that and embrace all that southern Oregon had to offer. The downhill dummy was one of those things. Entrants created dummies dressed in various outlandish costumes and makeshift vehicles, attached them to skis and snowboards, and sent them hurling down a ski jump. The winner took home bragging rights and a free ski pass for the year.

Andy had been begging me to sign Torte up for the competition for years. So when I approached him about entering the downhill dummy this year, he did a backflip in the middle of the dining room—literally—and promised me that he would work with Bethany, Steph, and Sterling to come up with a killer dummy.

I had no doubt about my team's creativity, and I was eager to see what they would construct. They had asked if I wanted to be involved in the build or be surprised. There was no question: I had to be surprised.

I removed a container of peppermint cream from the fridge and offered some to Ramiro.

"I can't wait to show your family everything the Rogue Valley has to offer, but I'm pretty sure I've overbooked us. Sorry. You know me."

He brushed a long strand of dark hair from his eyes. "It's fine, Jules. They're not ninety. They want to see where we live, and it's not like we can't cancel if it's too much, right?"

"Right." How was a teenager wiser than me?

"A moonlight snowshoe and snacks around a bonfire," Ramiro said, helping himself to a cinnamon roll. "It's so American. They'll love it."

"Good. And then we're going back up to the mountain the next day for the downhill dummy, assuming everyone isn't too tired." I filled my coffee cup with water and placed it in the microwave to heat for a minute.

"Sí. We can't miss it." He laughed and pressed his finger to his lips. "I am sworn to secrecy by Andy, but I will tell you the Torte dummy is so, so good."

"I can't wait. How's the soccer team's dummy coming together?" I removed my mug from the microwave and transferred the water to a bowl on the counter to cool. I would use it later to water my potted peace lily resting on the window above the farm-style sink. Then I poured myself a cup of coffee. It was a trick I had learned in culinary school to make my morning cup of Joe stay hot longer.

"It's pretty great." He plopped into a chair, letting his lanky limbs rest at his sides like long noodles.

He had seemed comfortable since the start of his stay with us, but as the months had gone on, he had become even more at ease. At first, he would ask if he could have a snickerdoodle or open a bag of tortilla chips. Now he helped himself to whatever he wanted. This was his home, and I loved that he felt empowered to raid the refrigerator and invite friends over after school.

"So they really launch the dummies down a ski jump?" He licked frosting from his finger.

"They do. It's utter carnage." The downhill dummy had been going strong since I was in high school. The event was popular with skiers, snowboarders, and the general public since no athletic skills were necessary to be a spectator, other than bundling in layers to watch an assortment of makeshift dummies sailing down the ski slopes.

"The goal is to get the most air, but the real winners are the dummies with the most outrageous crashes." I checked the pantry to make sure I had everything I needed for dinner. The Torreses' flight got in later this afternoon. I intended to start my day at Torte and leave early to meet Carlos and Ramiro at home before we caravanned to Medford to pick them up at the airport.

"Like a crash test dummy for cars?" He took another

bite of the cinnamon roll oozing with melty cream cheese frosting.

"Exactly. The bigger the crash, the better. Body parts, well, dummy parts, will be flying in the air." I twisted my long blond hair into a ponytail and kicked off my slippers.

"Cool."

Carlos came in through the back door with an armful of almond firewood. "Good morning." He took the wood to the living room to stack near the fireplace and returned to join us for coffee. "Julieta, do you want a ride to the bakeshop? I can take you and then go finish the list of errands."

"No, that's fine." I glanced out the steamy kitchen window to our backyard, where the manzanitas and madrones looked as if they had been crumb-coated—a term we used in the bakeshop, meaning frosted in a thin layer of buttercream. "It's a brisk winter morning. Perfect walking weather."

Ramiro rubbed his arms. "It's freezing. If I were going to school, I would take a ride."

We had timed it so that the Torres family was visiting during the last part of Ramiro's extended winter break. Classes would resume after they had returned to Spain. As for Torte, it was also our slowest time of the year. That meant my team could take the lead while I was with the Torres family. I would still check in but had penciled myself out of daily shifts.

"You two have fun on your errands." I took my coffee to the sink and turned to Carlos. "I might have you pick me up at Torte, depending on how the day goes, but I'll text you."

Carlos stood to kiss me. His dark eyes had a way of

always making my knees go slightly weak. This morning was no exception. As he pulled me toward his body, I could feel the heat radiating off his skin and smell a faint hint of chopped wood. His lips brushed mine before he released me with a flirty grin. "Have a good morning, Julieta, and let me know if you think of anything else we might need."

I surveyed the kitchen. Thanks to Carlos, it was better stocked than the industrial kitchens we had worked in on the *Amour of the Seas*. Food was our love language. Having house guests meant welcoming them with round-the-clock meals and snacks. Carlos had prepared a variety of homemade breads to make pintxos—skewered baguettes with smoked salmon and cheeses—along with bocadillos de jamón—ham sandwiches prepared with thin-sliced Serrano ham, cheese, olive oil, and tomatoes. Our cabinets were filled with staples to make soups and stews and pasta. We had enough food to feed a small army. And that didn't include everything I would bring home from the bakeshop. "I think we have enough food to feed the entire neighborhood or, better yet, all of Ashland," I teased.

I gave them both hugs and went to bundle up for my walk to the bakeshop. Frosty air greeted me outside as I made my descent down Mountain Avenue. A crunchy layer of light snow coated the sidewalks. Smoke puffed from chimneys. Holiday lights and Christmas trees still dotted the front windows of a few houses that wanted to stay in the spirit a bit longer. The campus of Southern Oregon University was utterly still, aside from a flock of turkeys huddled under a giant oak tree, as I passed the extensive grounds.

Once I turned onto Siskiyou Boulevard and headed past

the Carnegie Library, I could make out the soft glow of light illuminating the plaza. Storefronts featured warm winter displays of cashmere blankets, candles, books, and assorted teas. Like some of the houses in my neighborhood, many shops and restaurants had opted to leave their exterior twinkle lights on for another few weeks. Christmas trees and garlands had been replaced with crystal champagne glasses, sparklers, and lanterns to welcome the new year.

I crossed past the information kiosk and stopped to take in Torte's front window display. Decorating the windows and interior was another task I had handed off to my highly capable staff. Rosa, our front-of-house manager, and Bethany, our cake designer and lead baker, had partnered on many occasions to create compelling window displays to entice customers inside.

Once again, their vision for the new year took my breath away. White birch trees entwined with glittery white lights stood in each corner of the window. Oversized paper snowflakes hung from the eaves, and an assortment of white winter wonderland cakes were perched on glossy ceramic stands. Pale shades of silky buttercream in porcelain, ivory, and pearl made the cakes look iridescent.

The display was equally inviting and drool-worthy. They had sprinkled vanilla bean macarons and miniature cupcakes with shiny foil wrappers on the base of the window. Everything looked like it had been painted with a cloud of luster dust. I smiled as I used the handrail to navigate the slippery brick steps that led to the basement entrance.

I unlocked the door, flipped the lights, and turned on the atomic fireplace in the dining area adjacent to the open-concept kitchen. Working in the space that Mom and I had designed was one of the highlights of my day, but there was no debating that the basement was a good five to ten degrees colder than upstairs.

Before I started baking or making a pot of coffee, I heated the ovens and started a fire in the exposed-brick wood oven. That would help ensure my team didn't have to spend half the morning blowing on their fingertips to keep warm.

Once that task was complete, I gathered ingredients for the first bake on my morning task list—persimmon sweet bread. It was similar to banana bread but with a winter twist of persimmons, cloves, nutmeg, and cinnamon. The fruit offered a rich, earthy flavor to a breakfast bread.

I began by creaming butter and sugar together. Then I added eggs, the trio of warming spices, a touch of rum extract, honey, and persimmon pulp. Once I had a fluffy batter, I alternated between adding splashes of buttermilk and my dry ingredients—flour, salt, and baking soda. The batter was thick and smooth. I couldn't resist swiping a taste before I spread it into greased tins. Spicy notes came through, along with a touch of rum.

The final step for the bread was to thinly slice persimmons and arrange them on top of the batter to form a pretty pattern. Persimmons were harbingers of winter; their date-like flavor, soft sweet fruit, and bright orange color made them versatile and festive for baking.

As I was sliding the loaves into the oven, Andy came in through the back door. He was dressed in multiple layers with his ski parka, a pullover sweater, a puffy retro vest, and fingerless gloves. Ski passes dangled from his zipper while he tugged off his hat and tried to tame his hair. "Morning, boss. It's a cold one out there."

"That's why I'm baking bread." I grinned. "However, I didn't start the coffee. I decided I would wait for the A-team to arrive."

"I'm glad you did, because I have a winter roast that I want you to try." He removed a plastic tub of beans from inside his coat like a magician pulling a rabbit from a hat. "Stay put; I'll be back in a flash."

He darted upstairs. I loved seeing his enthusiasm when it came to coffee. He had decided to make a significant life change and drop out of college to pursue his passion. Thankfully his family supported his career shift. His grandma had helped him set up a roaster on her property, and Mom and I had been committed to sending him to courses and workshops on roasting techniques. Next on our list was to take him on a tour of some of the growing regions where we sourced our beans.

I could hear beans pulverizing in the grinder, followed shortly by their intoxicating scent.

Steph, Sterling, and Marty arrived shortly after Andy. It was hard to believe that we'd been working together for as long as we had. Turnover on the ship—and, quite honestly, in most professional kitchens—was a big problem. Fortunately, my team was like a second family. Everyone had their own roles and autonomy. Marty was the most recent hire. He focused on bread and pizza dough. Sterling had taken over savory items and had the official title of sous chef, although I felt it was time to offer him a promotion.

Steph worried me the most. Not because of her talent

or work ethic but because she had recently graduated from Southern Oregon University, and her cake artistry was unmatched. I didn't want Torte to hold her back, but I also wasn't ready to let her go. Yet another reminder of how lucky I was to have my relationship with Mom. I needed to ask her how she had managed her own grief when I had gone away.

I tried to push the thought aside as we went over specialty and wholesale orders.

"Bethany is delivering cakes to the Green Goblin later," Steph said, tying on a candy-apple-red Torte apron. "We crumb-coated them last night, so they'll be ready by noon."

"This old dude is ready for bread duty." Marty rolled up his sleeves. "Things are fairly slow for our wholesale orders. So many restaurants are taking a much-needed winter's nap."

He was right. Several businesses in the plaza opted to close shop for a few weeks in January, sometimes for the entire month. This was the one time of the year that small businesses owners could get away for a little respite or even complete tasks that couldn't be done during the rush of summer tourism or the holidays, like taking inventory or mapping out quarterly sales goals for the next year or just giving the space a deep clean or a fresh coat of paint.

"Are you making more of those buns you did yesterday?" Sterling asked Marty. He had grabbed an apron too, but instead of tying it around his neck, he opted to wear it folded around his waist with a dish towel tucked into one side. "They were so popular I thought I could make spiced chicken and a veggie chickpea mixture to stuff in your buns."

"Stuff in your buns," Marty chuckled. "You make it; I'll stuff 'em."

"What about a soup for the day?" I asked.

Sterling opened his sketchbook containing snippets of poetry, recipe ideas, and doodles. "How does a spicy Moroccan chicken stew sound?"

"Delish." I gave him a thumbs up. "Yes, please."

Andy came downstairs, balancing a tray of coffees with one muscular arm. "Okay, here you go. These should taste like snow."

"Snow?" Steph curled her lip, perfectly lined in a shade of violet that matched her hair and eye shadow. "Doesn't snow taste like nothing? It's just frozen water."

I had come to love and appreciate her sarcasm.

Andy shook a finger at her. "Hey, not a word from you. It doesn't taste like actual snow. I meant it should remind you of a snow day. I think I'm calling it a winter warmer."

"Then you should have said a snow day," she bantered in return, twisting fluted tips onto piping bags filled with blushing pink buttercream.

Bethany breezed in. "Sorry I'm late. I stopped by the grocery store to see if they might have any sprinkles. I know it was a long shot, but I ran out of the gold glitter after working on the window display last night, and I thought maybe with New Year's Eve, they might."

"Any luck?" I asked.

She shook her head, tugging off a rainbow parka and matching hat. "Nope. I struck out."

"I'm going up to Medford later to pick up Ramiro's family at the airport. I can swing by our supplier. Unless you need them sooner."

"That would be great. They're for an anniversary cake the couple picks up this weekend." She pointed to her purple sweatshirt with a silhouette of a rolling pin and the words LET'S DOUGH THIS on the front. "Check it out. It's a good one, yeah?"

"Love it," Andy replied with enthusiasm. His cheeks warmed, matching the color of Steph's buttercream. He cleared his throat. "As I was saying, I have a winter warmer for you to try. Hopefully, it will bring back fond memories of canceled school and sledding."

"What is it?" Bethany came closer.

"It's my spiced winter roast with white chocolate and a trio of house-made orange, raspberry, and cranberry syrups. I think it's a nice blend of the sweetness of raspberry with the tart cranberry and citrus notes of the orange. There's a house-made marshmallow to top it off." He passed around the drinks, avoiding Bethany's dewy gaze. "White chocolate can go way too sweet fast, so you'll have to tell me what you think."

I took a sip of his creamy latte. It tasted exactly as he described, and it felt like it was meant to be savored from a cushy chair in front of a crackling fire in a mountain lodge. "This is a snow day."

Andy grinned. "You like it?"

Everyone agreed. He returned to the espresso bar to add it to the daily special menus along with Sterling's soup and stuffed buns. Marty turned his attention to bread dough. Bethany and Steph began batches of muffins and cookies to stock the pastry case.

I teamed up with Sterling to chop onions, carrots, and celery for the buns. Mirepoix, the humble French flavor base, was the foundation for nearly every savory dish that came out of our kitchen. The unfancy veggie combination practically disappears after performing its part, but without the trio, soups and stews would lack depth and end up bland.

Sterling rolled up the sleeves of his slate gray hoodie, revealing tattoos from his elbow to his wrist. He smashed garlic cloves with the side of a knife blade, removed the peels, and began finely dicing them.

"What next?" I asked.

Sterling flipped a page in his notebook to the recipe. Like any good chef, there were notes in the margins with ideas for enhancing the recipes. "For the filling, I want to do tomato paste, turmeric, smoked paprika, chili powder, ginger, coriander, and salt and pepper. I made an update to add black sesame seeds to the tops. I'll brown some ground chicken for the meat option and then substitute that with chickpeas for a vegetarian version."

"Sounds delish."

"How do you feel about fresh peas?" He tossed the veggies in a pan with some olive oil.

"Love them, why?" I opened the spice drawers and began gathering everything Sterling had requested.

"Do you think it would be too much to incorporate peas? On the other hand, they could give a nice hit of sweetness and pop of texture."

"Let's do it." I handed him a container of turmeric.

While he made the filling, I rolled out a batch of Marty's dough and then cut it into circles. Next, we spooned two to three tablespoons of the chicken and chickpea mixture into each ring and then sealed them by flipping the sides and pinching them together.

We placed them seam-side down on a parchment-lined

baking tray and brushed them with an egg wash. Sterling finished each bun with a sprinkling of black sesame seeds for color and texture and slid them into the wood-fired oven to bake.

My persimmon bread had cooled enough to slice. I cut it into two-inch servings, arranged it on a tray, and put it in the pastry case upstairs. I touched base with Rosa, who managed the dining room, before I left for the airport.

Seeing Torte running so smoothly and my team working together like a stage director had choreographed us made my heart happy. I knew the bakeshop would be in good hands over the next few days while I entertained and got to know Sophia, Luis, and Marta. I hoped that they would love Ashland as much as I did. How could they not? It was an idyllic time to visit, with nothing much going on other than ample time to hang out and really get to know each other. Or so I thought.

# Chapter Two

The Medford airport was like stepping back in time. We waited with eager anticipation under the fluorescent lights with elevator-style Christmas music playing in the background. Its long concourse made it easy to spot the Torres family. Any remaining anxiety about meeting Sophia, Luis, and Marta was instantly eased the moment they walked off the plane.

Ramiro waved the welcome sign he had painted when he caught sight of his mom coming toward us. Sophia dropped her suitcase and sprinted to embrace her son. Tears spilled as I watched their tender reunion. Sophia squeezed Ramiro tight, kissing his cheeks and whispering in his ear. Carlos reached for my hand and clasped his fingers through mine. With his free hand, he brushed a tear from his eye, too. Airport greetings and goodbyes tended to make me weepy, and this was no exception.

Sophia finally released her grasp on her son and stood back to study him. "You are so tall."

Ramiro blushed and patted her on the shoulder. "Sí, Mamá. Jules has been feeding me."

Sophia grinned and turned to me. She was petite, with

flawless skin, long hair the color of toasted pecans, and a gentle smile. "Juliet, it's so wonderful to meet you after all this time." She reached out to hug me as Marta and Luis approached us with bags in hand.

Marta was a mini version of her mom, the exception being her hair, which curled in perfect spirals, just like her dad's. Luis clapped Carlos on the back before the two men embraced, and Ramiro scooped up Marta.

My chest expanded with warmth. I couldn't have scripted a better welcome. The Torres family was as delightful as Ramiro. Not that I should have been surprised. They had raised him, after all, but it was lovely to bond over our mutual admiration for what a great kid—or young man—he had become. Like Ramiro, Marta was witty, funny, and had an impish streak that endeared her to me immediately.

We spent the first day of their visit lingering around the dining room table, drinking Uva wine and snacking on endless appetizers and tapas. Luis was a poet. He had a number of his poems published and taught poetry at the University of Seville. Sophia worked in her family's restaurant, which is how she and Carlos had initially met. She knew what it was like to work side by side with family—the pros and the cons. We never seemed to run out of topics of discussion.

I had anticipated that I might feel a tinge of envy given her and Carlos's past and the fact that they shared Ramiro, but the opposite was true. Sophia was like the sister I'd never had, and I felt a deep kinship with her. I wasn't alone. Mom, the Professor, Lance, and Arlo had all joined us for dinner and a leisurely evening of port and desserts in front of the fireplace the night before our snowshoe trip. Everyone agreed that the Torres family was now our extended family.

"They're basically my new version of Ashland royalty," Lance whispered in my ear on his way out the door. "Consider me charmed. I'll be eagerly counting down the hours until our next soiree." Of course, as the artistic director for the Oregon Shakespeare Festival, Lance had a penchant for embellishing, which I was familiar with. Still, in this case, he wasn't wrong, and knowing that the people nearest and dearest to me felt the same about the Torres family was the icing on my cake, so to speak.

The next morning, I left everyone lounging in their pajamas and headed into Torte to bake some hearty snow snacks. No new snow had fallen on the plaza overnight, but the sidewalks were slippery from frost, and the mounting purple clouds hovering on the east hills made me wonder if more snow was on the way. I hoped that any impending showers wouldn't ruin our chances of seeing stars later.

Rosa was boxing up the last of the Christmas decorations in the dining room when I came inside. I never tired of seeing Torte's cheery interior with its red and teal walls, corrugated metal siding, cozy window booths, dining tables, and pastry cases packed with daily delicacies. She and Steph had changed the chalkboard menu, erasing our holiday line of dark chocolate peppermint bark mochas and spiced eggnog lattes and replacing them with Andy's winter warmer and an orange turmeric tea latte that Sequoia had been perfecting.

Mom and Dad had started the tradition of sharing a Shakespearean quote on the chalkboard. Today's was a passage from *The Merchant of Venice*: "How far that little candle throws his beams! So shines a good deed in a naughty world."

It was a fitting sentiment for a new year.

Since I wasn't scheduled to work, Andy frowned and motioned for me to back away from the espresso bar when I ducked behind the counter. "Uh, boss, what are you doing here? You're supposed to be on vacation."

"I know. I know." I held my arms up in surrender. "I've been good. You haven't seen me lurking around, have you?" I glanced around the bakeshop. A few customers shared avocado toast, sausage rolls, German apple coffee cake, and hot lattes at the booths. Two people were waiting for their drink orders, and no one was in line for pastries.

Andy scowled and twisted the dial on the espresso machine. Usually, we had two baristas at the coffee counter, but since things were slow, Sequoia had requested time off as she worked on finishing her training courses to become a massage therapist. I had zero qualms about Andy being able to handle drink orders on his own.

"I guess, but that still doesn't explain why you're here now." Andy poured oat milk into a stainless-steel pitcher and began steaming it.

"You won't even know I'm here. I promise." I made an X over my heart. "I'm just here to make a few things to take to Mount A tonight."

"Are you doing the moonlight snowshoe tour?" Andy perked up.

"Yes," I said, making room for Rosa, who scooted past me with a tray of individual champagne cakes.

"That's the last of the Christmas décor," she said as she placed the tray on the top shelf of the case. "Steph and I have packed away the final greenery. So it's only sparklers and champagne now." To prove her point, she had topped each cake with tiny silver and sparkling gold candles.

"Those are so sweet," I said, moving to the front of the counter to give them more room to maneuver. "And I love the quote you chose."

"It's a meditation for a new year—be a candle in the darkness, yes?"

"Yes," I agreed emphatically.

"My friend Shawn is helping out with the tours." Andy poured shots into to-go cups and handed drinks to the waiting customers. "I'm going to be up night-skiing later; maybe I'll catch you up there."

"Is Shawn your friend who's on ski patrol?"

Andy's passion for snowboarding rivaled his love for coffee. His snow reports started in September, long before there was any hope of powdery precipitation anywhere in the valley. It had become a running joke in the bake-shop that whenever the temperature dropped below fifty, Andy would be ready to break out his ski gear.

"Yep. He's rad." Andy handed me a steaming mug of coffee.

"Wow, what service. I didn't even need to ask." I noticed that he had grated fresh orange zest and added bits of dried cranberries to the top of the foam. "Is this the newest iteration of your winter warmer?"

"You know it. They've been selling well, so I had to level it up." He wiped down the steam wand with a dish towel. "If you're doing the snowshoe tour tonight, does that mean you're not going to be there for downhill dummy tomorrow? Because trust me, you have to be there. Our dummy is seriously epic. *Epic!*"

"No way. We wouldn't miss it for anything. I cannot wait to see what you all have come up with for a Torte-inspired dummy, and Ramiro's soccer team is entering, too. You're going to have some steep competition."

"Never. We've got it in the bag," he said with confidence. "Maybe I'll see you up on the slope tonight, but if not, don't be late for the dummy. Oh, and don't look in the storage closet downstairs either."

"I won't," I promised as I took my drink and went to the staircase. The bakeshop was divided into two levels. Our primary dining space was on the first floor, whereas most of our baking operations were in the basement. When Mom and I discussed expansion options with our architect, he suggested keeping a small area for bonus seating in the basement. I was so glad we had taken his advice.

Two couches, a coffee table, and some plush chairs made the space inviting. We kept an assortment of books and board games downstairs for customers to enjoy while sipping a hot mocha or Earl Grey tea latte. My favorite piece was the retro atomic fireplace. I loved the ambiance of its glowing orange flames and funky metallic design.

Marty was taking a tray of bread from the oven as I entered the kitchen. "Jules, what a nice surprise."

"That smells divine." I leaned closer and wafted the scent toward my nose.

"More buns. Buns, buns, buns." Marty bounced the tray with one hand. "They keep coming back for buns."

Sterling waved from the opposite side of the stove. "Hey, Jules, glad to see you. Just so you know, we made an executive decision and kept the special the same the last couple of days."

"Smart move." I resisted the urge to sneak a hot bun

from the tray. "Actually, I'm here to pack a dinner for snow-shoeing tonight. Maybe I should just steal your buns."

"No need to steal." Sterling poured olive oil into a Dutch oven. "I'll gladly make you a batch. Chicken or chickpea or both?"

"Both." I went to the sink to wash my hands.

"Have you seen the dummy yet?" Bethany asked as she spread thick dark chocolate brownie batter into a pan.

Steph swatted her with a towel. "Shhh, she's not supposed to see it, remember?"

"Oh, yeah. Sorry. I totally spaced that." Bethany gave me a sheepish smile. "Never mind. You didn't hear anything from me."

Their workstations were adjacent to one another with large storage drawers for sprinkles, decorating tips, flat spatulas, and extra mounted swivel lights for when they were doing fine detailed piping work.

"Is everyone coming up tomorrow?" I removed sugar and flour from the pantry and took them to one of the available mixers.

"It's the event of the season," Marty replied. "I've been told that I'll regret it for the rest of my life if I don't see these dummies flailing down the ski slope, and I have to say, when they put it like that, how can I resist?"

"Not just any dummy," Sterling corrected him. "A Torte dummy."

"Why can't we do a Merry Windsor dummy?" I asked as I added butter and sugar to the mixer and set it too low to cream them together.

"Now, that is a missed opportunity." Marty tsked and shook his head.

Richard Lord, my archrival and the self-declared king

of Ashland, owned the aging hotel at the far end of the plaza. I tried not to let him get under my skin, but his constant harassment and accusations made it hard to ignore, which I'm sure was exactly what he was hoping for.

"Next year." I added vanilla and almond extract to my fluffy butter mixture.

"What I want to know is exactly how dangerous is the dummy downhill?" Marty stacked glossy golden buns on cooling racks. "Has anyone ever been injured? It seems like if the dummies catch enough air and break apart, they could hit a bystander."

Bethany sprinkled chunks of dark chocolate and toasted pecans on her brownie batter. "They rope off the bottom of the ski jump for that reason. There have been some insane crashes in years past, but that's part of the fun."

"As long as no one from Torte gets strapped into skis," Marty commented.

"No way. Only dummies." Bethany finished the brownies with toasted coconut and another layer of batter.

"That would be gnarly." Sterling shuddered. "I can't imagine a human getting strapped into the contraption we've made."

The team chuckled. Sterling caught my eye and winked. His soulful sea-blue eyes were one of the reasons there was almost always a group of young teenage girls hanging out in the basement under the guise of playing Catan and getting hot chocolate refills, giggling every time Sterling passed by with an order to go upstairs. I hated to break it to them that he only had eyes for Steph.

I focused on baking. Whatever I brought for our midnight outing needed to be able to be packed and carted around the rim of the mountain. I decided on three cookie options. A classic winter shortbread with fresh citrus zest and sparkly citrus sugar, spiced ginger cream sandwich cookies, and chocolate marshmallow cookies to dip in hot chocolate. Additionally, I would pack an assortment of Sterling's savory buns and sausages to grill over the fire.

The base of the shortbread came together quickly. I grated lemon and orange zest into the dough and mixed the juice with coarse sugar for the top of the cookies. I floured the counter and rolled the dough into a large rectangle. Then I cut out snowflake shapes, brushed them with an egg wash, and sprinkled them with citrus-infused sugar.

Once those were in the oven, I made a batch of our spiced ginger cookies. The soft, chewy cookies packed a spicy punch with ginger, cinnamon, nutmeg, cloves, and a tiny hint of black pepper. I would fill them with a sweet cream to offset the spice.

The last batch of cookies was a seasonal favorite amongst guests and our staff. I used our classic chocolate as a base and mixed in marshmallows and mini chocolate chips. We would make hot chocolate later at home and pack it in thermoses. Carlos suggested bringing miniature bottles of peppermint schnapps, rum, and Bailey's for any adult who might be in the mood for a nightcap.

When everything had finished baking and was packed neatly into containers, I said my goodbyes and told everyone I would see them on the slopes, either later this evening or tomorrow, for the dummy downhill.

The house was quiet when I got home. I kicked off my boots and left them in the entryway. It smelled like someone had been cooking.

Carlos waved to me from the living room. He was reading in front of a dwindling fire. "How was Torte, mi querida?" he whispered.

I set the packages on the coffee table. "Good. Everything is shipshape, as usual. Where is everyone?"

He motioned upstairs. "Napping. Jet lag, and they want to be awake for the moonlight tour."

"Smart." I curled up next to him and tucked my feet under the blanket. "I feel like we haven't had much time alone. How is the visit for you? I'm really enjoying having them here."

"Sí." He massaged my back. "I was nervous, like we talked about before they came, but it has been better than I expected."

"Good." I leaned into him, letting the aroma of his cologne and garlic and onions envelop me. "Have you been cooking?"

"How did you know?"

I took in a deep breath, inhaling a faint hint of herbs. "I can smell it on you."

"Is this a bad thing?" He kissed the top of my head.

"Never." I let myself relax deeper into his arms. "What did you make?"

"A torta for later."

"Yum. We are going to have a literal feast." I told him about what I had baked.

"Perfection." He kissed the top of my head again and got up. "I'll put everything away so you can rest, too."

I protested, but he knew me well. Between the radiant heat of the fire and the warmth of the blanket, I found myself drifting off. The next thing I knew, movement overhead and footsteps stirred me awake. I glanced at my watch. I had slept for almost an hour.

Ramiro appeared in the hallway wearing ski pants, a turtleneck, and wool socks. "Oh, sorry, I didn't know you were napping."

"Neither did I." I stretched and tossed off the blanket. "I can't believe I actually slept."

"Me, too. It's one of the things I miss about Spain that surprises me—siestas. You should have them in America."

"Agreed." I made sure the fire was out by poking the last of the embers and shutting the iron screen. "I suppose I should probably go layer up. It looks like you're ready for the snow."

He grinned. "I need boots and my coat, and I'm ready."

I went to change, feeling the hum of eager anticipation buzzing through my body. A mountaintop snowshoe adventure awaited. I couldn't wait to let the moonlight be our guide as we trekked into the darkness on a winter family adventure.

# Chapter Three

Mount A was less than a thirty-minute drive from Ashland. We piled into the car, and I took the wheel. Carlos was a good driver, but I had more experience driving in winter weather conditions. Fortunately, the clouds I had seen earlier had broken off, revealing crisp, clear moonlight.

The curvy, narrow road that took us to the lodge was an adventure in itself. Boulders the size of the car clung precariously to the volcanic cliffs to our right. The road veered off to the left, dropping hundreds of feet down into the canyons below. Marta squealed twice as I steered around tight hairpin turns. We could see the lights from the lodge and lifts before either came into view.

Massive snow berms enclosed the parking lot. I pulled into a space directly in front of the ski patrol offices. Their red flag with a white cross flitted in the wind, sending a signal that help was available to anyone on the mountain who might need it. Behind the building, the ski lifts radiated light. Skiers and snowboarders zoomed down runs in colorful gear. Other riders queued at the base of the lifts, waiting to hop on the next chair.

The bunny hill and lodge were on the opposite side of

the slope. A small path had been cut through the snow to the three-story lodge, which resembled a ski chalet with its dark wood exterior, sloping roof, and massive stone chimneys. The ski park was founded in the mid-1960s. It paid homage to OSF by naming all the chair lifts, ski runs, and trails after Shakespeare's characters and plays—Sonnet, Windsor, Titus, Brutus. My namesake had two designated runs, Upper and Lower Juliet.

"This is exactly how I pictured it," Marta exclaimed, getting out of the car first. Bethany had loaned her a pink snowsuit that she had outgrown. It reminded me of a stick of bubble gum and perfectly matched Marta's pink polka-dot hat.

We were scheduled to meet Hero, our tour guide, in front of the ski patrol offices, but first I needed to check in. Carlos and Luis stayed to unpack the trunk while Sophia and I went to the lodge.

"Do you ski much in Spain?" I asked as we navigated the narrow path covered in boot prints.

"Not often. We've taken a few trips to the Pyrenees, but the best skiing is in Switzerland, which isn't that far away." The cream snow jacket and matching ski bibs she had borrowed from Mom glowed under the lights and made her look like she was in soft focus.

"That's one of the things I miss about the *Amour of the Seas*. Whenever we had an extended port stay in Europe, it was so easy to travel from country to country." My feet sunk into a pocket of soft snow.

"It's true, but also our country is only about twice the size as the state of Oregon. The US is massive. You could probably spend years traveling here."

"That's one of our goals. I've never been to the Midwest, and there's so much I want to show Carlos here on the West Coast." We made it to the lodge and stomped snow from our boots before going inside.

"You both seem very happy," Sophia said as I held the heavy doors open for her. "I haven't had a chance, but I've wanted to apologize to you for a long time." Her chin quivered like she was fighting to hold back tears. "Too long."

"Apologize, why?" I stopped at the entrance and grabbed her arm. "You don't need to apologize to me."

"I do." She kept her head angled toward the wood-planked floors, but her eyes met mine. "I feel bad about how things happened with Ramiro. It was a difficult time with my family, and now, with some hindsight, I wish I would have handled it better."

"Oh, me too, Sophia. Me too." I placed my hand over my heart. "It's not your fault, and trust me, I've had a lot of growth and work to do myself. I'm glad that we're all in the space we're in now. I'm truly thrilled to have you here, and I hope you know that."

"I feel very welcomed." She squeezed my hand. "And thank you for taking such good care of Ramiro. He has changed for the better in the months he's been here." Her voice broke as she spoke.

"The thanks are all mine," I gushed. "We feel so lucky that you trust us with him. It must be hard to have him halfway around the world."

"You'll know if you have your own children, but it's bittersweet." She paused while a group of youngsters in neon ski suits stomped past us up the next set of stairs toward the rental shop and concessions. "I want him to be independent and get to experience traveling and living in new places, but sí, I will confess that I've had a few teary nights without him at home. I suppose I must get used to it, as Luis keeps reminding me that Ramiro will be starting university soon. It goes by in a flash."

I knew what she meant. It felt like yesterday in some ways that I had left Carlos on the ship, yet it also felt like we'd spent a lifetime in Ashland together.

A woman about Mom's age brushed by us. She had a clipboard tucked under one arm and appeared to be in a hurry because she accidentally bumped my shoulder and barely paused to apologize before running outside.

"I wonder if we're late?" Sophia asked.

"I guess we should check in." I started toward the stairs. "Really, though, thank you for this chat and for everything." I gave her a quick hug before we headed upstairs.

Memories of my teen years rushed to the surface as I surveyed the busy chalet. Twenty-foot windows offered views of the ski runs and bunny hill on the main floor. Dark wood pillars served as barriers between the concession area and dining tables. Wide, oak-plank distressed floors with an antique finish forgave any scuffs or weathering from ski boots.

The focal point of the second floor was the oversized circular fireplace in the center of the large room. Skiers gathered around every side of the roaring fire with its shingle-tiled chimney that stretched to the third floor. The upper level was open with balconies and alcoves with ample seating for skiers and boarders to take a break between runs and cozy up with something hot to drink. Ski memorabilia and vintage travel posters hung on the walls. An old wooden lift chair was mounted on the peak of the A-framed ceiling for decoration.

Condensation dripped from the windows. There was the

sound of boots and music above us and a familiar smell of grilling burgers mingled with hot apple cider. Mount A might not be a luxury getaway, but the rustic lodge and family atmosphere made it one of my favorite places on the entire planet. That was saying a lot—I'd spent a decade sailing from one tropical port of call to another.

"We check in this way," I said to Sophia, leading her through the crowd to the ski rental shop. There was a short line. When it was our turn, we were greeted by a young guy about Andy's age wearing a black ski parka with the signature ski patrol white cross.

"Jules, right?" He thrust out his hand. "Hero. I'm going to be your guide tonight."

"Yes, so great to meet you. I didn't realize you were on ski patrol." I motioned to Sophia. "This is Sophia; she and her family are visiting from Spain. We're all very excited about the tour."

He was younger than I expected. His broad shoulders and emergency training gave me confidence that we were in good hands. "Excellent. Obviously, I can't control the weather, but it's looking like the moon is cooperating. The forecast is calling for clear skies. We'll try to do a constellation lesson and some star navigation while we're out there. When we go over our safety protocols, I'll give your group some snowshoeing tips and techniques."

I was impressed with his professionalism.

"Is your party here and ready?" Hero asked, typing notes into a laptop.

"Yes, everyone is outside."

"Okay, great." He leafed through papers attached to the clipboard and offered me a pen. "You can sign the liability waiver, and then we can gather outside to go over safety precautions and get everything packed into the sled. I'll meet you in front of ski patrol."

"Sled?" Sophia asked. "I thought we were snowshoeing."

"Yes, you'll be on snowshoes. I'll be tethered to a sled with our emergency gear, blankets, food, supplies, and everything we need to rest at the winter shelter on the other side of the mountain. You look like you've got good layers on. That's important because you're going to want warmth and flexibility with your outerwear. We want to minimize sweat when we're exerting it out there. Don't want to let hypothermia set in."

I signed the paperwork.

Hero made more notes on his computer and photo-copied our waivers. "If you'll give me a couple of minutes, I need to check in and register our route with ski patrol, and then I'll meet you by the lifts."

"It's very official," Sophia noted.

"I know. I'm quite impressed."

We went back outside to wait with everyone. Hero returned shortly with a sled full of snowshoes and trekking poles. He gave us a brief demonstration on how to secure the snowshoes to our boots properly, adjust our trekking poles, get up from a fall, and traverse a steep path. Then he explained that we would follow a well-groomed trail, but it wasn't lighted. "We'll be using the moon, which is full tonight, and then each of you has a headlamp. I have additional batteries and backups in the sled. It's important to be mindful of our environment. We're going to be in the backcountry, away from the busy slopes." Hero motioned behind him to the ski runs. "We're going to be walking amongst the old-growth forests. As we go, I'll point out constellations and set a manageable pace for everyone, but don't hesitate to speak up if it's too fast or too slow."

We attached the headlamps and put on our snowshoes. Hero's flashlight and headlamp combo were bright enough to direct a plane in for a landing.

I shielded my eyes as he gave us a final word of caution.

"Under no circumstances should you ever veer off the trail. We are in mountain lion and bear territory, and there are some sheer drop-offs that are deadly. Understood?"

We nodded in solemn agreement.

My protective instincts kicked in as I looked at Ramiro and Marta. It wasn't that I was worried one of them would venture off trail, but I hadn't considered that a moonlight snowshoe might come with danger.

Sophia must have sensed the tension in my body. She patted my arm. "They will be fine."

"Am I that obvious?" I locked my poles into position.

"Carlos says you wear your emotions not only on your sleeve but in your entire body."

"That's probably why I've never been good at poker."

She laughed as we fell into step behind Hero.

"Just holler if you have any questions," he said, leaving the ski slope and pointing us toward the cross-country trails.

It was impressive to watch him practically glide over the snow with the sled attached to his waist.

The air sucked my breath away. It was like stepping into the walk-in freezer at Torte, crisp, ice-cold yet oddly invigorating. At this elevation, it felt like I could stand on my tiptoes and pluck stars from the endless sky. Moonlight reflected off the snow, casting a soft aurora of white light all around us. The only sounds were our snowshoes sinking into the deep powder and our labored breathing. At nearly seven thousand feet, the air was thinner up here.

"You can group up like this while we're on this forest access road," Hero told us. "But once we reach the trailhead, we'll go single file. Does anyone want to volunteer to be the sweeper?"

"What's a sweeper?" Ramiro asked.

"The person at the back of the pack. Their job is to make sure no one gets left behind," Hero replied.

Had people often been left behind?

I didn't like the sound of that either. I wasn't sure what the reason for my skittishness was, but the calm and quiet trip I had imagined was sounding more and more hazardous. Steep drop-offs, potential cougar encounters, leaving one of our party behind in the dark.

I let out an involuntary shiver as I trekked next to Carlos.

"It's peaceful, isn't it, Julieta?" His eyes drifted overhead. Stars bled together in a glittery show of dazzling light. "I have never seen so many stars in my life. Is that the Milky Way?"

A faint trace of the wispy galaxy cut through the moonlight. Without a full moon, it would have been even more defined, since there was no light pollution for hundreds of miles.

"It's incredible," I agreed.

He was about to say more when heavy footsteps and a booming voice broke through the stillness.

"Hey, Hero, out of my way, slow guy. Make way for the speed team, and then you can have your kiddie lane back." A guy on cross-country skis called out behind us.

Hero froze. He turned around and shone his light at the group on our tail. "Fitz, what are you doing here?"

Fitz puffed out his chest. "It's a free mountain, my dude." He could have passed for Sasquatch with his colossal frame and black ski gear. He had to be well over six and a half feet tall with thick hair that escaped from the sides of his dark balaclava.

"Did you register your tour with ski patrol?" Hero asked. "I didn't see any other tours slotted for tonight."

"You're such a suck-up, man." Fitz rolled his eyes and motioned for the small group behind him to press forward.

"Uh, no. It's called mountain regulations," Hero countered. "You have to have official permits to offer guided tours, my *man*. You can't just have people pay you under the table. What are you doing out on cross-country skis, anyway? This trail is reserved for snowshoe tours tonight."

Fitz flashed Hero a hang loose sign. "Like I said, it's a free mountain. Let's go." He intentionally pushed past us, forcing Hero off the trail. "Catch you on the flip side."

Hero stared at them. Fitz was leading two women along the narrow trail. They looked like they might be a mother and daughter.

I recognized the older woman. She had bumped into me in the lodge earlier. It was odd, because she still had her clipboard under one arm. How was she managing to cross-country ski with a clipboard, and why?

The younger woman's ski gear was well worn, with dozens of lift tickets attached to the zipper of her faded coat. She looked like she could give Andy a run for his money with the number of passes she had accumulated.

"Sorry," the younger woman said with an apologetic smile as she glided by on thin, narrow skis.

"Who was that?" Ramiro asked Hero after the group had moved on.

Hero smashed his fingers together like he was forcing himself to remain professional by modeling a calm stance. "Fitz Baskin. Don't get me started on the guy. I don't know what he's up to. He's new to the slope, and I guess he's trying to take tours out, but who knows? Everything he does is shady. He doesn't get the proper permits, doesn't record his itinerary and route map with ski patrol, and charges everything under the table. Ski tours aren't permitted tonight. I'm the only tour on the mountain. If he's not careful, he's going to get someone killed."

"Why do you say that?" Carlos caught my eye and made a face.

"Because it's dangerous out here. Like I explained before we left, we're in the wilderness at night in the bitter cold. I'm prepared if someone were to take a fall and break an ankle or if a storm rolled in. I have emergency supplies and gear. I always bring a locator beacon, I'm trained in first aid and CPR, and ski patrol knows what time I'm expected back. They'll send a crew to find us if we don't show up at the lodge by nine tonight. Fitz does none of that. He's not professionally trained or prepared. He's putting everyone who goes out with him in danger."

Hearing Hero rattle off his training and safety protocols made me glad I had chosen him as our guide for the night. I didn't like the thought that other people on the mountain could be in danger, but I was relieved that Hero took his role seriously. It sounded like we were in good hands and didn't need to worry about anything other than staying on the trail and staying warm.

# Chapter Four

Under the canopy of moonlight, the mountain was even more beautiful than I could have imagined. Stars erupted in the sky. It was as if the whole world had gone quiet except for the soft footsteps on the fresh snow. My heart rate climbed as we hiked the rim of the canyon. Sweat formed on my brow, and my cheeks warmed from the exertion and sting of the cold wind. Each step became a moving meditation. My awareness of my surroundings was crystal clear—the aroma of the pines, the way the stars mingled, the distant cry of a lone wolf on one of the peaks nearby.

Our party was merry as we traversed the cliffside under Hero's watchful gaze and the warming hut finally came into view. It had taken a little over an hour to reach our destination. We probably could have made it faster, but we stopped frequently to take photos and enjoy the majestic views.

The hut was officially known as the Grouse Gap Shelter. Its covered pavilion, central fire pit, and picnic tables offered a shady respite for Pacific Crest Trail hikers in the summer and a spot for cross-country skiers and snowshoers to thaw their frozen fingers in the winter.

When we reached the warming hut, Hero gathered stacked prechopped wood and started a fire. The hut had an open-sided covered structure with a giant rock fire pit in the center. There were ample benches and tables for groups to warm themselves in front of the fire.

I placed a gingham tablecloth and battery-powered lanterns on the table closest to the flames and then began unpacking platters of steaming buns, cookies, and camp mugs for hot chocolate. It felt like we were in the land of hobbits, with the smoke curling up the chimney and the glow of moonlight on the snow.

"This is ready, everyone. Come enjoy." I waved a gloved hand over our spread and encouraged them all to dig in.

There was no hesitation. We had worked up an appetite on the first leg of our journey. Any thoughts of danger faded away as we snuggled under blankets at the table and sipped spiked hot chocolate.

The sound of our laughter echoed in the vast canyon below. I could make out the hazy lights of the ski slope in the far distance.

Sterling's spiced chickpea buns melted in my mouth.

"Everything is so wonderful," Luis said, helping himself to another stuffed bun. Tiny icicles had formed on his beard.

Marta tugged off her pink gloves and warmed her hands over the fire. "My favorite is the ginger cookie. What's in the middle?"

"Fluffy cream. You can't go wrong with buttercream and a soft, spicy cookie, in my professional opinion," I replied with a smile.

"Sí, she is the professional," Carlos added, giving Marta a conspiratorial wink. "We have no choice but to trust her."

Hero didn't participate in the conversation and refused my offer of food. Instead, he stood at the far edge of the shelter like a guard keeping watch over the mountain.

While Carlos passed around the thermos of hot chocolate and mini bottles of booze for a second round, I checked one last time before packing up any leftovers.

I put my gloves back on and walked over to Hero. "Are you sure I can't entice you with a warm bun or shortbread cookie?"

He forced a smile but didn't pull his eyes away from the side of the dark slope. "Thank you, but no. I'm fine. I'm trying to figure out what's happening down there." He unzipped his backpack and removed a pair of binoculars.

"Is everything okay?" I followed his gaze to a tiny grouping of lights moving through the darkness way down below. Their headlamps looked like a line of fire snaking down the mountain.

He blew out a long breath and shook his head. "No. I can't believe it. Well, yeah, I can. It's Fitz. He's way off the trail. This guy is a joke. Why would he take people down there? I think I'm going to have to call ski patrol."

"That's Fitz down there?" I squinted at the tiny dots on the treacherous hillside.

The snowshoe and cross-country trail we had followed wound around the rim of the mountain. The trail hugged the ridgeline the entire way. Fitz and his party were at least a half mile, if not farther, down the steep snowy embankment.

"How did they get down there on skis?" I scrunched my eyes tighter to try to make out their figures in the darkness.

"Your guess is as good as mine. The slope isn't stable. There's no trail there. It's super rocky terrain."

"I know. I've hiked up here in the summer, and it's like a canyon of massive, loose boulders."

"Uh, yeah, because it is a freaking canyon." Hero nodded and then shook his head in disbelief. "It's completely idiotic to go off trail in the daylight, but at night, it's downright deadly. Fitz is a moron."

His uber-professional manner shifted as his anger mounted.

"Do you think they're having a hard time getting back up?" It was hard to tell how far off the path they were.

"I'm sure of it. They're on skis. That's not what cross-country skis are designed for." He yanked off his black ski hat and ran his fingers through his hair. "I'd love to just leave him to freeze in the cold. I can't stand the guy, but he's not alone down there. I swore an oath to serve and protect, and there's no way I'm leaving innocent bystanders stranded."

Serve and protect? Was that part of the ski patrol code? "What should we do?"

He pounded his fist on his thighs and then reached for his bag. "I don't have a choice. I'm going to call it in."

"Are you a member of ski patrol?"

"I mean, I did the training and everything, but I'm doing guiding now."

He didn't exactly answer my question. Not that it mattered. I was happy to be in his capable hands. I just couldn't figure his connection to the rescue group.

A flare exploded in the sky, sending orange sparks shooting hundreds of feet in the air, followed immediately by a boom so loud that it felt like it shook the entire canyon. Both Hero and I startled.

"That's it. I'm calling it. It shouldn't take long for ski

patrol to get out here," Hero said, retrieving a satellite phone from his pack. "They're obviously in distress. Ski patrol will have to respond on snowmobiles. I'm really sorry to ruin your tour, but we're going to need to hang out until ski patrol arrives so I can show them the exact area to focus their rescue."

"Of course. It's not a problem." I watched the sparky remnants of the flare drift back to the ground. "We'll add a few more logs to the fire and polish off the rest of the food. Are you sure I can't bring you a plate or at least a cup of hot chocolate?"

"No." He was already punching numbers into the satellite phone. "Thanks, though."

I returned to the table and explained our predicament to everyone.

"It is quite amazing that Hero warned Fitz about safety and submitting his route info to ski patrol, and now he's stuck off the trail." I bit into a hot cocoa cookie.

"I understand why Hero would be angry with him," Carlos said. "This is a foolish decision."

Hopefully, Hero was right, and ski patrol wouldn't take too long. We were toasty warm with our blankets, drinks, and a crackling fire, but Fitz and the two women we had seen with him were totally exposed on the mountainside. If he hadn't bothered to follow basic protocols, I doubted he had prepared for a situation like this.

Hero paced in front of the shelter, watching the flickering lights down from us. Fitz had put him in a terrible position, too. Carlos distracted Ramiro and Marta with stories of his kitchen antics on the *Amour of the Seas*.

I wasn't sure how much time had passed, but I heard engines roar as two snowmobiles plowed toward us. They sounded like jets taking off. It was a striking contrast from the pervasive quiet of the mountain.

The sound grew stronger as they approached the warming hut, kicking snow in every direction and causing us to cover our ears.

"Hero, what's up, man?" the first ski patrol member asked after parking his snowmobile near the warming hut and jumping off. He pushed his ski goggles to the top of his head. Even if we weren't aware that ski patrol was on its way, the first responders were easily recognizable in their reflective red jackets with white cross patches on their chests and shoulders.

"It's Fitz." He pointed down the hill. "He's gone off trail again, and I think they're stuck. What a stupid move to go out of the trail boundary like that."

"How did he get down there?" The guy grabbed his own binoculars to get a better look.

Hero gave them a brief recap of our interaction.

"Oh, hey, you're Jules from Torte?" the first guy asked once Hero had explained what happened. "My buddy Andy works for you."

"You must be Shawn?" I extended my hand.

"Yep. Andy's riding right now. I saw him a few minutes before we got the call." Shawn looked the part of ski patrol with his uniform, long brown hair that stuck out from beneath his beanie. and windburned cheeks.

"I'll have to find him when we get back to the lodge."

"Why did Fitz think that was a trail?" another member of ski patrol asked.

Hero stroked his throat like he was forcing himself to swallow. "Dude, why are you asking me? Have you met the guy? He's the worst. He should be banned from the mountain. Actually, you know what you need to do."

"What?" Shawn asked.

·He licked his lips and fixed his stare at the other side of the slope. "Send him out on avalanche duty, but just let him free ski out of bounds and see what happens."

I winced at Hero's dark humor. At least, I hoped it was humor.

Hero huddled with Shawn and his partner to formulate a rescue plan. I figured I could probably pack up the remains of our late-night snacks. Now that ski patrol was on the scene, we should be able to make our return trek to the lodge.

"Okay, everyone, I need to check in with you," Hero said, calling us together as I put the last cookie tubs on the sled. "Ski patrol is sending reinforcements but could use my help and gear. How do you feel about getting back to the lodge on your own? Or do you want to wait it out here? Just know that it could be a few hours. It's going to be challenging to get down there to make a rescue."

"I feel confident about going back as a group. We follow the ridgeline, right?" I looked at Carlos, Sophia, and Luis. "What do you think?"

Everyone nodded.

"I'll send you with extra gear, and ski patrol will probably meet you halfway. Like you said, you follow the same route back, and it should be very well marked now that the snowmobiles have come through. I will refund half of your deposit."

"You don't have to do that," I protested. It wasn't Hero's

fault that Fitz had gone off trail and put himself and his party in harm's way.

"Don't worry about it. Trust me. Fitz will pay for this."

There was something about his tone that gave me pause.

We organized our gear and packed up the rest of the supplies and food that Hero would bring with him on the sled once they had completed their rescue.

As anticipated, the return trip was easy. We followed the snowmobile tracks and used our flashlights and lanterns to make sure no one came too close to the edge. It felt like we made it to the lodge in half the time it had taken to get to the warming hut. Part of me was relieved to be surrounded by lights and skiers again, but the other part couldn't stop thinking about Fitz and the stranded women. I hoped that Hero, Shawn, and the rest of the ski patrol could get them out safely. But I couldn't shake a looming feeling that something terrible was about to happen.

# Chapter Five

The rustic three-story lodge looked like a beacon shining in through the darkness. My shoulders relaxed at the sight of skiers and snowboarders traipsing inside for hot chocolate and popcorn. "Should we go sit by the fire for a while?" I suggested.

"Is it okay if we ski? The runs are open for another hour." Ramiro put his arm around Marta. "You want to come with me? Some of my friends are here."

Carlos deferred to Sophia, who agreed and sent the kids off with a reminder to meet in the main lodge dining room when the lifts closed.

We proceeded inside. Sophia and Luis went to find seats. Carlos offered to get everyone drinks, and I needed to let the staff at the ski shop know we were back safely. I had promised Hero I would check in so they could radio him. He had enough to worry about without wondering if a second rescue would be needed.

As I headed toward the rental shop, I spotted a familiar face coming my way. "Andy," I exclaimed, throwing my hands out.

His cheeks were flushed from the wind and the cold.

He propped his snowboard in one arm and hugged me with the other. "Boss, you made it. How was the tour?"

"Well, it took a bit of an unexpected turn." I told him about Fitz and Hero. "We met Shawn, though."

"Wow." Andy raised his eyebrows. "Shawn can't stand that guy."

"Fitz?"

"Shawn has had to save that guy's a—" Andy stopped himself when he noticed there were young ears around us. "Oh man, Shawn is probably foaming at the mouth."

"Why?" I scooted to the side to make room for a crew of middle schoolers waiting to return their skis and boots.

"He hates Fitz. I've heard that guy's name at least twenty times this past week—and none of it is good. It sounds like Shawn isn't alone. Everyone on the mountain would like to see him go."

"Go where?"

"Anywhere but here." Andy shrugged.

I was beginning to sense a pattern. Fitz seemed to be Mount A's version of Richard Lord.

"Don't worry," he said. I'm sure Shawn and the team will be able to bring everyone back safely."

I appreciated Andy's confidence in his friend.

A staff member announced on the speaker that the lifts would close in thirty minutes.

"I should let you get out there before the lifts close," I said.

"Gotta go drop into some awesome lines and rip a few more turns while I can. Can't wait to show you Torte's dummy tomorrow." Andy gave me a salute.

I found Carlos, Sophia, and Luis seated at a table beside the fireplace. The lodge, with its giant dark timber beams, reminded me of a holiday movie set. The circular stone fireplace took up at least a quarter of the large gathering room. I peeled off layers and glanced at the walk-up counter on the far side of the room that sold pizza slices, burgers, fries, and drinks.

"Would anyone like a cup of tea?" I asked.

"Sorry, I can get it," Carlos said, starting to get up. "We bumped into the vintner from RoxyAnn, and I got distracted. They want us to bring Sophia and Luis out for a tasting. I told them we would love to do a tasting as long as that works with your planning for the rest of their time with us."

"Yes, that would be great, and don't worry about tea." I waved him off. "I'm already up, and you all look so comfy in front of the fire. It's no problem. Tea all around?"

"Tea would be nice," Sophia said with a smile.

Everyone nodded.

I went to get in line with the crowd of skiers queued up for snacks. When I reached the front of the line I noticed a familiar face behind the counter, Kendall Hankwitz. Her family had managed the lodge for as long as I could remember. They lived in a cabin on the south side of the mountain and owned the entire slope of lush evergreen forest. I had heard that over the years, several lucrative offers had come in from developers interested in the premier land. The Hankwitz family had turned down every offer in favor of preserving the wild space, luckily for us and the mountain. I couldn't imagine how different Mount A would feel if it was developed with luxury condos and expensive resorts. It was one of the places you could go and truly get away to disconnect from technology and reconnect with nature.

Within a quarter mile, on our snowshoe trek, we had been out in the backcountry with only the stars and the moon to guide us. Where else could you get lost in nature only thirty minutes away from town?

Kendall had been a few years ahead of me in school, but our parents had served on the chamber of commerce board and partnered for various weddings and events at the lodge over the years.

"Juliet, nice to see you. What can I get you?" Kendall waited, ready to punch my order into her tablet. She was sporting a red buffalo plaid shirt with the Mount A logo stitched on the front pocket, jeans, and snow boots. Kendall looked like she belonged in an advertisement for the ski lodge with her makeup-free complexion and casual mountain style.

"A pot of tea. We're just back from a snowshoe tour and could use some extra warming."

"No problem." Kendall turned to fill a teakettle with boiling water. "How was the tour? Did you go out with Hero?"

I studied the menu. The lodge offered classic ski food—burgers, fries, hot dogs, nachos, and healthier options like hummus plates and veggie wraps. "Yes, we did, and it was great for the most part."

"For the most part?" Kendall filled a small basket with a variety of individually packaged teas. "That sounds worrisome."

"Do you know Fitz?"

"Oh no, what did he do now? That man is wreaking havoc on my mountain." Kendall's smile vanished.

I told her about Fitz leading his party off the trail and getting stuck halfway down the cliffside.

"I swear, Juliet, there aren't many people I can't tolerate, but Fitz Baskin is one of them."

"Do you know him well?"

She handed me the basket of tea. "I wish I could say that I didn't, but unfortunately, he makes it his mission to be known."

"He sounds like Richard Lord."

"Exactly." She snapped her fingers. "Maybe he's Richard's long-lost son. They have the same entitled attitude about everything. Fitz acts as if Mount A belongs to him and him alone. He doesn't abide by any rules or safety protocols. Ski patrol has found him skiing out of bounds too many times to count. He's going to trigger an avalanche in the backcountry."

That matched what Hero had said about him.

"I heard he's trying to start his own tour-guiding company."

"He's trying to get a piece of everything. First, he was obsessed with getting on ski patrol. He wanted a job here in the lodge. He's got all kinds of side gigs going on. None of them make sense, and he's certainly not qualified for any of them. I can't believe he talked anyone into going out on a nighttime tour with him. He's so shady." She used a pot holder to hand me the kettle. "Be careful; it's very hot. Take this with you."

"Will do." I grabbed the pot holder from her. "What do you mean by shady?" I glanced behind me to make sure I wasn't holding up the line. That was the exact word Hero had used to describe him.

"He's always scheming about something and hanging

around the lodge. I don't trust the guy. He cares about one thing, and one thing, alone—himself." She frowned. "I would steer clear of him if I were you."

"Don't worry. I have no plans to partner with him," I assured her. "I just hope that the women he took out with him are okay."

"Me too. Maybe this will finally wake everyone up. I've tried reporting him to the forest service, ski patrol, even the Better Business Bureau, but there's not much else I can do."

It was clear that Kendall had strong feelings about Fitz. I didn't blame her. It sounded like he had managed to make an impression on everyone he had come in contact with, and not a good one.

I wanted to ask her more about how the lodge was faring, but a commotion broke out behind us.

"Well, speak of the devil," Kendall said through clenched teeth.

I glanced behind me to see Shawn dragging Fitz up the stairs.

"You're done, dude. Done." Shawn pulled Fitz with one arm like he was a doll. I was surprised by how easily Shawn was shoving Fitz up the stairwell. Fitz had to be at least a half-foot taller than Shawn, but Shawn was in control. "That's it, Baskin. You're off this mountain for good."

"Don't touch me, man." Fitz yanked away from him and threw his hands up.

"You could have killed them. This is it. You're on our list at ski patrol, and I'm reporting you to the authorities."

Fitz laughed in his face. "Go ahead. What are they going to do? Put me in a time-out?"

Shawn stepped closer. For a second, I thought he was going to throw a punch, but he regained control. "My job is to keep everyone safe. I'm not going to let you put anyone in danger again. We just risked our own lives to save you; that's not happening again."

"I didn't ask to be rescued. We were fine, and you know it, dude."

Shawn's jaw clenched so tight it made my head hurt. "Don't mess with me. You're not going to like how this ends."

"Try me." Fitz lunged forward like he was going to strike.

"It's over." Shawn ducked out of the way. "You're done. Done." He fumed as he turned and walked downstairs.

Fitz laughed again and looked around to see if he had an audience.

Kendall leaned over the counter. "See what I mean? The guy is a menace. He has to be stopped."

# Chapter Six

The remainder of the evening was refreshingly drama-free. Once Fitz realized he didn't have a captive audience, he took off. We enjoyed our tea while Ramiro and Marta finished their runs. By the time the lifts closed, I was fighting to keep my eyes open. Carlos drove us home, and I proceeded to fall asleep the minute my head hit the pillow.

As usual, I was the first person awake the following day. I pulled on a pair of thick cabin socks and tiptoed downstairs to make a pot of coffee. My mind drifted to Fitz and the strange turn of events last night as I sipped the strong brew and thought about what to make for breakfast. I wondered what—if any—authority Shawn had as head of the ski patrol. Could he actually ban Fitz from the mountain?

After my conversation with Kendall and listening to Hero's take on Fitz, I had a feeling that if Shawn had the authority to keep Fitz away from the slopes, he would be labeled Superman. The downhill dummy competition commenced at noon, so I would soon find out.

I decided to make an assortment of quiches for breakfast. The protein-packed egg dish should tide us over until after the downhill dummy. We had made plans with Lance and Arlo to stop at Caldera, Ashland's largest craft brewery, on the way back for lunch and beer tasting.

I began with the piecrust, forking butter and flour together, along with a splash of my secret ingredient—vodka. Once the dough came together, I formed it into a ball and covered it with plastic wrap to sit while I concentrated on the fillings.

I whisked eggs and heavy cream together, along with salt and pepper. For the first quiche, I added shredded Swiss cheese, diced ham, and tomatoes—an American breakfast classic. The second quiche would be vegetarian with spinach, sun-dried tomatoes, roasted red peppers, and a trio of Italian cheeses. For the last quiche, I opted for spicy chorizo with sautéed onions, hot peppers, olives, and mushrooms. Quiche was such a versatile and easy dish. I often made it for dinner and paired it with a salad and a glass of wine.

I sprinkled flour on a cutting board and rolled out the crusts. Next, I draped them loosely over two glass pie plates. I used my pastry shears to trim the edges and poked the bottom of the crust with a fork to allow air to escape while baking. I crimped the sides to create fluted edges and filled each crust with the egg mixture. I placed them in the oven to bake and poured myself a second cup of coffee.

A text message dinged on my phone. It was from Lance. "Are we on for dummy and lunch?"

It was early for Lance to be up. I responded right away and made plans to meet at the lodge. Soon the aroma of the baking quiches and coffee stirred everyone from their beds. We enjoyed a languid breakfast of quiche slices, berry and yogurt parfaits, and of course, copious amounts of coffee. It was nice not to worry about Fitz and the spectacle he had made last night. It wasn't my problem, to begin with, but I've always tended to overthink and get sucked into other people's issues. I suppose on the pro side, this tendency made me empathetic, but it also made my head swirl.

A few hours later, I found myself back on Mount A. Last night's moon-drenched twilight had transformed into sapphire skies. In the daylight, the 360-degree view from the summit gave us a pristine shot of Mount Shasta to the south and the entire Rogue Valley to the north. A dusting of new snow had fallen overnight, filling in boot prints and making the lodge look as if someone had sifted powdered sugar on its slanted roofline. A bumblebee-yellow snowcat groomed a trail as riders in a kaleidoscope of colors zipped down the runs. Orange flags used to direct emergency helicopters where to land flapped in the slight wind.

The energy for the dummy contest was palpable and buzzing like the entire crowd was on a caffeine high.

The downhill dummy would take place adjacent to the lodge where a one-hundred-foot temporary ski jump had been constructed. Its ninety-degree angle made my stomach drop. It was good that only dummies would be launched from the precariously steep slope. The launch platform and viewing area for spectators were roped off with red and white plastic flags. I was sure the organizers didn't want to risk an errant piece of wood or boot flying through the air and knocking out an unsuspecting crowd member.

Mom, the Professor, Lance, and Arlo were all waiting for us near the top of the ski jump.

"It's about time." Lance waved us over with two gloved fingers. His retro rainbow ski suit looked straight out of the '80s with its pastel stripes and belted waist.

"I love the suit," I said to Lance.

He stretched out each arm and turned in a complete circle. "The downhill dummy demands a fashion risk, isn't that right, Arlo?"

Arlo put his hand on Lance's shoulder. "Absolutely, dear." His red, white, and blue stars-and-stripes American two-piece snowsuit was equally colorful. "To think I had planned to leave the house in basic black Gore-Tex pants."

"As if Lance would ever let that happen," I teased.

"And be outdone by these young ones? Never. Someone has to teach them." Lance swept his mint green glove toward the ski slope. "An event like this requires a visual disaster like only eighties fashion trends can attain. I couldn't miss out on that. It's my civic duty to model appropriate dummy wear. Would you expect anything less, darling?"

"No. Never." I grinned.

Arlo stifled a laugh.

Mom and the Professor squished closer to make room for everyone. Like us, they had gone for waterproof pants and snow boots, but I had to credit Lance for making a bold statement with his gear.

Spectators lined both sides of the ski jump. Participants and their handmade contraptions gathered at the top of the launch deck. I could see a long row of entries. A tent had been erected near the starting line, with audio and video equipment and prominent speakers. Members of the ski patrol took turns serving as the MC.

"It's you, folks. Your applause and cheering will crown

this year's winner, so don't be shy. We've got a sound monitor that will chart how much noise you make for each dummy. Let's do a practice round. Can I get a *hey, hey, it's the downhill dummy*?"

The crowd roared in response and began chanting, "Downhill dummy, downhill dummy," in unison.

"Rad! Rad!" The MC applauded our efforts. "Now for the serious stuff. We're gonna need you to keep the ski jump clear at all times. Stay behind the ropes, people. The crash site can get gnarly, so keep it clear or risk losing an ear."

"Losing an ear?" Lance muttered. "Surely he can do better than that. Do they not teach iambic pentameter in school anymore?"

"Watch out for our team of volunteers in those bright yellow vests downslope. Give us a wave, would you, volunteer crew?" the MC continued, blaring a whistle on a bullhorn that sent a piercing sound reverberating off the summit. "When you hear this, it means we're about to send the next dummy down, so get out of the way. Got it? Let me see a wave for that."

A small group of volunteers with large black trash bags and yellow vests waved and nodded from the bottom of the jump.

Skiers in helmets and onlookers in knitted hats with pom-poms on the top squeezed forward and angled their phones at the ski jump.

The countdown began. Then huge applause thundered as the first entry sailed down the slope past us—an inflatable T. rex on a polka-dot snowboard. As it hit the bottom berm, it caught so much air that it looked as if it was going to land on top of one of the hundred-foot evergreen trees. But, instead, it crashed at the bottom of the jump and deflated in slow agony like a balloon with a pinprick hole.

Next was a wicked witch on a flying ski broom, followed by a miniature snowcat that the ski patrol had constructed from cardboard and spray-painted bumblebee yellow. Not surprisingly, it crumbled immediately on impact. Caldera Brewing's dummy was an old keg with bride and groom dolls strapped to the top and a chain of empty beer cans trailing behind it.

"There's Ramiro." Sophia pointed to the launch area, where Ramiro and his soccer team stood waiting to let their red and white Grizzly goal dummy fly loose.

We cheered as the team huddled and did their AHS cheer before letting their floppy goalkeeper catch some serious air.

"Everyone is so creative," Carlos said. "But Ramiro's is my favorite by far, not just because he's my son."

"Not so fast, you dashing Spaniard." Lance raised his index finger. "Just wait until you see the OSF dummy."

"What is it?" I asked.

"No cheating. You'll have to wait like the rest of the groundlings."

I felt a buzz of anticipation when Sterling and Andy appeared above us. Steph and Bethany helped them get the Torte entry into position. Unfortunately, it was covered with a large white sheet, so I still couldn't tell what they had created.

When Bethany yanked the sheet away, I gasped.

A six-tiered cake with Torte's signature red and blue logo and intricate buttercream piping sat atop a pair of skis designed to resemble the flat spatulas we used in the bakeshop. Piping bags and cookie cutters were strung along the sides of the cake, and a blond doll in a Torte apron was fastened to the top tier.

"I see a strong resemblance." Lance touched the side of my cheek. "Oh, yes, from this angle, it's quite striking."

I punched him in the arm playfully.

"Get ready, darling. You're about to take a nasty tumble." Lance winked and rubbed his hands together in eager anticipation of my impending doom.

I clapped until my hands stung as the cardboard cake came hurtling toward us. Piping bags and cookie cutters littered the packed snow like confetti. The cake held up well, considering it soared overhead and landed on its side, shattering one of the spatula skis. To add to the fun, Bethany and Steph had baskets of individually packaged Torte cookies that they threw to the crowd, which made everyone cheer louder.

"Well done. Well done." Lance's gloves muffled his attempt at clapping.

Carlos jumped up and down and whooped like he was at a soccer match.

I cheered so loud that I thought my voice might give out.

It was an impressive entry, and the fact that the cake hadn't smashed into pieces was a testament to my team's construction. I wasn't sure if Torte would win the competition, but they were winners in my book.

Between each dummy, the volunteer cleanup crew in eye-popping yellow and orange reflective vests and hard hats would race out and pick up stray debris and any pieces of the entries left on the mountainside. It was almost as enjoyable to watch the volunteers scurry like alpine mice to clean up the ski jump as to watch the dummies themselves.

The contest was winding down. But, as Lance had insisted, OSF's dummy was equally impressive. Set designers had made a replica of the Elizabethan stage, complete with Barbie doll actors in regal paper gowns and tunics. The theater had to be nearly six feet tall, made from hand-painted cardboard, and decorated with maroon velvet curtains and LED stage lights.

"Bravo! Bravo!" Lance screamed, jumping up and down as his Shakespearean theater came hurtling down the hill.

The choreography between launching the dummies and cleaning up the slope was like watching set changes at OSF.

"Hey, hey, my shredders and powder blasters, get ready for our last dummy today. Put your hands together for Steep Slope, made by our ski patrol team. We aim to keep you safe and riding in smooth style, and this one is steep!" The MC kept the energy up for the final dummy.

Hero, Shawn, and a few other ski patrol members in red jackets stood ready to launch their dummy.

I spotted Kendall standing a few feet away with a tray of hot chocolate samples. Having so many people on the mountain must be a boon for business. I knew from personal experience that whenever there were events in the plaza, like the Halloween or holiday parades, the crowds would funnel into Torte for treats and coffee.

The dummy Hero and his friends got into position was by far the largest and most intimidating structure of the day. From my vantage point, it appeared to be nearly twenty feet tall. It was an evergreen tree made from a combination of aluminum pipes and actual tree boughs.

"I wouldn't want pieces of that coming unattached," Lance said, making a face and inching away from the flags.

"I know. It looks like those pipes could turn into missiles," I said.

"All clear," one of the volunteers shouted, and waved to the MC, signaling that it was safe to send the ski patrol dummy down the hill.

"Okay, let's give it up for our last dummy," the MC said, and blew his air horn.

Everyone jumped up and down and cheered. I had a feeling it was not only because this was the final entry but also because, after spectating for an hour, all of our toes were starting to get cold. I bounced with everyone, shouting through my hoarseness.

The wobbly evergreen tree on skis zoomed by, tilting like a toddler learning how to walk. I didn't think it would stay upright once it made it to the berm and really took off.

My prediction came true. The pipe tree hit the snowbank and caught colossal air. I craned my neck to follow its trajectory.

It circled in the sky like a tornado before slamming down below. Unfortunately, the angle was so steep that I couldn't determine where it landed.

However, people lower than us on its flight path must have gotten a good view because there were wild cheers and applause, which quickly shifted to something else. Something much more sinister. Screams began to break out.

Carlos looked at me with wide eyes. "What is it?"

People shouted for help and covered their eyes.

We pushed down the perimeter to get a better look.

Fear pulsed through my body as I caught sight of the scene. There was carnage across the bottom of the ski jump. Pipes and evergreen boughs littered the ski jump like shrapnel from an explosion.

My knees buckled as I realized that a person was lying on the ground beneath the damage.

"Get help!" someone near me screamed. "He's not breathing."

# Chapter Seven

My feet felt like lead. I trudged down the steep slope, not noticing whether Carlos or anyone was behind me. Who was beneath the wreckage on the ski jump? Why would someone have set out across the slope where the dummies were falling?

The crowd had pressed forward toward the flimsy barricade, which was nothing more than colorful flags strung up to mark the danger area.

"Give us space. Back up. Back up," one of the yellow-vested volunteers directed while another waved frantically for ski patrol.

A blur of red jackets zipped past me.

The Professor ducked under the flags and offered his assistance.

I couldn't determine who had been injured, but, with dread, I noticed a pool of deep red fanning against the hard-packed snow.

"That doesn't look good." Lance stuck out his tongue. "It looks like they were impaled with one of the pipes."

I stood on my toes to get a better view but then changed

my mind. I didn't need a visual of life-threatening injuries running through my head. "Can you see who it is?"

Lance shook his head. "They have the victim surrounded."

"What do you think happened? Did they not hear the air horn? Or did it go off too soon? Was it one of the volunteers picking up pieces from the OSF dummy who didn't get out of the way in time?"

He shrugged. "Your guess is as good as mine. Either way, it's a gruesome sight. There's an inordinate amount of blood pooling around the person. I don't think the injuries they've sustained are survivable." Then, in a show of protection, he positioned his body to shield my view. "I would most definitely avert your eyes, darling."

"It's so horrible. With kids around . . ." I trailed off, noticing that parents had already caught on and were ushering youngsters into the lodge and toward the sledding hill. Hopefully, they were none the wiser about the tragic incident.

I also hoped that the person who had been hit was okay. Just because there was a lot of blood didn't mean the person was dead. Between the Professor and ski patrol, who were trained first responders, they were in competent hands, if there was any chance of survival.

Lance's mouth fell open like he wanted to look away but couldn't pull himself to do it. "Uh-oh."

"What's uh-oh?" My throat burned like I had chugged scalding hot coffee.

"It doesn't look good. They've stopped CPR." He placed a trembling gloved finger to his open mouth.

"Maybe the person is okay." Had the temperature dropped again, or was it just me?

"I don't think so, Jules." He adopted a strained smile. "There's too much blood. It looks like a scene from *Macbeth*."

If Lance was calling me Jules, this couldn't be good.

A wave of sadness washed over me. What had started as a carefree day had taken a dark turn. I almost couldn't believe it was real. I wanted to pinch myself in hopes of waking up from a nightmare.

The crowd around us had thinned some. Probably because families had fled the scene. I scanned the sea of neon snowsuits for Carlos and spotted him higher up the slope. He caught my eye and motioned with his head that they were going to the lodge. I waved and held up a finger to let him know I'd be there in a minute.

"I suppose we should go join everyone in the lodge. There's not much we can do here."

Lance sputtered. "As if. We shall do no such thing. We are basically the second line of defense in situations like this. I'm speechless that you would suggest leaving our posts."

"When in your life have you ever been speechless?"

"This is a serious moment; I'm surprised you're being so flippant." Lance raised his brow and addressed me in a scolding tone.

I knew his banter was a protective mechanism, so I dropped it.

The Professor had moved away and had his phone to his ear.

I glanced at the MC station, where Kendall, Shawn, and Hero were all hanging around, watching things unfold from a higher vantage point. I couldn't be sure, since I had only seen them briefly and in the dark, but it looked like the two women who had been with Fitz last night were chatting with Hero.

The distinct whir of helicopter blades grew louder and louder. We watched as Life Flight landed on the helicopter pad next to the ski patrol chalet. I dug my fingers into my ear to block out the thumping sound of its blades spinning. The ground vibrated as it touched down, sending snow shooting out in every direction.

More first responders exited the chopper and went to assist ski patrol and the Professor.

I wasn't sure how long Lance and I stood waiting for an announcement or maybe to be told to vacate the area, but after what felt like an hour, the Professor ambled over, his fur-lined boots disappearing into the snow with each step.

His posture sagged slightly, another sign that the situation below us must be dire. He pressed his lips flat. "I know that we're all stunned. Did you happen to notice anything out of the ordinary before the accident?"

"Not really." I shook my head. "But I wasn't paying close attention to anything other than waiting for the next dummy to fly down the slope."

Lance seconded my statement. "It appears that someone had a nasty run-in with a dummy."

The Professor sighed as he gave a slight nod of acknowledgment. "I'm afraid that it's more than a run-in. The person is deceased. We have yet to notify next of kin, so I would ask that you keep this information as quiet as possible for the short term."

I had figured as much, but hearing it from the Professor gave me pause. A fun afternoon had turned deadly. I wanted time to speed up but felt trapped in the moment.

"Do you know who the victim is and how it happened?"

Lance asked, taking off his '80s pastel ski gloves and dabbing his forehead with the back of his hand.

"We'll be taking statements from witnesses. Obviously, there is no shortage of observers. Unfortunately, it appears he was in the wrong place at the wrong time." He stole a brief glance toward the accident scene. "Perhaps there was a miscommunication between the volunteer safety crew and the organizers. That's part of what my team will have to determine in our investigation."

"Was the person a volunteer?" I asked, noticing for the first time that the cleanup crew was all gathered at the far side of the base of the ski jump.

The Professor shook his head. "I don't believe so. He's been identified. We won't be releasing his name publicly until his family can be notified, but since this is a public crime scene and you'll likely hear rumors, the man's name is Fitz Baskin. Do either of you know him?"

"Fitz?" I couldn't contain my shock. "Fitz is dead?" The sudden feeling of cold spread through my body again.

"I'm afraid so." The Professor offered me a solemn nod. "I take it this means that you knew him."

"Not really." I told him about the rescue last night, trying to make sense of what had happened.

The Professor unzipped his down jacket and took notes in his Moleskine journal, which was like another appendage. I always saw him with a notebook or pen, whether he was hiking, dining out, or working a case.

Once I had finished telling him everything I could remember, the sound of a woman shouting interrupted us.

We turned to see Kendall storming down the hill. Her red plaid shirt stood in contrast with the bright white snow.

"I need to talk to you right away." She pointed her index finger and made a beeline for the Professor.

Where had she come from? The last time I saw her, she was handing out hot chocolate samples near the entrance to the lodge. She must have abandoned her tray of warm drinks and sprinted down the hillside.

She was breathless by the time she reached us. "I know who did it." She clenched her ribs with one hand and caught her breath before pointing to the launch area. "I know who killed him."

"Killed him?" The Professor's eyebrow arched ever so subtly.

"I saw it happen." Kendell held her palms up. "Look at my hands. They won't stop shaking. I can't believe it. I can't believe he killed Fitz. I mean, don't get me wrong, I was not a fan of the guy. He was awful. He was vile, but he didn't deserve to die."

The Professor placed his hand on her forearm and modeled controlled breathing. "Let's take a moment and slow down." He inhaled deeply, closed his eyes, and then gently released his breath. "Good, that's it. Nice and slow."

Kendall regained some composure as she breathed in rhythm with the Professor. She didn't take her eyes off of the launch platform, though. Every few seconds, she would steal a glance in that direction as if she was worried that whoever she thought had killed Fitz might escape.

"What leads you to believe that this wasn't an accident?" the Professor asked in an even tone. He flipped to a new page in his notebook and waited for Kendall to say more.

"I witnessed the entire thing." Her voice cracked as she

glanced above us again. "I can't believe he did it. Why would he do something so awful?"

She wasn't making sense. I could tell the Professor felt the same way because he continued practicing methodical breathing.

"I understand that this is an extremely stressful situation. However, it would be helpful if you could perhaps start from the beginning and walk me through exactly what you witnessed."

"Okay, yeah. Yeah, I can do that." Kendall bobbed her head in agreement. "I came outside to get a better view of the dummy launch. We thought it would be good promotion for the snack bar and restaurant to bring out little tastes of our hot chocolate. I had one of my staff members put together trays of our spiced white hot chocolate, apple cider, and our dark peppermint hot chocolate to hand out to spectators. I was standing right up there." She pointed to the spot where I had seen her before Fitz's accident.

The Professor waited for her to continue.

"The drinks went quickly. I was about to return to the lodge to refill my tray when I tripped on something."

"You tripped?" Lance asked.

"Uh, yeah. On the wires." She grabbed a fistful of her hair and clutched it like a security blanket. "I didn't realize what was happening, but there were clear heavy suspension wires attached to the ski patrol dummy. It was so heavy they needed extra reinforcements to hold it in place before the launch."

"You tripped on wires?" The Professor suggested.

"Yes." Kendall blinked like she was having difficulty processing precisely what she had seen. "Yes, that's right.

I tripped on the wires. I was on the ground, flat on my face. As I said, the tray was empty, so nothing spilled, but it landed a few feet away. I got up to grab it and realized that someone was cutting the wire holding the dummy. They must have intentionally sent the dummy down the ski jump while Fitz was standing there helpless, completely oblivious that a hundred pounds of aluminum pipes were hurling toward him."

The Professor nudged her. "Who cut the wire?"

She swallowed hard and craned her neck in the direction of the launch pad. "Shawn."

"Ski patrol Shawn?" I asked.

"He did it." She folded her arms over her stomach and hunched forward like she was going to be sick. "He killed Fitz."

# Chapter Eight

Kendall's revelation changed the Professor's demeanor instantly. His gaze flitted around the mountainside, never settling on one spot for long. Lance nudged my ribs with his elbow. Kendall tore off her flannel shirt and tied it around her neck while fanning her face like we were standing in the middle of a blazing hot desert, not an arctic summit.

"Do you need medical attention?" the Professor asked her with concern.

She scooped a handful of snow and pressed it on the base of her neck. "No, hot flashes. They're the worst."

"Ah, I see." He offered her his arm. "Shall we have a further chat in private?"

Kendall followed him up the hill to the landing platform.

Almost immediately, a frenzy of activity broke out above us as Kendall pointed wildly to Shawn, shouting, "You killed him! You killed him," repeatedly.

"There has to be a mistake," I said to Lance. "Shawn is one of Andy's good friends. What possible motive could he have to kill Fitz?" As the words escaped my lips, I thought back to what Andy had said last night about Shawn despising Fitz. But not liking someone didn't mean that he was a murderer.

"That I can't answer." Lance let out a low whistle. "However, why would he be fleeing if he's innocent?" He directed one long finger toward the platform.

"Fleeing?" I turned just in time to see Shawn grab his skis and run toward the chair lifts.

"Where does he think he's going?" I asked. People were scattered everywhere on the mountain, and the lifts weren't operating. Shawn's only option was to ski out of bounds, straight down the undeveloped side of the west slope.

It looked like that was exactly what he intended to do, as he strapped on his skis, pulled his goggles over his eyes, and sprinted away as if he was entering an Olympic cross-country ski race.

I watched as the Professor directed other ski patrol members to go after him. A snowcat rumbled to life.

This couldn't be happening. Why would Andy's friend kill Fitz? It didn't make sense. However, there was no denying that Shawn was attempting to get away. His behavior didn't match someone who was innocent.

Shawn was a strong skier but was he a match for the snowcat?

"We should have a bucket of buttery popcorn with us for this show," Lance said.

The snowcat was gaining on Shawn but running out of time as Shawn neared the tree line. If he made it to the densely forested slope, the snowcat would never catch up. It was too big and bulky to maneuver through the tightly packed towering pines.

The buzz on the mountain turned to an awed silence when the cat caught up with him just as his silhouette was about to disappear into the forest.

Everything unfolded quickly. Shawn's ski patrol buddies surrounded him and wrangled him into the snowcat. Then teams of police officers arrived, including Thomas and Kerry. The Professor huddled everyone together to give them directions as Life Flight took off.

Thomas and I had grown up together. Our families had been inseparable, as had we. That was until we broke up right after graduation. At the time, I thought I would never recover from the heartbreak of losing my boyfriend and my best friend, but the universe had other plans for me. If it hadn't been for Thomas telling me he needed space, I probably wouldn't have boarded a plane for New York to attend culinary school or spent a decade sailing through azure seas to faraway ports of call. I wouldn't have met Carlos. I might have felt stuck in our little hamlet.

Instead, like so many things in my life, the ache of losing my first love had cracked me open to new parts of myself that I never knew existed. I was grateful that both Thomas and I had grown into ourselves and found lasting love with other people. I was also thankful that since returning to Ashland, we'd rekindled our friendship, and I had gained a bonus friend in his wife, Kerry.

After the Professor conferred with his team, he took the mic and addressed the crowd. "I'm sorry to inform you that there will be some delays in releasing you this afternoon. I'm quite sure you understand the severity of the situation, and you have our deepest gratitude in advance for your cooperation. We'll do our best to complete our investigation as quickly and thoroughly as possible. Please hold tight."

"This is so unbelievable," I repeated as police officers fanned out and gathered spectators into groups.

The snowcat had backed up and was returning toward the lifts. Every empty red chair swung in the breeze. Sun glinted off the radar dome. The giant ball was always a topic of conversation, especially for anyone venturing into the ski area for the first time. The National Weather Service tracked dangerous storms and improved air traffic safety at its state-of-the-art radar station perched atop Mount A's highest point of over 7,000 feet. The shiny white sphere could be seen from the plaza on a clear day.

Lance fiddled with the flags that marked the ski jump. "Agreed. You know what this means, don't you?"

"No, what?" I didn't like the touch of what sounded like eagerness in his tone.

"We're on the case, darling." He released the flags and brushed his gloves together. "It's obvious that the police are in dire need of our assistance."

"How so? It sounds like this is going to be an open-and-shut case." I motioned to the base of the lift, where the Professor and two uniformed officers were waiting for the snowcat. "If it turns out that it was intentional, Shawn just tried to flee the scene. What is there to investigate?"

"Please." Lance sounded dismayed. "Have you not heard yourself?"

"What do you mean?"

"You just said how impossible it is that Shawn could be a killer. It's our civic duty to see that justice is served."

I watched as the snowcat chugged in front of the ski patrol offices. The officers helped remove Shawn from the cat, and then the Professor took him by the arm and secured him in the backseat of Thomas's squad car. From my vantage point, it didn't look like Shawn was putting up a fight. So why had he raced off to begin with? It didn't make sense.

I wasn't sure what that meant in terms of Fitz's death, but there was no mistaking that the Professor was taking him into custody.

"See? My point." Lance twisted his hand with a flourish. "Where shall we start?"

"I don't know." That was true. "It was pretty clear that Fitz didn't exactly warm anyone's heart last night. Hero was furious with him. Rightfully so. Fitz not only put his tour group in danger, but everyone who came to help him."

"He sounds like a true narcissist."

"Yeah. I didn't talk to him for more than a few minutes, but in that short time, he was incredibly abrasive," I agreed. "Kendall also made it abundantly clear that she's not a fan, but I'm not sure what happened during the rescue. When Shawn and the other ski patrol members showed up, we returned to the lodge. I have no idea whether their interactions were contentious or if something happened during the rescue that could have triggered Shawn, because he and Fitz got into a fight back at the lodge. Shawn banned Fitz from the mountain. I don't know if he has the authority to do it, but he sounded serious."

"What about his tour group?" Lance unzipped the top of his retro ski suit, reached into an interior pocket, and removed a silver flask engraved with his initials. "Fancy a nip?" he asked after taking a small slug.

"No thanks. My head is already spinning."

"Suit yourself, it's Arlo's homemade whiskey, and I must say it's not bad for a first attempt at distilling." He returned the flask to his interior pocket. "Anyway, you were saying?"

"I never met Fitz's tour group. They passed by us briefly. I think it's a mother/daughter duo, but I'm not sure. The older woman seemed to be here in some official capacity. She had a clipboard with her when I bumped into her in the lodge before the tour and again out on the ridgeline. Maybe she's training to be a guide or was evaluating Fitz." I looked around to see if I could find her, but there were so many pockets of people being interviewed by the police that she could have been anywhere.

"Then that's where we shall commence our inquiries." He zipped his ski suit up to his chin and looped his arm through mine. "Onward."

"What are we going to do? We can't just march up to them and start asking a bunch of questions," I protested. "I already told you I don't know either of the women."

"As if that has ever deterred us before. Follow my lead and march in step behind me like a good soldier." Lance lifted his legs in exaggerated steps as we trudged up the steep slope. "Do you see them?"

I paused, happy for a minute to catch my breath. Maybe it was from standing in the cold for so long, but every step felt like it took double the effort.

He cut a path through the snow to the women who had been in Fitz's party last night. They were standing a few feet away from the launch platform.

In true Lance fashion, he sauntered up to them and extended a hand. "I don't believe we've had the pleasure. Let me introduce myself; I'm Lance Rousseau, artistic director at OSF. You may be familiar with my work, but there's no need for formalities."

The women looked at each other like they were trying to figure out how to respond.

"And this is my dearest friend, Juliet Capshaw Montague, owner of the exquisite Torte bakeshop in Ashland," he continued, oblivious to their confusion. "We couldn't help but notice that you both look quite out of sorts, understandably. We wanted to offer our deepest condolences for your loss and see if there might be any way we can be of service."

Both women stared at us in silence like he was speaking a foreign language.

"Excuse me?" The older woman cleared her throat and ignored Lance's extended hand. "Your condolences. Why are you offering me condolences? I barely knew the man." She tapped her clipboard.

Was she judging the dummy contest?

"Oh, is that so?" Lance pressed his hand to his chest. "My apologies. We had heard otherwise. We were under the impression that Fitz was your mountain guide last night."

The woman scowled as she stuck a pencil into the top of her clipboard. "You're mistaken. I was on duty last night. Fitz wasn't my guide. I don't know how anyone could call him a guide. He nearly killed us."

"Ruth isn't exaggerating," the younger woman interjected. "He took us way off the trail. Although I guess it's our mistake for following him. If it hadn't been for ski patrol, we might still be stranded. I can't wrap my head around why they're arresting one of our rescuers." She paused to peer over her shoulder at where the police cars were gathered in the parking lot. "I'm January, by the way."

"January, charmed." Lance shook her hand. "How were you acquainted with Fitz? Are you here for a family holiday? A winter ski break?"

"Us?" January scrunched her face and used her thumb to point from herself to Ruth. "We're not related."

"Oh, my mistake again." Lance made a clicking sound with his tongue. "It's one of those days."

"It's shocking," January said, tugging at one of her braids. In daylight, she was even younger than I had thought last night, but her faded ski suit had seen plenty of action from the looks of its patches and small tears. "Is he dead? We heard rumors. Is it true?"

Lance reached for a handkerchief. He had to be one of the last men in the world who carried a silk handkerchief. "Indeed, the police have confirmed it."

January waved off his offer of the handkerchief. "Nah, I'm good. I'm with Ruth on this one. I can't say that I'm sad to hear that he's dead. He tried to kill us, so it's hard to have a lot of sympathy for the guy."

"Do you really think he tried to kill you?" I asked. Ruth had alluded to the same. Could that explain why Fitz had gone so far off the trail last night?

January glanced at Ruth. They shared a strange look. "That's what we were just talking about. We've been trying to figure out what to do next. We're both sure that Fitz intentionally took us off the trail. He was going to leave us out there in the freezing cold to die." She rubbed her arms with fraying gloves at the memory. "We told ski patrol last night. They thought we were being hysterical because we were nearly hypothermic. I found Ruth at the start of the competition because I want to go to the police. Fitz should never be allowed to guide another tour."

"Looks like someone agreed with you," Lance said.

"Huh? What?" January wrinkled her nose.

I wanted to punch Lance in the arm, but that would be too obvious. No one had said foul play was involved, except for Kendall, but Ruth and January couldn't know that yet.

"We can't just leave it, you know?" January went on. "That wouldn't be cool for anyone else who ended up out in the backcountry with Fitz, but since the bros at ski patrol are so worthless, I told Ruth we should tell the cops." She ran her zipper up and down as she spoke, like she was trying to get it unstuck. "We were about to call the cops when we heard the screams and word started to spread that it was Fitz." January folded the edge of one of the lift tickets attached to her zipper and gnawed on her lip.

"What made you think that Fitz tried to get you lost?" Lance asked.

Ruth jumped in. Unlike January, her ski gear looked like it had come straight from the rack and had never been worn. "We don't think that he tried to get us lost. We *know* that he succeeded. If it hadn't been for Hero and then the ski patrol team, we would have been abandoned on the mountain. Fitz had it planned all along."

"But why?" Lance pressed. "That doesn't sound like a viable business model. Why would he want his clients to get left behind?"

"What are you talking about? He wasn't out on the mountain to guide us," Ruth replied with a slight tinge of annoyance. "As I said, I wasn't a client. I'm assessing the entire ski region—the lodge, the lifts, the trails, the campsite, everything. Fitz was recommended by lodge staff and a few others because of his extensive knowledge of the backcountry trails. We weren't tourists out for an adventure, we were working."

"Are you working together?" I addressed January.

She ran her fingers on the folded edge of the lift ticket like it was a security blanket. "No. I've been doing a bunch of gigs, trying to make enough to pay to ride, and I heard that there might be space for some new tour guides, so I tagged along. I thought I might learn something new, but it turns out Fitz is a real prick."

"What was Fitz doing, then?" I asked them.

"I have no idea." Ruth held out her clipboard to show us a page of notes. "I've been documenting everything we witnessed last night." She rolled up the sleeve of her down jacket. "See these bruises? That's from ski patrol having to hoist me up the ravine. I'm bruised and sore all over. I intend to share my feedback about Fitz Baskin and his unprofessional actions with the authorities, regardless of whether he's dead."

This was a huge twist, but I still couldn't understand Fitz's motivation for putting them in harm's way.

Lance voiced my thoughts. "Do you have any idea why he led you both so far off the trail?"

"We were pawns in some strange game he was playing, and I will do anything and everything in my power to see that he is brought to justice," Ruth said with force as she stuffed her phone back in her pocket.

"But he's dead," January said.

"Exactly. Just one of the ways that man is going to pay."

# Chapter Nine

Lance choked back a cough. "Apologies. This brisk air is making my throat quite tickly."

I had a feeling there was another reason for his choking fit—Ruth. She had learned that Fitz was dead, and her first reaction was to make sure that he "paid."

January rubbed the tops of her thighs. "I'm losing feeling in my legs. I think I might go and warm up in the lodge."

Ruth yanked the younger woman's wrist so hard that January's entire body lurched.

"Jeez, what are you doing?"

"We have a few more things to discuss, remember?" Ruth held her gaze.

January's teeth chattered. She ran her hands together like they were two sticks over a fire. "Can we talk inside? I'm so cold."

January was toothpick thin with wiry hair and translucent skin. I didn't think she was exaggerating about being cold, mainly because the holes in her gloves were the size of quarters and pretty much rendered them useless.

Ruth huffed, sending fog out like a dragon breathing

fire. "Fine, but we need to finish this discussion in *private* so that I know how to proceed and can finish my report." The way she emphasized *private* made it clear that she was done with Lance and me.

"I think that's our cue to leave you," I said to the two of them. "If you can fill the Professor in on your experience with Fitz last night, I think it will be beneficial to their investigation."

"Thanks for that gem of wisdom," Ruth snarled, and dragged January away. "I'm here on professional business; it's not like I wouldn't speak with the authorities."

"Well, that was certainly enlightening, wasn't it?" Lance raised his brow and pressed his finger to his chin. "The question is, could either of them be our killer?"

"I don't know what we just learned from that conversation. I'm still confused. Why were they out with Fitz last night? Ruth was assessing the ski area, and January was shadowing him. It doesn't make sense, does it?"

"Nothing ever makes sense at the beginning, darling. Does it?" He patted my cheek. "Chin up. Don't let those frown lines in."

"What do you think his angle was? Why did he agree to take them out, and what would have motivated him to try and intentionally strand them on the cliffside?" As I asked the question, I let out an involuntary shudder. "If we hadn't been at the shelter last night, I wonder if he would have succeeded. Maybe one or both of them were seeking revenge."

"I wondered the same thing." Lance nodded with enthusiasm.

"We'll have to talk to Hero. On our guided trip, he was complaining about Fitz not following the rules and trying to undermine mountain protocol. Still, he also made it sound like Fitz was doing everything he could to garner business, and he definitely seemed to think that Ruth and January were part of Fitz's tour group. Something doesn't add up."

"We can't let a few little niggling questions stop us." Lance caught sight of Arlo near the entrance to the lodge and waved. "Let's keep this on the down-low for the time being, shall we?"

I wasn't entirely convinced Lance comprehended the meaning of *the down-low*, but I wasn't about to argue with that idea. My role at the moment was to continue to host the Torres family. Running off to try and solve a murder with Lance probably wouldn't make me the most gracious host, so I followed him to the lodge. Rows and rows of colorful skis and snowboards cluttered the entrance, propped on racks and against the lodge. With the lifts shut down, no one was skiing. I wondered how anyone would find their skis when and if the lifts opened again.

"There you are. I lost you two in the shuffle. I wonder why?" Arlo's face told me he knew exactly where Lance and I had vanished to.

"Us? We simply got lost in the mix." Lance was laying it on thicker than a layer of buttercream.

"Sure you did." Arlo put his arm around Lance. "Give me the news. I know you were snooping."

"Ouch." Lance stabbed his heart with his thumb. "Daggers to the heart. Us, snooping? I resent the implication. Never. Juliet and I were merely offering our services should they be needed."

Arlo laughed so hard he snorted.

Even Lance couldn't hold character. He broke into a fit

of giggles before elbowing Arlo. "This is serious, you understand? It's highly likely that Doug and his team will want to loop us in."

"Loop the artistic director of the local theater and the baker into their investigation. Right. Right. That makes sense." Arlo's deep brown eyes squinted with skepticism.

Lance pretended to fume. "I'll have you know that Juliet and I are semiprofessionals. You can't know every line in *Macbeth* and not have a penchant for solving crime."

"I never doubted otherwise." Arlo caught my eye and winked. "But you need sustenance for your sleuthing, I assume, which means I can count us in for lunch at Caldera?"

I had almost forgotten about our lunch plans. "That's right; I should go find Carlos, Luis, and Sophia."

Arlo nodded toward the lodge. "Carlos told me they were returning their ski rentals since the lifts are shut down."

"Okay, I'll head that way. Should we meet you at the brewery in thirty or forty minutes?"

"We'll save you seats." Lance blew me a kiss and left with Arlo.

I knew there wasn't anything else I could do in the short term, but so many questions remained. I wanted to hear more from Kendall about what she had seen and her impressions of Shawn. She must know all of the ski patrol team. They worked directly with the lodge. I also wanted to speak with Hero. He seemed to know Fitz better than anyone else. Maybe he would be able to offer insight into why someone would have resorted to murder.

"Julieta, over here." Carlos waved and walked toward me. "I was coming to look for you."

"You found me." Relief flooded my body at the sight of him. Being in Carlos's presence had a way of centering me.

He held out a gloved hand. "Are you okay?"

"I mean, I'm as good as I can be, given what we just witnessed. I'm more concerned about Marta, Ramiro, Sophia, and Luis. This wasn't the whimsical weekend experience I was hoping for. First last night. Now this."

"Sí, they are fine, though, and we are all safe and together, which is what matters." He squeezed my hand.

"Yeah. You're right." I returned his grasp. "Do you still want to meet Arlo and Lance for a late lunch?"

"Yes, let me gather everyone. Do you want to come with me or meet at the car in a few minutes?"

I noticed that Hero was finishing being interviewed by a police officer in front of the ski patrol offices. This was my chance to talk to him while everything was fresh. "Let's meet at the car. I'm going to have a quick word with Hero."

"Okay, but be careful, mi querida." Carlos gave me a knowing smile before heading back inside.

I hurried over to Hero. "Hey, how's everything going?"

He shook his head in disbelief, running his hands through his hair until it stuck out in all directions. "Not good. Not good at all."

"I can't believe Fitz is dead," I said, staring at the rows of skis sticking out of the snow and goggles and hard hats hanging from fencing attached to the side of the building.

He looked at me in surprise and then readjusted his chest radio harness. "I can. Everyone I know wanted to kill him, but the cops took the wrong guy."

I hadn't mentioned anything about murder, but I didn't

say that to Hero because I wanted to hear what he had to say. "You mean Shawn?"

"Shawn is a good dude." He tried unsuccessfully to smooth his hair down. "If it weren't for him, Fitz might already be dead. You were there. Think about it. If Shawn had wanted to kill him, he easily could have done it last night. No one was around. It was dark. Cold. They were on a cliff. Shawn could have pushed Fitz off, and there would never have been an investigation. It would have been called an accident. There's no way he did it. He risked his life to save Fitz last night, and the police arrested him—that's messed up. I don't get it."

"I don't either," I admitted. Hero's point was valid. If Shawn was the killer, why would he have chosen such a public place and, frankly, an unreliable method? How could the killer have guaranteed that Fitz was in the right spot at the right time to cut the wires? Whoever killed him had put the other volunteers at risk, too. If they had cut the wires earlier, someone else could have been hurt. The event had to be precisely timed. They must have been ready and waiting to snip the tether at just the right moment.

"Shawn's trained to save people. That's his entire job. So why would he do it?" Hero's eyes drifted to the red and white ski patrol flag hanging from the eaves of the small chalet.

"Did they know each other? Could something have happened between them during the rescue last night?" I suggested.

"Fitz was hard to ignore. If you spent any time on Mount A this season, you know the name and probably do everything you can to avoid him. Shawn knew him. Shawn got super upset about Fitz skiing out of bounds and taking his group with him, but there's no way he killed Fitz because of that."

"What about you?"

Hero recoiled. He tapped his chest harness. "Me? You think I killed him?"

"No, I wondered how you felt about Fitz playing by his own rules." It was odd that Hero's posture had suddenly become defensive. Had I hit a nerve?

"I told you last night; I was not a fan of the dude. It's not like any of us are corporate, but there are rules, and you have to follow them. Fitz didn't care. Fitz was in this for a money grab and who knows what else."

"Yeah, about that. I heard talk that Fitz might have had another angle or maybe a separate project going on. Did you know anything about that?"

"The guy was a scammer." He pointed to headquarters behind us. "Ski patrol caught him out of bounds all the time. I don't know what he was up to. I know he tried to steal my clientele and bad-mouth my tours."

This was news.

"He did?" I waited for him to say more as I watched wispy clouds snake above Mount Shasta on the far horizon.

Hero kicked snow with his boot. "He tried to get under everyone's skin. It was his thing. I wasn't worried about it. I don't know how he managed to book January and Ruth. They were threatening to sue him last night. I thought that was going to be the end of him. I didn't realize he would . . ." Hero paused, realizing what he was about to say.

In the distance, I spotted Carlos and our crew heading

for the car. "Look, I should let you go, but if you need anything, stop by Torte. I really appreciated your professionalism last night, and I'm glad you were our guide."

Hero gave me a small smile. "Thanks, yeah, maybe I'll do that."

As I walked to the car, I wondered just how much of Hero's business Fitz had tried to steal. Hero didn't seem like the murderous type to me, but then again, if his livelihood was in jeopardy, I couldn't rule him out as a potential suspect either.

"Jules, Jules," a voice sounded nearby.

I turned to see Andy barreling toward me. He ran with his snowboard hanging over his right shoulder. His windburned cheeks were streaked red.

"What's going on?" I asked, concerned that I had missed another accident or worse.

"It's Shawn. I can't believe it. They're taking him to the police station."

"I know, I heard." I touched his arm to console him.

"You have to do something, Jules," he pleaded, glancing at the waiting squad cars barricading half the parking lot. "Please, Jules. You have to help him."

"I'm not sure what exactly I can do."

"Jules, please. The Professor is your family. You have to talk to him. Let me talk to him. Shawn is one of my best friends." His voice cracked. Tears welled in his youthful eyes. "Please, Jules, do something."

I reached out to console him. "I'll do my best. You know the Professor as well as I do. He's thoughtful and methodical. He won't do anything rash."

"Jules, I get that, but Shawn doesn't have any money for a lawyer or anything. He's a ski bum. He's not a slacker.

He works hard on ski patrol. He feels the lifestyle. He does odd jobs, any additional work he can get just to be on the slope. He needs our help. He doesn't have family here." His words came tumbling out together, matching the pace of rapid breaths.

It was obvious that Andy was in distress.

I held my hand up. "Okay, I promise. It's going to be alright. I'll talk to the Professor and see what I can do. We're heading to Caldera for lunch. Do you want to join us?"

"No, thanks. I'm going to stick around and see what else I can learn. Maybe one of my friends on ski patrol has heard something. I can't just sit around and do nothing. I have to help my friend."

"I get it." I squeezed his hand. "I'll see you back at Torte, and we'll reconvene after I talk to the Professor."

Andy leaned in to hug me. "You're the best, boss."

I proceeded toward the car. I already felt compelled to learn as much as I could about Fitz and what might have led someone to want to kill him, but hearing Andy so passionate about wanting to help his friend was a clear sign that I was going to need to find some opportunities to slip away from my hosting duties over the next few days.

# Chapter Ten

Caldera Brewing was like a second base camp for skiers and snowboarders. Its proximity to the mountain provided a perfect resting and refueling stop after a long day of fresh powder.

"So many beers," Sophia exclaimed as we entered the restaurant.

One of the brewery's showpieces was its vast collection of beer bottles and cans from around the world. Shelving started halfway up the wall and stretched to the ceiling in order to display over four thousand unique bottles.

"Did they brew those?" Luis asked.

"No, the head brewer has collected them over the years," I replied. "But it is rumored to be the biggest collection in the state."

Carlos pointed to the bar with its purple accents and keg barrel planters. "They have over thirty beers on tap, so don't worry, we'll have plenty to taste."

Our lunch conversation revolved around Fitz. Thankfully, while Marta and Ramiro went to wash their hands, Sophia told me that neither of them had seen anything.

That was a relief. We sampled beer tastings and devoured Caldera's famous beer cheese soup, pulled pork sliders, and white truffle mac and cheese.

"I'm so glad that no one else was injured," Sophia said, holding a grapefruit beer to her lips. "It could have been much worse."

"Our soccer coach thinks this might be the last year the dummy happens." Ramiro plunged a spoon into his hot chocolate and swirled around the whipped cream on top. "I'm glad I got to see it."

"Are they thinking of canceling future events because of today?" I savored my Ashland amber, a red ale with a hint of Oregon hops.

"Sí. We may have just watched our first and last downhill dummy." Ramiro's shoulders drooped as he nodded. "They're saying it's too dangerous."

It would be a shame to cancel the annual event because of the actions of one person. Before Fitz's accident (which sounded less and less like an accident), I hadn't had a single safety concern. I dropped the subject and focused on enjoying our time together. I pushed the thought aside and savored my soup and bread.

After lunch, everyone decided it was time for a siesta. An afternoon rest sounded inviting, but I knew myself well enough to understand that I needed to do something after witnessing Fitz's death. I needed to bake.

We said goodbye to Lance and Arlo, and I had Carlos take me to the bakeshop after he dropped everyone else back at the house for a nap.

"I'll walk home and see you all for dinner." I opened the car door.

Carlos reached for my hand and caressed it with his

thumb. "I can pick you up, mi querida. I know that you're upset about Fitz. I don't want you to be alone if you don't want to."

His touch brought flutters to my stomach. "Thank you, really. It means a lot to me, but honestly, I think a walk will be good for me."

He leaned in to kiss me. Part of me wanted to go with him, curl up in his arms, and pretend like Fitz's death hadn't happened. But I knew I wouldn't be able to rest until I moved some of this negative energy out of my body, and the best way I knew how to do that was to bake.

"Call me if you change your mind." He blew me a kiss and drove off.

I let out a slow breath before going into Torte. Hopefully, between baking and a leisurely walk home, I could process what had happened. I almost felt my blood pressure returning to normal as I crossed under the red and blue awning. Bethany and Rosa's frosty winter display made me hungry for something sugary.

Sequoia was steaming oat milk for our raspberry matcha latte. "Hi, Jules. We weren't expecting to see you today."

I squeezed behind the espresso bar. "I know. There was a development on the mountain."

"Really?" She finished the drink and handed it to a customer. "Your tone sounds ominous."

The dining room wasn't crowded at this hour. A handful of customers enjoyed late lunches and afternoon coffee pick-me-ups, but there wasn't a line at the pastry case.

I gave her a quick recap as she wiped down the counter. Her fluid motions always reminded me of a dancer, whether she was frothing milk or cleaning up a spill.

"How is Andy doing?" She twisted one of the colorful friendship bracelets on her wrist.

"Not well. His friend Shawn was taken in for questioning. I almost wondered if he might make an appearance here at some point. But, when I left him on the mountain, he was going to talk to some of his friends on ski patrol."

She finished with the counter and turned her attention to refilling canisters of teas. "One of Andy's friends being a killer is not possible in my universe. Or any universe, for that matter."

"Killer? I think I missed something." Rosa scooted around the counter carrying a tray of apple tarts, chocolate croissants, and chai cookies.

I filled her in and took the empty tray out of the pastry case.

She placed the fresh one in the case. "That is absolutely terrible. Do they have any idea who did it?"

"No. Well, at least not that they're saying. The Professor, Thomas, and Kerry are up on the mountain now. They detained everyone and were taking statements before letting anyone go."

Rosa positioned a cookie so that it was in perfect line with the others. Our iced chai cookies were a winter favorite. I was tempted to grab one for myself.

"Is there anything we can do?" Rosa placed both hands over her heart. Her kind eyes welled with empathy. "I feel so awful for everyone who witnessed it and for our Andy."

"I know. Me too. They did a good job of getting the kids out of the way, so hopefully none of them saw the accident. Still, it has to be traumatic just being there and picking up the energy of the adults around them." I glanced at the chalkboard menu where a youngster with black braids was playing a game of tic-tac-toe against her dad. We provided spaces for customers of all ages at the bakeshop. Watching little ones doodle on the chalkboard or nibble on dark chocolate chunk cookies the size of their head was one of my favorite parts of the day.

"How's everything here? It looks pretty slow." Aside from the tic-tac-toers, there were two groups at tables and no one at the counter.

"Fine, nothing eventful." Sequoia strummed her fingers on the espresso machine. Her nails were painted slate gray with yin and yang symbols. "We had a brunch and lunch rush, but as you can see, things are pretty chill now."

"Yes, this is the last tray of baked goods for the day," Rosa added. "We're going to begin a slow cleanup."

"I'll go downstairs and see if Marty needs anything." With Bethany, Sterling, Steph, and Andy taking the afternoon off, we ran with a skeleton crew for the closing shift.

Marty didn't greet me with his usual jovial smile or a bear hug. Instead, he drew his eyebrows together and rubbed his chest. "I heard."

"You did? How?"

"Andy texted." He pressed his lips together. "Terrible. Terrible."

I washed my hands and tied on an apron. "It was awful, and there were so many spectators."

"I was eager to hear about the Torte dummy, but now . . ." Marty didn't finish.

"I know. I still can't believe it happened. It feels like a bad dream." I assessed the kitchen. Marty pulled a tray of rustic bread from the wood-fired oven. The scent made me inhale deeply and pause for a moment.

"I can only imagine," Marty said, resting the tray on the bread rack. "I take it you need to bake?"

"Am I that obvious?"

"Baker to baker, yeah." He caught my eye and gave me a reassuring smile. Then he took off his oven mitt and stoked the fire. "Baking is my escape from grief. I can't quite put words to it, but the kitchen is where I seek solace. I thought that might change with time, but it hasn't. You know how they say that time heals all wounds? Don't believe that lie—it doesn't." He ran his finger around his wedding ring, his voice cracking softly as he continued. "Time changes us. Time morphs us. But for those of us who have loved and lost, grief comes with us. So whenever I find myself overcome with sadness or flooded with memories, this is where I come, too."

"That's so well said." My eyes watered. I blinked away salty tears, moved by his words. "It's true. We're lucky that way, I suppose."

"Name another profession where you can knead away your demons and end up with a delicious loaf when you're done." He returned and stoked the flames again.

"Marty, have I told you lately how much I appreciate you?"

"There's no need. I feel it right here every day." He tapped his chest. "Torte is the most heart-centered place I've worked."

"That's good to hear. Heart-centered is the only way I want to operate in the world."

Marty moved to the stove to check on the pot of soup. "So what's your baking escape going to be?"

I rolled up my sleeves. "I think I'm going to go bake

another batch of chai cookies. Mainly because I want to take some home with me."

He placed a lid back on the Dutch oven. "There are probably two or three more servings of soup left for any stragglers. I'll let Rosa know. Then I'm boxing up this bread order for the Green Goblin and calling it a day, so the kitchen is all yours."

While Marty loaded bread into delivery boxes, I compiled the ingredients I needed for my chai cookies. The base began with a mixture of butter creamed with granulated white sugar and brown sugar. Then I added chai spices—cardamom, cloves, cinnamon, nutmeg, ginger, and black pepper.

I had been baking a version of these chai cookies for years, but Bethany had updated the recipe to mirror Taylor Swift's take on the spicy classic. Bethany, who always had her finger on the pulse of social media trends, suggested we name the cookies the Spicy Swifties. Not surprisingly, they flew out of the case.

After I had whipped in the spices, I added eggs, vanilla, flour, baking soda, and salt. Then I scooped the dough into two-inch balls on parchment-lined baking sheets. The next step involved flattening the balls and dusting them with cinnamon. I placed the trays in the oven to bake and started on the glaze.

Glazing cookies is a simple way to give the humble dessert something extra special. For today's glaze, I knew I had a few bottles of eggnog left over from our holiday baking, which I combined with more powdered sugar and a touch of vanilla. I whisked it until it was smooth and almost translucent.

When the cookies had baked and cooled, I dipped them in the glaze and finished them with a touch of nutmeg. I couldn't resist trying one. The buttery sugar cookie base melted in my mouth and was followed by a symphony of spices with just the right amount of sweetness in the glaze to balance every bite.

"Hey, boss." Andy startled me.

I mumbled a hello through a mouthful of cookie. "Sorry, I didn't hear you come in."

"That's because I snuck in the back." He motioned to the basement door and began peeling off layers.

"Did you come straight from the mountain?" I held out the tray. "Cookie?"

"I can't resist your cookies."

"Any luck in talking to your friends on ski patrol?" I was glad that there was no one in the dining area downstairs so that Andy and I could talk in private.

"Not really. None of them think Shawn did it." He reached for a cookie and broke it in half. "They all hated Fitz, too, so it's not like Shawn was the only one. I heard that Fitz didn't register the tour and that there might be a lawsuit coming."

"A lawsuit?"

He held up a finger while eating part of the cookie. "Did you meet either of the women with Fitz? January and Ruth?"

I nodded. "Yeah, I spoke with both of them."

"This is so good and hits the spot right now." Andy took another huge bite. "I've seen January on runs and stuff, but I don't know her well. It sounds like she's your classic winter snow bum. In town for the season, hanging out on couches, and getting odd jobs when she can to support her habit."

"You mean snow habit, right?"

"Yeah." He laughed. "One of the women on ski patrol thinks there's something more about January. I guess there are some rumors about her hanging around too much."

"What does that mean?" I was tempted to have a second cookie with the way Andy was devouring his.

"I'm not sure. She seemed to hint that January was into Fitz, but nobody else agreed."

"Interesting." I made a mental note.

"Ruth has been on the mountain for a couple of weeks. She says she's doing an assessment, but no one knows who she's working for. Apparently, she's been taking notes everywhere—in the lodge, ski patrol offices, campsites; one of my friends said they even saw her up at the weather station a few days ago."

"But no one knows who she's working for?"

"Nope." Andy polished off the last bite of the cookie. "Can I have another?"

"No need to ask." I pushed the tray closer.

"Here's the thing, I saw her in the lodge right before I left. I went in to grab a sandwich for the drive home, and she was behind the concession counter. Kendall accused her of snooping. It was a super awkward interaction and got me thinking, what if that's the lawsuit? Maybe that's why she's been hanging around everywhere. Do you think she could be taking notes for a case?"

"It's possible. If she's had access to the lodge and ski patrol office, I would assume that Kendall or whoever is in charge knows what she's doing and why she's there. She mentioned wanting to make Fitz pay when I talked to her earlier, so maybe there is a connection. We should let the Professor know."

Andy bobbed his head in agreement while he swallowed another bite. "My friends said they're going to tell the police everything. They want to clear Shawn ASAP."

"That's good."

His phone buzzed. "Shoot. I gotta run. Bethany is making dinner for me. She said I need some comfort food tonight."

"That's sweet, and she's right." I grabbed a to-go bag and filled it with cookies. "I'm sure she's baking, but spiced cookies are essential comfort food."

"Thanks, Jules." His voice was thick with emotion. "And thanks for everything. I know I kind of freaked out earlier. It's just that Shawn is such a good guy."

"Don't worry about it. I appreciate that you're concerned for your friend, and like I said on the mountain, I'll do whatever I can to help."

He took the bag and gave me a two-finger salute. "Thanks again. I'll see you soon."

"Say hi to Bethany," I called as I packed up some cookies to share with everyone at home and scooped the remaining dough into balls to chill overnight. One of the many things I learned during my years in culinary school and as a pastry chef for the *Amour of the Seas* was the value of pre-prep when filling pastry cases. Cookie dough could be prepped the night before, or even weeks before, and frozen. Then we would simply remove the dough balls from the walk-in tomorrow morning, and ta-da, the cookies would be ready to bake.

I thought about what Andy had learned. If January was hanging around all the time, what was the reason? And who was Ruth working for? There was a lot to uncover, but it could wait.

Baking and talking to Andy had put me in a much better headspace, and I wasn't about to ruin that.

Rosa and Sequoia assured me they didn't need extra help closing the bakeshop, so I took my chai cookies and bundled up for the walk home.

Baking had served its purpose. I felt calmer and more connected to my body. I still had no idea who had killed Fitz or why, but those questions could wait until tomorrow. Tonight I intended to curl up with our new extended family and not think about murder.

# Chapter Eleven

The next morning, I woke with a new resolve. We had scheduled a wine-tasting tour with Luis and Sophia later in the day. They were taking Ramiro and Marta shopping and then out to brunch. Carlos was checking in on the tasting room at Uva, so I decided to do some window shopping of my own in the plaza.

Many shops had post-holiday sales in effect, and I was hoping that I might find Thomas, Kerry, or the Professor at the police station. I also wanted to stop into Torte and see how Andy was faring and whether he had heard anything new about Shawn.

I strolled along Main Street. It looked like a scene from a Dickens novel, with snowy rooftops and glowing lights illuminating each storefront. New Year's Eve decorations were on display at London Station. Buckets of sparklers, champagne glasses, and party hats filled the front windows.

We had planned to return to Mount A for the New Year's Eve firework show, but with yesterday's turn of events, I wondered if it would be canceled.

I was about to pop into the store and pick up some noise

makers and glow sticks for Ramiro and Marta when I saw Shawn walking straight at me. He had his ski patrol jacket slung across one arm. His heavy ski boots thudded on the dry sidewalks. Had he come from the police station?

Maybe the Professor had kept him overnight.

"Shawn, how are you?" I asked as I met up with him.

He looked at me like he couldn't place who I was for a minute.

I started to reintroduce myself, but he rolled his shoulders and shook out his hands. "Jules, yeah, hi. Hey, sorry. I'm kind of in a daze."

"Were you at the police station?"

"Yeah, they had me locked up last night." He rubbed his eyes like he was trying to wake up. "How do you know that?"

The Professor must have had solid evidence connecting Shawn to the murder. He wouldn't have kept him overnight unless he had a good reason.

"The Professor is family, so I tend to hear things."

"Oh, right. Does everyone in town know that I was arrested?" He ran his hands through his shaggy hair. "It's a long story, but someone has to believe me."

"Do you want to talk about it? We can walk to Torte, and I can get you something warm to drink and eat."

"That would be cool." He followed me past London Station.

"Did the Professor explain why he detained you?" I asked as I fell into step with him.

"They had a witness come forward who claimed that they saw me messing with the dummy that killed Fitz."

That matched what I had heard.

"I didn't do it, though. I don't think they believe me

because a bunch of other people said that they saw me and Fitz get into it, but dude, I didn't kill him. Why would I? Because I don't like the guy? No. I don't like him. Yeah, we fought, but what's the big deal? It's a black eye. He deserved it. And he swung at me first."

This was not information I had heard. Shawn admitted that he and Fitz had fought.

"I take it you and Fitz weren't close, then?" I waved to the owner of the used bookstore, who was stacking books in the shop's front window to spell out *Happy New Year*.

"No, that's what I tried to explain to the cops." He paused and stared at his feet as we waited to cross Pioneer Street. The OSF welcome center windows had been covered in brown paper. Lance would do a reveal party in a few weeks to show off the posters and costumes for the new season.

The light changed for us. We stepped out into the street, and Shawn tied his jacket around his waist. "It's going to come out anyway, so I might as well tell you. Andy said you're cool, and your mom is married to the detective, so you probably know more about what's going on than anyone else. Do you think you can help me?"

"I can try."

His eyes darted in every direction like he was making sure we weren't being watched. Then, as we stepped into the street, he lowered his voice. "Look, I'll tell you the truth. Fitz was paying me on the side."

"Paying you for what?"

"He wanted to know how to access trails and runs that were out of bounds."

"Why? For his clients?"

Shawn shrugged. "I don't know. He didn't say. That was

part of our deal. I was supposed to keep it secret and not say a word. I wasn't going to blast that around. I could lose my job on ski patrol if it came out that I was showing Fitz off-limits areas, so I was fine with our arrangement."

We stopped talking as a group of shoppers passed by us.

"Do you think that's why Fitz was off trail the night you had to rescue him?"

"I have no clue what that guy was up to. I don't think it had anything to do with guiding. That wasn't a legit business, that's for sure. He was doing something else, but I have no idea what."

"Hero made it sound like Fitz was trying to steal his clientele," I said as we passed the pizza shop. I wondered if they piped out the delicious aromas of simmering tomato sauce and garlic dough.

"Fitz couldn't care less about snowshoeing tours. That's not what he was up to. I know that much without a doubt." He cinched his coat tighter around his waist.

"But you don't think he was trying to start a tour company?"

He let out a half laugh. "No way. Whatever that dude was up to, it wasn't quiet constellation tours of the winter sky. I should have asked him more. I knew what I was doing was wrong, but the money was good. He paid all cash under the table. Ski patrol is a lifestyle. I would never want to do anything else, but it doesn't pay much. I saw a chance to save for a bigger apartment, and I took it. Stupid. Dumb. Call me anything you want. I'm calling myself much worse."

"I'm not judging you, Shawn," I assured him, although internally I wasn't so sure that was true. "I'm trying to help.

I want to get to the bottom of the mystery of what Fitz was doing on the mountain. What exactly did he want you to show him?"

"That's what I don't get, which is what I told the police." He raised his voice and then realized he was speaking loudly. His tone quieted as the blue police station awnings came into view. "He only wanted to see trails on the west slopes. Nothing else. He was obsessed with getting out in the backcountry on that side of the mountain. I warned him that it was dangerous and that we were in avalanche territory, but he didn't care."

"Could there be a reason for that? Maybe he thought he could build a client base by offering tours on that side of the mountain."

"No, it's all private land. The forest service owns some of it, but most of it is owned by the Hankwitz family. So technically, it's trespassing to be in any of the areas Fitz was interested in."

Something didn't add up.

We made it to Torte. Andy's eyes practically bulged out of his head at the sight of his friend.

"Shawn, man, you're here. So good to see you." He abandoned the espresso machine and ran around the counter to give his friend a clap on the back. "This is great news. Did the police let you go?"

"For the moment. We'll see." Shawn sounded dazed. I wasn't sure if it was from lack of sleep, stress, or something else.

"Why don't you go find a seat at one of the window booths, and I'll get you a cup of coffee and a ham and cheese breakfast burrito," I suggested.

"Yes, I'll hook you up, man." Andy hugged Shawn

again before returning behind the bar. "I knew you would help him. You're the best, Jules."

"Don't get your hopes up. We're just talking. He was at the police station all night, so I'm trying to see what I can find out, and then I'll follow up with the Professor."

"Still, Jules, I appreciate it. A lot." He poured a splash of heavy cream into Shawn's coffee. "Tell him to come to see me before he leaves."

"Will do." I took two coffees and a burrito to the table.

Shawn's eyelids struggled to stay open. He slumped over the table on one arm. Was he about to pass out?

"Here. Hopefully this will help." I pushed the coffee toward him.

He looked at the mug as if I had offered him a steaming cup of arsenic.

I leaned across the table. "Shawn, are you good?" I knew that in times of severe emotional turbulence—like being the prime suspect in a murder investigation—shock could set in. Shawn's behavior made me wonder if he was on the edge of having a meltdown.

He dug his fingers into his jawline and made small circles. "I guess it's finally sinking in. I'm a suspect in a murder case. How did this happen?"

"That's what we're going to try and figure out," I assured him. "What did the Professor say when he let you go?"

Shawn's hands left red marks on his cheeks. "He told me not to go far. They offered me a lawyer last night because they might have more questions for me. I need to follow up on that today, I guess."

"You told them everything you've told me about Fitz's odd behavior and taking money from him, right?"

"Yeah. I don't know if they're going to tell my boss. If they do, I'm fired for sure." He returned to massaging his face again, ignoring his coffee and breakfast burrito. "It's my fault. I shouldn't have done it. I knew it was dangerous. The west slope is off-limits. It's a sketchy area even for a professional skier—lots of tree wells and untracked snow. I get the draw of an untouched powder field, but skiing out of bounds can turn deadly quickly. The minute you step out of the gates of a ski resort or away from the parking lot into the side country, you're taking a risk. I explained that to Fitz. You have to be prepared with the gear and a plan. A lot can go wrong in unpatrolled areas, but I needed the extra cash, and Fitz didn't care. The weird thing is he didn't seem to care about the skiing either."

I took a sip of Andy's winter roast to buy myself a minute to process what Shawn had said. "You obviously spent a lot of time with Fitz. Is there anything else you noticed? Was there anyone else he had much contact with?"

Shawn picked up his coffee but put it down again before drinking, like my question had triggered a memory. "Yeah, January."

"What do you know about her?"

"Not much. They hung out all the time." Shawn became more animated. He hit his fist on the table twice. "Why didn't I think of that earlier? I should have told the police about her."

"Do you think she was training the night of the snowshoe trip? Perhaps Fitz was showing her backcountry trails?"

"Not at all. She's a rider—a snow junkie. She was hanging around him constantly." He put his hand to his head. "You know what? I totally spaced this, but he complained to Kendall about it. I overheard it the other night. We were all at the lodge having pizza after closing. We do that sometimes. Kendall likes to feed us with any leftovers. It's a nice perk. Anyway, Fitz showed up and crashed our party. I tried to tune him out, but he was ranting about January."

"What exactly did he say about her?"

Shawn's energy was almost palpable; I could feel the buzz of excitement.

"He complained that January was lurking. He called her a leech, said he couldn't shake her. That she was constantly following him, day and night, whether he was skiing upper Tempest or in the backcountry. I don't know if it's true, but he was super frustrated that night, and according to him, he told her to stop stalking him or he would put an end to it himself." He tapped his fingers on the table like he was playing the drums.

"Stalking," I repeated. "Fitz claimed that January was stalking him. That is certainly a new twist."

Shawn guzzled his coffee. "Yeah, that's what he said. I can't believe I didn't remember that until now. I guess I was in shock that the police wanted to question me, but yeah, he kind of went off on her."

"And you're sure this was before he took her on the tour?"

"I don't remember the exact day, but it was probably three or four days before the snowshoe trip."

"Why would Fitz have taken January on the tour if he was accusing her of stalking him?" I asked out loud, not expecting Shawn to have the answer. "You helped with their rescue. Did you have a chance to talk to her that night?"

He shook his head and finished his coffee. "No. I was in emergency mode. It didn't even cross my mind. When you're out on a call like that, your adrenaline kicks in, and my only focus was getting them off the mountain before hypothermia set in. It was a rough extraction, too. The other woman took a bit of a fall and ended up with some minor bruises. I was tasked with providing first aid for her."

It sounded like a reasonable explanation. I knew that Shawn was Andy's friend, and I wanted to trust that he was telling me the truth, but I also didn't want to lock myself in on a theory that could prove not to be true. There were some glaring holes, like how Shawn had overlooked sharing such critical information that could potentially lessen suspicion of him with the police. And was January stalking Fitz? Or was that a convenient lie?

Shawn reached for the rest of his breakfast burrito. "Hey, thanks for listening. It helped to talk it through. I'm going to say hi to Andy and then tell the Professor this. How much do I owe you?"

"Nothing. It's on the house."

Whether everything Shawn had relayed was true or not remained to be seen, but January was suddenly on the top of my list. What was she doing on the slopes that night, and could Fitz have threatened her life? Was that why he had taken them off the trail? If so, that gave January a pretty clear motive for wanting to kill him—revenge.

# Chapter Twelve

I didn't stick around Torte long. I knew that the kitchen was my personal siren song that I wouldn't be able to refuse, so I said a quick good-bye to the team. I took the long way around the plaza past A Rose by Any Other Name, Puck's Pub, and the Green Goblin to give Shawn time to speak with the Professor.

Window boxes and storefronts were a dazzling show of radiance with New Year's Eve balloons and streamers. Snowflake banners and blue icicle lights hung from the antique lampposts. I wandered toward the entrance to Lithia Park and ruminated on the idea that January might have been stalking Fitz.

A slippery path took me through an archway of leafless trees toward the lower duck pond. In the summer months, the pond would be packed with families enjoying picnic lunches or artists sketching the tranquil lake. A peekaboo view of the Elizabethan jutted up behind Japanese maples. Two ducks cut a path through the waters, hoping I might have a slice of bread for them. Feeding the wildlife that inhabited the park was strictly forbidden, though.

"Sorry, friends, I don't have anything for you," I said

to the ducks as I circled the pond, my thoughts returning to January. If she *was* stalking Fitz, how had she managed to tag along with him? What had happened out on the trail? Could Hero and I have witnessed it wrong?

What if January had been the one to take them off course? Maybe she was furious that Fitz didn't reciprocate her feelings. Maybe she had wanted to harm him. Could that be why Fitz fired the flare gun?

But then again, there was Ruth. She had backed up January's story.

I sighed with confusion, retracing my steps back to the park's entrance.

Enough time had passed for Shawn to speak with the Professor, so I looped around the Lithia bubblers and crossed the street. The front of the quaint police station was decked out with New Year's signage and flyers about ride shares and free transportation for the night.

I peered in the front window just in time to see the Professor pulling on his olive parka with pumpkin orange lining and a furry hood.

"Juliet, how nice to see you." The Professor opened the door before I even had a chance to touch the handle. He was dressed in a pair of slacks. I recognized the cable-knit scarf around his neck as Mom's holiday handiwork.

"I have cookies." Not one to show up at the police station empty-handed, I'd brought him a bag of spiced chai cookies.

"Ah, what a gift." He patted his trim stomach. "As the Bard says, 'appetite, an universal wolf.'"

"Given the hours and stress of your job, I would be worried if you didn't have an appetite."

He moved out of the way so I could step inside. "Do come in. It's quite brisk out here."

"Were you just leaving?" I hesitated. "I'm not intruding, am I?"

"You could never intrude, my dear." He motioned to the back. "Shall we go have a chai cookie and chat in my office?"

"As long as you have time. I don't want to keep you from the investigation."

"Follow me." He led me to his office. It was toasty warm from the old wall-mounted radiators. "It's not up to Torte standards, but Thomas made a fresh pot of coffee not long ago. Can I pour you a cup?"

"No, thank you. I've already hit my caffeine intake for the day. I've just come from Torte."

"Do you mind if I drink without you?" He took off his parka and hung it on a wooden rack near the door. "These cookies are calling to be dipped in coffee."

"Of course not. I couldn't agree more. What's a cookie without something to dunk it in?"

He excused himself briefly while I took a seat in the plush chair next to his desk. The Professor's office didn't look like a traditional detective's office. Playbills and posters from a variety of OSF performances hung on the walls. His desk was tidy and organized, with framed pictures of Mom and me, a collection of fountain pens, and a box of tissues. I picked up a photo of the Professor in full Elizabethan garb from a reading he had done with the Midnight Club years ago. His hair had grayed a bit, and the lines around his eyes had deepened, but otherwise, the same kind, wise face stared back at me from the frame.

I felt so grateful to have the Professor in my life. He and Dad had been dear friends. They met and connected over their mutual love of the Bard. Not long after, they formed the Midnight Club, a group of Shakespeare and theater aficionados that gathered in the darkest hours of the night to perform sonnets and soliloquies and try out new plays. They had also bonded in the early years of the Professor's detective career. Dad had even helped with his first case, which I learned after discovering Dad's old journals documenting how he had sniffed around for information about an unsolved murder at the grand opening of the Cabaret Theater. Under the guise of catering intermission desserts, he had nearly cracked the case.

Knowing that I'd inherited my tendency to sleuth from Dad deepened my desire to see justice served. After he died, it took me years to realize the extent of the hole he left. The Professor had seamlessly filled some of the gap while at the same time making space for Dad's memory.

"Apologies." He cleared his throat, coming back into the room with a cup of coffee.

I returned the photo to his desk.

"Ah, the good old days when midnight was barely the start of an evening." He sat across from me. Your father and I used to go out for a beer and burger *after* our midnight antics. I can't fathom doing that now. My rocking chair and book are usually calling me by the dinner hour."

"Try working baker's hours."

"Fair point." He opened the bag like he was unwrapping a precious heirloom and helped himself to a cookie. "I suppose you didn't stop by to reminisce. Not that I would ever decline a little stroll down memory lane."

"I wish. I'm here with some news."

He shifted into detective mode, sitting straighter and reaching for a pen.

"I bumped into Shawn this morning."

"Yes, yes. He said as much."

"Did he stop by again?"

The Professor nodded and waited for me to continue while he dunked the edge of a spiced cookie into his coffee.

"And he told you about January?"

"In fact, I was on my way to Mount Ashland when you came in." His eyes drifted to a bamboo-framed clock with an original rendering of Queen Elizabeth I. "January and I are scheduled to have a chat this afternoon."

"So I am keeping you." I started to stand up.

"No, no. Sit." He raised his coffee cup. "This gives me a moment to allow what I've learned to percolate and enjoy a delectable Torte sweet."

"Well, maybe I don't need to tell you what Shawn said. I was worried he wasn't going to follow through and actually come back."

"I would appreciate your perspective." He paused to open his desk drawer and proceeded to remove a rosewood fountain pen set. "A gift of thanks for tracking down a missing cat. I must put it to use." He pulled the pen from a blue velvet box.

"It's so elegant."

He ran the stainless-steel nib over a scrap of paper to get the ink flowing. Then he opened his notebook and held the pen ready. "Anything you can add would be of interest. At this stage, there is no detail too small. No stone shall go unturned, as they say."

I told him everything about my conversation. Then,

when I was done, I said, "I can't figure out why January would have been on Fitz's tour if she was stalking him. I mean, I suppose it makes sense that she would have signed up for the tour. I'm stuck on why Fitz would have agreed to let her come."

"That is a question we must pursue. There are others. For instance, was there a second snowshoe tour, or could Fitz have had another reason for venturing on the trails with January and Ruth? I do not believe that everything is as it seems. It's like the mountain. The snowpack can hide obstacles beneath it, like rocks and small trees. It's a precarious balance, isn't it?"

Was he alluding to something buried on the mountain or merely speaking in metaphors?

"It would give January a motive," I continued. "I happened to be looking in that direction right before the accident, and she was near the ski patrol dummy."

The Professor flipped to the front of his notebook. "Yes, we've had that confirmed by several witnesses. Unfortunately, Shawn, Kendall, Hero, and Ruth were also nearby."

"I saw them all, too."

"Did you happen to see anything else? Take a moment. Sit with that question."

I followed his advice. Had I seen anything else? I hadn't been expecting to witness a murder, so it wasn't as if I had homed in on the group of suspects. I replayed the sequence of events. We were waiting for the final entry. I glanced up at the launch pad and saw the group above. No one stood out. Kendall had been balancing a tray of drinks. Everyone else seemed to be watching the competition.

Or were they?

A flash of a memory that I couldn't quite grasp surfaced. It was like trying to catch a bubble without it popping.

"Have you remembered something?" he gently nudged.

"Maybe. I can't bring it up, but yes, I feel like there might be something I'm missing."

"Don't perseverate on it," the Professor cautioned. "It will likely come if you give it time."

What was it? What had I seen?

The Professor closed his notebook and returned the fountain pen to his top drawer. "I keep hearing the Bard's famous phrase 'Lord, Lord, how this world is given to lying' repeat in my head."

"Is there anything I can do to help?"

He savored a bite of cookie before responding. "Continue to listen, observe. Share anything that you think could be of importance. I'm sure I sound like a broken record, but do remember that no detail is too small. It might also be helpful to share that with your staff. After taking each of their statements, I told them this, but a reminder certainly wouldn't do any harm. I often find witnesses reluctant to come forward with information that they might deem trivial when what they share could crack an investigation wide open."

I pushed my chair back and stood. "I should let you go. I'll make sure to remind my team and get back to you if anything else comes up."

"That would be much appreciated." He stood as well and walked around the desk. "I'll see you out."

We strolled to the front.

"Your mother and I are eager to have everyone for our annual New Year's Day buffet." He held the door for me after putting on his parka.

"We're looking forward to it. Can I bring anything?"

"Perhaps a dessert?"

"Count on it." I hugged him as we parted ways. Mom and the Professor had started a tradition the year before they got married of hosting a New Year's Day buffet. The festivities always started in the afternoon and ended up lasting well into the night. This year the event was serving as a send-off party for the Torreses. It was also a chance to cook a meal for the team at Torte. We tried to take advantage of the slow season for staff gatherings and parties.

I needed to check with Mom about what she was making and then coordinate a dessert. Since I still had time, I decided to pop back into Torte to see what we had stocked in the pantry.

As fate would have it, Mom was in the kitchen. "You are just who I wanted to see," I said, reaching to hug her.

"Well, I could get used to that kind of greeting." Mom measured sugar on a scale.

In a professional kitchen where even now, during the slow season, we were baking dozens upon dozens of pies, cakes, and tortes every day, we relied on scales for accurate measurements. Scooping cups of sugar and flour by hand would not only take twice as long, but it would potentially throw off the consistency of the bake. Precision is essential when it comes to producing quality pastries day after day. Not to mention that weighing dry ingredients means fewer dishes to wash, which is a win in any kitchen.

"I wondered what you plan to make for your New Year's Day feast." I peered over her shoulder. A growth spurt had sent me shooting over her in my early teens. I had inherited my height from Dad's side.

She cracked her knuckles before giving me a sheepish

smile. "Well, I must warn you that our feast has expanded a tad more. I may have invited a few other people."

"Okay, that's great. The more, the merrier. Who's coming?"

"The entire team, as usual. Along with Janet and my mahjong group. Some of Doug's Shakespeare friends and I mentioned to Lance and Arlo yesterday that I was making meatloaf, mashed potatoes, and homestyle green beans. Their faces were pitiful, like little hungry puppies. I couldn't *not* invite them."

I laughed. "Wise decision. You'd never hear the end of it otherwise."

"They're basically surrogate members of Torte anyway, and Lance is a partial owner in Uva." Mom winced as she lifted a heavy bag of flour.

"Let me do that." I swooped in.

She stretched her fingers. "Thanks, honey. This cold weather makes my arthritis flare up. It's nothing to worry about, though."

"I know, but let the young ones around here do the heavy lifting."

Years of working in the bakeshop had taken their toll on Mom's hearing and hands. In culinary school, we studied the environmental and occupational hazards of bakeries and restaurants. Sharp knives, boiling liquids, and open flames were some of the obvious culprits. Sound exposure from the constant whirl of industrial mixers, blenders, and espresso machines was at the top of the list. Rarer were issues like bakery-induced asthma from ongoing exposure to allergens in flours, yeast, nuts, and eggs, and skin conditions like dermatitis and eczema from constantly touching dough and excessive handwashing.

One requirement for every new staff member at Torte was to read an article from *Bakers Journal* titled "A Career to Die For" that outlined the risks and signs and symptoms to look out for. I tasked my team with being proactive, encouraging them to come to us should any ailments arise so that we could make adjustments to the kitchen and connect them with early interventions.

Knock on wood, everyone at the bakeshop was healthy, but that was also due to our regimented cleaning and safety protocols.

"You don't need to justify it to me," I said to Mom, refilling the flour canister and returning the bag to its spot in the walk-in. "I'm happy to include them, and I know Sophia and Luis will be, too. Do you have any requests for dessert?"

"Something that goes with meatloaf. I'm making my world-famous simmer sauce to go along with it," Mom suggested. "Marty is bringing bread, and Sterling is bringing a salad. I explained that we didn't need anything, but I would never refuse extra dishes. Bethany and Steph said they would put together some movie snacks. Lance won't show up without wine, and I bet Andy will have a new winter roast for us."

"So basically it's Torte 2.0—Torte light." I laughed. "It sounds like we need a classic American dessert to pair with your spread. What about a couple of cheesecakes? Maybe a traditional vanilla with a cherry compote and a chocolate option layered with caramel sauce?"

"You can't go wrong with cheesecake." Mom poured the sugar into one of the industrial mixers.

"I'll make them fresh tomorrow." I glanced around the kitchen. Trays of sourdough and rustic wheat rested on the cooling racks near the wood fireplace. Bethany and Steph had headphones in as they concentrated on intricate design work. "I'm not staying. We're taking Luis and Sophia wine tasting in a little while. I thought I would swing by and make sure everything was okay since I was doing some shopping on the plaza."

"Shopping?" Mom's eyes crinkled.

"Does shopping for information count?" I confessed.

"Were you at the station?" She cracked eggs into a bowl and then added them to her sugar mixture. That was another tip I always imparted to new staff—never crack an egg directly into a batter or dough. That way, if you happen to get a bad egg, it won't ruin an entire batch. Breaking eggs in a separate bowl also makes it much easier to retrieve any pesky eggshells.

"Yeah, I just came from there."

"Did Doug already leave for the mountain?"

"I think so. I caught him on his way out. Why?"

She pointed upstairs. "We have a visitor who just showed up in the dining room, but I was under the impression Doug intended to have a conversation with her at the mountain. I'm positive she was supposed to be at the lodge."

"January?"

Mom pressed her lips together and nodded.

January had ditched her meeting with Professor. That could mean she was guilty and trying to avoid being questioned by him, or it could mean that she was flaky and forgot they were supposed to connect. There was one way to find out—go upstairs and talk to her myself.

# Chapter Thirteen

I went upstairs and searched for January. I didn't spot her at first because she was seated at a two-person table with a shabby beanie pulled over her eyes and her face buried in a tattered paperback that looked as if it had spent some time in a hot bath. I filled a coffee carafe with a fresh roast and went over to her under the pretense of refilling her cup.

"Can I top you off?"

She didn't reply.

I leaned closer. "Would you like more coffee?"

Still no response.

Was she asleep?

I tapped her shoulder, which caused her to nearly fall off her chair. "Sorry, I didn't mean to startle you. I wondered if you wanted a refresher."

She tugged an AirPod from her ear. "Huh?"

"Coffee?" I held the carafe over her cup.

"Yeah, sure. Thanks." She took her headphones out and put them in a case. Then she yanked the beanie off her head.

"Is everything okay?" Her expensive headphones

seemed out of place, given her secondhand ski gear and the stories I'd heard about her trying to pick up gigs to cover the cost of a lift ticket. Not that I was judging.

She reached for her coffee. "Do you want the truth? Because you probably won't like it. Nothing is okay. Nothing is ever going to be okay again."

Was she referring to Fitz? Her wistful tone and blood-shot eyes made me wonder if there was truth to the rumors that she had been stalking him. She sounded like someone who was grieving. I took it upon myself to sit across from her. "Is there anything I can do?"

January wadded her beanie into a ball and played with her hair, tying it up into a ponytail and then releasing it again. "I'm not supposed to be here right now. I'm supposed to be up on Mount A."

"Are you having transportation issues? I can show you where the ski bus picks you up. It's right over there." I pointed out the window toward the Merry Windsor hotel. I doubted that January needed a ride, but I figured I had a better chance of her trusting me if I kept our conversation light to start.

"No, I have a car." She let her hair fall again. "It's the police. I'm supposed to be meeting with the detective right now, but I can't do it." She took off her upcycled ski jacket and hung it on the back of the booth.

"Why?" I couldn't believe she was opening up without any prompting. I barely knew her. It was great from my vantage point that she was being so forthcoming, but it also made me wary. Why would she confess everything to a stranger with a pot of coffee?

"I know that if I talk to him, he's going to arrest me. They think I did it."

The Professor hadn't mentioned anything about making an arrest.

"You see, there's more about me than anyone knows, and I'm afraid that when it comes out, everyone is going to be convinced that I killed Fitz. I get it. It looks like I have a motive on paper, but I didn't do it."

"What motive?"

She yanked a strand of hair so hard that I thought she was going to pull it out.

"Listen, you don't need to tell me if you don't feel comfortable, but I'm here, and I'll do what I can to help you."

January took a sip of coffee and then fanned her mouth. "That's hot. That's my karma, burning my tongue." She waved a hand over her face. "Look at me. I'm a hot mess. A hot, hot mess."

"I don't know if it will help, but sometimes even taking a deep breath can center me." I modeled the breathing technique for her.

She responded by sucking air through her nose like a shop vac. "I lied. That's the problem. I lied, and now karma is catching up with me."

"Do you mind me asking what you lied about?"

"My job. What I do. Everything. That's why I know that if the police find out, which I'm sure they probably already have, I'm in big trouble. That's their job, right? They have access to all of my personal information." She didn't seem overly concerned that the few tables around us might overhear our conversation.

"So you and Fitz knew each other in a professional capacity?" I prompted. Was that why Shawn thought January was stalking Fitz? Maybe they were secret business partners. That also opened up the possibility that January could have killed Fitz to get him out of the picture.

Different scenarios flooded my mind. What if Ruth had witnessed January cutting the wire tether that sent the dummy downhill early and was trying to scapegoat Shawn instead? Or what if Ruth had overheard a conversation between January and Fitz that night? And did Fitz have a death wish? He seemed cavalier about venturing into dangerous territorties.

"No, not exactly." As she inhaled, she threw her head backward. Then she arched her back and stared at me with her golden-hazel eyes. "I'm an environmental activist. I work for the UEP." She fumbled through her fringed purse to show me a badge with her picture and the United Earth Protest group logo. "I'm not a ski bum. I'm here undercover."

"Undercover? You're working with the police?" If that was the case, why would she be worried that the Professor would arrest her?

January shoved her UEP badge in my face. "No, I work for the UEP. We're here to stop development on the mountain."

I was familiar with the climate justice group. They had made headlines for staging sit-ins in the forest and dismantling tractors and equipment to stop old-growth trees from being felled. Some might have viewed their tactics as radical, but with the rapidly changing climate, widespread pollution, and shrinking biodiversity, I understood the urgency behind their mission.

January rested her badge on the table. "I've been working undercover, posing as a seasonal skier, hanging around the mountain, trying to get as much information on what's going on with deforestation as I can for the UEP."

Now I was perplexed. What connection did that have to Fitz's murder?

I took a slow breath. Mainly to try to reoxygenate my brain cells. Nothing January was saying made sense. "Is there logging happening on Mount A?" Oregon had a long history of logging forested lands. Lance's family fortune had been amassed from the timber industry back in the 1970s and '80s, much to his dismay. But as far as I knew, the deciduous forests surrounding the ski park were protected lands. There hadn't been evidence of vast swaths of hillsides being clear-cut. If anything, the current threat to our forests in the last decade had been megafires. Wildfires had burned through acres upon acres of the Siskiyou Mountain range, leaving behind charred, barren landscapes.

Sustainability and preserving the state's vast wildlands was an issue near and dear to my heart and one that I had discussed at length with Lance. He believed that we needed to return forest management to indigenous women who historically had overseen prescribed burns, and find more harmonious ways to thin overly dense portions of the forest. Women had traditionally been responsible for maintaining village areas with fire, and recently there had been a move toward training indigenous women fire brigades.

"What is UEP doing?" I asked January.

"It's better if I don't say. The planet is at a crossroads, and marching and nonviolent protests aren't doing enough. If we don't curb this senseless destruction of natural lands and our dependence on fossil fuels, there's going to be nothing left. We're heading toward a mass extinction event, and no one seems bothered by it." She gestured with her hands as she spoke.

"I agree," I said with sincerity. "I'm just unsure how this fits in with what happened to Fitz."

"Me either. That's what I've been trying to get to the bottom of. I've been pulling all-nighters, following him and some other people I won't name around the lodge and ski park." She laced her fingers together. "It sucks that he's dead. I thought I was finally getting close and that maybe I'd have actual evidence to bring to my boss so that we could then formulate a plan to put a stop to him."

I didn't like the sound of "put a stop to him."

"Now the police are going to think I'm a violent anarchist and arrest me for a murder I didn't commit. I think I should get out of town, like, right now. I can go off the grid. I've done it before. I can do it again." She patted the side of her cheek like she was trying to talk herself into the idea. "They won't be able to find me, so what can they do? They can't arrest me if I'm off the grid. It would take years for them to catch up with me. I know these forests better than anyone."

I could tell she was seriously considering the idea by the way her gaze drifted from the espresso bar to the plaza, like she was calculating how long it would take her to disappear.

"That's not a good idea. You need to be honest with the Professor, especially if you're innocent."

"I *am* innocent. That's my point. They're not going to believe me. No one is going to believe me, and I'm going to end up in jail for a crime I didn't commit." She picked up her coffee and then put it down again without taking a drink.

"But running will make it worse," I said carefully. "Innocent people don't tend to flee crime scenes or investigations." I tried to reason with her, but I wasn't sure there was any hope.

"You don't understand," she wailed. "I have a record. I did some jail time. Don't get me wrong. I don't have any regrets about it. We have to raise awareness and take action on the climate now. We don't have time to wait. We're already on the brink of complete civilization collapse. The time for timid appeals to those in power is gone. I feel solid about my stance, but my previous record is not going to look good to the police. They must already know about it by now, which is why I'm sure they wanted to meet me on the mountain. They're going to arrest me."

"Do you mind me asking why you spent time in jail?"

She piled her hair on top of her head. "It was an oil rig protest. I chained myself to the boat for five days. Finally, the oil company had us forcibly removed, and when I fought back—just protecting myself—I accidentally hit one of the guys in the face, and he fell overboard and ended up in the hospital. I wasn't inciting violence. They were."

Listening to January's story felt like making puff pastry dough—there were so many layers. I couldn't decide whether I believed her or not.

"I didn't kill him. He was up to something. That much I know, but I didn't kill him. That's what I was talking to Ruth about. She was the only other person with us that night. I hoped she might come to my defense and back up my story, but she's worthless."

I wanted to keep her talking not only to see what else

she might reveal but also because the longer she spent with me at Torte, the less opportunity she had to go "off the grid," in her words. "How could Ruth back up your story?"

"She saw how everything went down. Fitz led us off-trail on purpose. I know he was trying to get rid of me. He must have figured out who I was working for. He was trying to kill me. I am one hundred percent positive that he wanted me dead, and if it hadn't been for your group seeing us, I might be."

# Chapter Fourteen

I bought myself a minute to process everything January had said by going to refill the coffee carafe. She was convinced that Fitz had intentionally led them off the trail in an attempt to silence her. Didn't that give her more reason to kill him?

Everything kept circling back to revenge.

Was January sincere, or did she have the ultimate reason to want Fitz dead?

I did a quick spin around the dining room with a fresh pot of coffee while making sure to keep an eye on her. I didn't want her to bolt. Once I had finished refilling drinks, I shot a quick text to the Professor to let him know January was at the bakeshop.

Hopefully, I could keep her here until he arrived. I felt slightly guilty for turning her over, but the Professor was investigating a murder, and I wasn't going to take any chances.

"We have a special quiche this morning. Can I get you a slice?" I asked January.

She hesitated.

"It's on the house."

"Uh, okay. Sure. I guess some food might help."

I went downstairs to get her a piece of Sterling's bacon, cheddar quiche, and an apple tartlet. When I returned to the table, Ruth had taken my seat.

"Good morning." I greeted her with a smile as I handed January her breakfast. "Can I get you anything?"

"Coffee—black—now." She massaged her temples and barely acknowledged me. The deep purple bruise she'd suffered during their snowshoe rescue was flecked with spots of green, and her eyes were red and puffy like she hadn't slept in days.

I gave her a bit of a pass for her dismissive attitude because it looked like she might be in pain. Normally I would have pushed back. Mom and I had implemented a strict policy of kindness at Torte. We treated everyone who came through our front doors like family. The bakeshop was a welcoming and safe space, and we expected that our guests would treat us the same way in return. Unfortunately, working in the service industry meant that on rare occasions, we would have customers who felt entitled to treat my team disrespectfully. I made sure that everyone on my staff felt empowered to hold firm yet kind boundaries when it came to rude customers.

In this case, I made an exception. I wanted to hear Ruth's perspective on what had happened on the trail with Fitz, so I brought her a coffee.

She managed to mutter thanks and clutched the coffee cup tight as I squeezed into the booth next to her.

"Are you feeling okay?"

Ruth popped her jaw and twisted her neck from side to side. "I feel worse today. I think I might have a concussion from the fall the other night."

"Have you seen a doctor?"

"No." She cracked her neck again and took a slow sip of coffee.

January stabbed her quiche with her fork. "You probably should. You hit that rock hard. Fitz never should have let you be out in front. I don't know what he was thinking."

"You fell?" I hadn't heard that Ruth had taken a fall, only that she'd gotten a bit bruised in the rescue effort.

January answered for her. "I don't know why Fitz told you that ledge was safe. It's a good thing your ski caught. Otherwise it could have been a lot worse." She flinched at the memory. "I thought you were going to fall all the way down the canyon."

"That sounds terrifying," I said to Ruth.

Her hand went to the base of her neck. "Fitz was worthless. Ski patrol gets the credit for our rescue. I'm sore, but at least I'm alive."

"Fair point," I agreed. "Speaking of that night, can I ask why you both were out with Fitz?"

January choked on her quiche. She pounded her chest with one hand. "Sorry, I swallowed wrong."

Ruth closed her eyes as she attempted to stretch her neck. "I already told you; I was doing an assessment for work."

"An assessment of what?" I asked.

January's phone buzzed. She glanced at the screen, dropped her fork, and grabbed her things. "Sorry, I've got to go. Thanks for the coffee." She left half of her quiche untouched and raced out the front door.

What had changed so drastically? I'd thought January had calmed down a bit and was actually going to stay put until the Professor arrived. Was she worried about Ruth learning that she was working for the UEP? Or was I missing something?

Ruth watched her go. "She's so skittish."

"How so?"

"She was like that the night of the snowshoe. Every little sound made her jumpy." She squinted as she spoke, as if the lighting was hurting her eyes.

I wondered if she was trying to change the subject. She hadn't answered my question about her assessment. "Is that why you went? Were you including information about the tours in your report?" I had about a dozen other questions for her, like who she was working for and why she needed to assess the entire ski park, but I thought it was best to start slow.

"Fitz had nothing to do with my work. I was supposed to join Hero's tour to make notes on the condition of the rim trail and Grouse Gap Shelter at night. My report had to be extensive. That's why I've been allowed unlimited access to the ski park and lodge. But I got caught up in a conversation with Kendall and missed the start. She's the one who suggested I tag along with January and Fitz. It's not a smart idea to go out alone in the dark—well, or even daylight, for that matter. Talk about a mistake. Fitz had no idea what he was doing. January told him we simply needed to follow the rim trail, but he wouldn't listen. He kept taking us farther and farther off the main trail. That's when I fell." She stopped and massaged her neck. "It could have been worse. Like January said, my ski caught between two boulders. If it hadn't, I might have ended up at the bottom of the ravine."

"Wow, I had no idea."

"Thankfully, ski patrol was able to get to us." She lifted the sleeve of her fleece. "They bruised me up too, but only because they had to in order to pull me out."

"You know the hospital takes walk-ins. It's only a few blocks away." I pointed in that direction. "It's probably a good idea to have someone look at your injuries."

She started to say something but stopped herself. "It's fine. Ski patrol gave me things to watch out for. I'm just sore."

I changed the topic. "Did you notice anything odd about January that night?"

"Odd how?"

"Were she and Fitz doing the tour together? Do you know why January was with him?"

Ruth tilted her head like she was mentally weighing my question. "Now that you mention it, no. It never came up."

"Did you get the impression that January was stalking him?"

"Stalking?" Ruth sounded incredulous. "Not in the slightest. Watching him like a hawk, yes, but stalking him, no. If anything, she was as disgusted by his behavior as I was. I can't fathom why Kendall suggested I tag along. They were in a huge screaming match earlier in the day."

"Fitz and Kendall?" I was so glad that Ruth had stopped in. This was another nugget of information that I had yet to hear anywhere else.

Ruth made a face and then winced in pain, massaging the side of her neck with her uninjured hand. "It was ugly. If you were within a hundred-yard radius of the lodge that afternoon—inside or out—you would have heard them. Kendall went ballistic on him. She threatened to kick him out of the lodge permanently, which is why I'm just now realizing how odd it was that she recommended Fitz as a guide to take me to the warming hut."

The ski bus rumbled past the front window. Ruth shot up. "That's my ride. I have to go. I need to get up to the lodge to . . ." She paused and searched for the right word. "Well, let's just say I have a few last things to wrap up, so I should get to it."

Once she was well out of earshot, I called the Professor. I wasn't taking any chances. I wanted to relay what I had learned while it was still fresh and make sure he knew that January was talking about going off the grid.

His phone went straight to voicemail. I left him another message to inform him that January was gone. The question was how far she could get between now and whenever the Professor showed up. Then I took a minute to sit alone and collect my thoughts.

My morning had taken a turn for the worse. I had thought I was getting somewhere with January, but now I was more confused than I had been from the beginning of our conversation. I cleaned up the table and tried to piece together the essential parts of what I had learned.

She wasn't simply someone looking for a snowy moonlight adventure. She was working covertly for an environmental protection group, trying to get info on Fitz. Even as I considered it, this sounded outlandish. Maybe it was intentionally ridiculous or a cover for the truth.

There was another possibility, which was that Shawn's theory was correct. Perhaps January had a crush on Fitz and had been stalking him. Maybe that night, he had refused her once and for all, which had set her off. If he had refused or perhaps even threatened to go to the authorities and take out a restraining order, that could explain her being involved in his death.

If she was in love with him and he had turned her down, it wasn't out of the realm of possibility that she might have snapped and cut the wires in a moment of passionate rage. She could have wanted to scare him or hurt him. Maybe she saw him on the bottom of the slope alone and seized the opportunity. On the other hand, it might have been that she never meant to kill him.

But Ruth had basically blown up that theory. I needed to learn why Kendall and Fitz had fought and why Kendall had sent Ruth out onto a dark, cold mountain with him.

I had learned one other bit of new information, which was that Ruth had no affiliation with Fitz. She said she needed to include the Grouse Gap Shelter in her assessment, but I still didn't understand her role or who she worked for. She hadn't exactly been forthcoming about why she was on the mountain.

Had she been intentionally evasive? She had managed to answer some of my questions and avoid others. Was that just because she was stiff and sore from her injuries, or could she be hiding something?

I sighed as I took the dishes downstairs.

One thing that I needed to find out was whether January was telling the truth about her employment. If I could confirm that she was working undercover for the UEP, that would give me direction. The question was how. I couldn't exactly call the UEP and ask.

Mom was frosting champagne and cherry cupcakes with white chocolate buttercream. "You look like you could use something sweet. Cupcake?"

The celebratory New Year's Eve flavors were a favorite. "I wouldn't turn down a cupcake."

I took the dishes to the sink, washed my hands, and pulled up a bar stool near the island.

"Any news?"

"I don't know. I'm more confused than ever." I removed the paper wrapper and bit into the tender cupcake. The subtle champagne flavor with a bright, cherry pie center and rich white chocolate buttercream was a winning combo in my book. "January just took off in a hurry shortly after Ruth showed up. I was trying to keep her here until the Professor arrived, but now I have no idea where she went. She was talking about going off the grid to try and avoid being arrested."

"Off the grid?" Mom used a flat spatula to smooth the top of the buttercream and then placed a sugar-dusted cherry on top.

I filled her in on our conversation. "Do you know anything about the UEP?"

"No, but I'm sure Doug is looking into every angle. She's right that he will be aware of any prior arrests, and to your point, it does seem like an elaborate story to fabricate if the truth is that she had a crush on Fitz."

I couldn't answer with my mouth full of the light sponge cake.

"Doug texted me a while ago that he's returning to town, so I'm confident that he and Thomas and Kerry will be able to track her down and determine her connection with UEP. Going off the grid isn't as easy as it sounds in this day and age. Even here in Ashland, there are cameras throughout the plaza. I don't think she'll be able to get far, and running certainly won't help her cause."

"I wonder if she was worried that Ruth would find out that she's working for the UEP. It seems weird that she took off right as I asked them about their snowshoe trip with Fitz, doesn't it?"

"Yes, I agree." Mom scooped more fluffy buttercream into the piping bag. "But, honey, aren't you supposed be on vacation? I know you're taking Sophia and Luis on a wine-tasting tour later. This isn't your responsibility."

I started to protest.

"Hear me out." She gave me her best mom look as she deftly swirled frosting on a cupcake. "I know how attached you get to wanting to solve a puzzle like this, and I know you feel connected to wanting to make some sense of this tragedy, but maybe the best thing you can do is take a break. Enjoy your family time and sip some wine, knowing that Doug is doing everything possible to make an arrest. The investigation is in his skillful hands."

"You're right." I polished off my cupcake, having made sure to reserve enough frosting for my final bite. Bethany had created an informal poll in the bakeshop on the best way to eat a cupcake, and I had been shocked to learn that most people broke the small cakes in half, eating the bottom first and saving the frosting for last. I preferred a balanced cake-to-frosting ratio in every bite.

It was rare for Mom to be so direct. She tended to be an active listener who asked open-ended questions geared toward self-reflection.

"I don't know that there is a right or wrong in this situation, but I can see the stress on your face." She paused decorating the last round of cupcakes and met my eyes.

Instinctively I put my hand to my cheek.

"You look fine, honey. I'm only cautioning that this is

already a stressful time, post-holidays, having the Torres family visit, and now this. Try to enjoy yourself, and knowing you, you'll probably have a lightbulb revelation when you're not forcing your brain to make connections that might not exist yet."

"That's good advice."

"I can't take credit for it. Doug always says that his breakthrough moments happen almost without fail when he's not focusing his full attention on a case." Her dimples creased as she offered me a smile.

"Noted." It was what I needed to hear at the moment. If I didn't leave things alone and give it a break, I would spend the rest of the day, and likely the entire wine-tasting trip, perseverating on Fitz's murder.

I tossed my cupcake wrapper in the garbage and kissed her on the top of her head. "Thanks for that. I'm taking your advice and finishing my shopping before enjoying a leisurely afternoon and evening at some of our beautiful Rogue Valley tasting rooms."

"I'm glad to hear it. Tell Sophia and Luis hi from me, and we'll see you all at the party tomorrow."

"Perfect," I said good-bye to the rest of the team and left the bakeshop before I had a chance to change my mind and get sucked in further. I was glad that Mom felt comfortable giving me a nudge. It was exactly what I needed.

As I crossed the street and headed past the Lithia bubblers, I bumped into Kendall. She had a stack of paperwork tucked under one arm. She barely registered me as our shoulders connected.

"Ouch." She scowled and then looked up. "Oh, oh, Jules, sorry I didn't see you there."

"You look like you're in a hurry."

"I am. I have to get to the police station right away."

"Why?"

"I have information about Fitz and what was going on at the mountain that the police need to hear immediately." She clutched the papers tighter.

So much for my resolve. It was like the universe was testing me. What did Kendall know? And was she about to reveal who had killed him?

# Chapter Fifteen

"The Professor is on his way down from the mountain," I said to Kendall.

She rolled her papers into a long tube. "Do you have any idea when he'll get here?"

"I would think it should be soon. Is it an emergency? We can try to get ahold of Thomas or Kerry." I glanced around the plaza in hopes that one of them might be on foot patrol.

"No, it has to be Doug. I need to speak with Doug." She unrolled the papers in her hands and then rolled them into a tight cylinder again. "I have some info about the lodge that he needs to hear as soon as possible. It really can't wait."

I could tell from her piercing gaze that she wouldn't speak with anyone other than the Professor. "I thought he was up at the lodge."

"Not now." She tapped her Mount Ashland Lodge flannel. "I was just there and didn't see him. No one has seen him. That's why I came into town."

"Maybe you passed each other on the way here," I suggested.

She chomped on the inside of her cheek. "I wonder where he is. I need to speak with him as soon as possible—it's a matter of serious urgency."

I wasn't sure what to say about the situation with January. His focus might be on finding her when he got back into town. "Are you sure you can't speak with Thomas or Kerry? They're working on the investigation with him. You know Thomas. He'll keep whatever you need to tell the police quiet."

"Yeah, maybe." She didn't sound convinced.

I reached for my cell. "Why don't we call and at least see if he's nearby?"

Kendall tapped the roll of paperwork on her palm as if she was mulling it over. "Yeah, okay. I guess that's better than doing nothing."

Thomas answered right away. "Jules, what's going on? Do you have some jelly-filled donuts for me?"

It was our running joke. We had made a tiered donut cake for their wedding, and whenever our brioche donuts made the rotation, I always brought a box to the police station for Kerry. Whether or not she shared with any of her coworkers was entirely up to her.

"I'm in the plaza with Kendall. Are you or Kerry around?"

"Kerry's in Medford. I'm not far. What's going on?" His tone shifted.

"Let me hand the phone to Kendall." I handed her my cell and stepped closer to the bubblers so she could speak privately with him. The natural sulfur waters were shut off for the winter, but the pungent aroma lingered in the porcelain basin.

Kendall's conversation with Thomas didn't last more

than a couple of minutes. She hurried over to me and gave me back my phone. "Thanks for getting me in touch with him. I'm heading to meet him at the station now."

She didn't offer more, and I didn't push it. I wanted to ask her about January and Ruth, but the way she was moving her feet from side to side indicated that she wasn't going to hang around for long.

"You know the coffee is always brewing at Torte, and I'm here if you ever need a listening ear or a warm muffin."

She forced a small smile. "I doubt that there's anything that can be done at this point. I think it's too late, but we'll see what Thomas has to say. I've got to get over there now." With that, she hunched her shoulders and power-walked past the information kiosk. She barely bothered to check for traffic when she ran across the street and vanished inside the police station.

What did she mean by that? There was nothing that could be done. About Fitz? His killer?

I could see that Kendall was visibly shaken. She didn't want to share whatever she knew with anyone other than the Professor. Was she worried about her personal safety? Could she be in danger? Maybe she had witnessed something she shouldn't have, or perhaps she had overheard a conversation with the killer.

I was glad that she was going to Thomas for help. If she was in harm's way, he would protect her. With that thought in mind, I crossed the street and came face-to-face with Richard Lord.

"If it isn't Ashland's resident snoop. What are you doing lurking around my property?" he snarled as he tipped his black plastic bowler hat to me. I was surprised to see him wearing an ill-fitted suit and tie. Richard was notorious for his outrageous golf outfits.

Maybe he was getting in the New Year's Eve spirit early. A gold vinyl HAPPY NEW YEAR banner hung above the hotel front porch announcing a midnight champagne toast. Although in classic Merry Windsor fashion, that banner had last year's date crossed out and this year's written over it in black Sharpie.

The Merry Windsor Hotel was the last place on the planet where I would choose to lurk. The building's aging façade looked as if it might crumble into pieces at any minute. Richard had tried to hide the cracks in the foundation and chipped paint on the fake timber siding with cheap plastic banners announcing Shakespeare-themed brunches and Sunday *family* dinners.

*Hmmm, I wonder where he got that idea?*

Richard accused me of copying him and spying on him and his staff at every turn. The opposite was true. He had a penchant for lingering in front of the bakeshop to see what we were featuring in our front window display and then doing his own (albeit lame) version of the same display. He had blatantly ripped off our concept for Scoops, our pop-up summer ice cream shop, and offered whatever was on Torte's menu at the Merry Windsor.

For years he had been complaining about our popular Sunday Suppers, where we picked a theme, pushed tables together in the dining room, and served a three-course meal family-style once a month.

The Merry Windsor had attempted a variety of iterations of the concept, but none had stuck. Maybe Richard thought a neon blue banner touting his Sunday family dinner would pull guests in. He wouldn't be able to fool locals. Everyone in town knew that Richard's concept of fresh and handcrafted involved microwaving frozen lasagna and slathering copious amounts of cheap butter on stale bread.

"Last time I checked, the sidewalk is a public space," I said to Richard.

He shook a finger that was so swollen it looked like a sausage in my face. "Don't be a smart aleck with me, young lady."

"I'm not. I'm stating the obvious." I studied him for a minute, feeling an unfamiliar concern for his well-being. Richard's cheeks were red and puffy, which wasn't anything unusual except that they were taut and weirdly shiny, as if he had had a botched plastic surgery job. "Richard, are you feeling all right?"

I couldn't say what I was thinking, which was that his face looked like an overripe tomato about to burst.

"How dare you insult me, Capshaw." His puffy lips made me wonder if he'd been stung by a bee, but the bees weren't active in this winter weather.

"Richard, I'm serious." I stepped closer and made sure my tone was gentle. Was it possible he could be having a heart issue?

"I'm fine. Leave it alone, Capshaw, and get off my property," he growled. "I'll call the cops if you keep loitering."

I held out my arms in a show of surrender. "Look, I'm walking up the street, but seriously, Richard, take care of yourself."

He muttered something under his breath that I couldn't make out.

Richard Lord was not my favorite person, but I didn't wish him ill, not literally, anyway. If the Merry Windsor kitchens got a bad review, that was one thing, but his health was another.

I decided to run over to A Rose by Any Other Name and give Janet a heads-up. She was a neutral party when it came to Richard. The same journals that led to my discovery of Dad's early sleuthing days also gave me an understanding of why Richard always seemed to have it out for Mom and me. He had been in love with her in the early years when my parents first opened the bakeshop. She had refused his advances, and he had held a grudge ever since.

Janet, who owned the flower shop, had been best friends with Mom since Thomas and I were in preschool. She had managed to act as a referee and buffer between Mom and Richard over the years. Richard wasn't prone to spending money on anyone but himself, but he did order a weekly bouquet for the Merry Windsor's lobby from A Rose by Any Other Name, with the cheapest flowers, of course. Janet joked that the only reason she kept carnations in stock was for Richard. But he also tried to stay in her good graces because of Thomas. He tiptoed on the edge of legality when it came to overworking and underpaying his staff, ignoring building codes in the plaza, and pretty much everything else. Although they both saw through his act, he was smart enough to behave in front of law enforcement.

The flower shop was aglow with New Year's Eve arrangements. White lilies, roses, and hydrangeas were twisted together with gold ribbon and winter greenery to form an archway around the front door. The window boxes were filled with magnolia leaves, pinecones, birch branches, and gold and silver balls. Janet was visible through the frosty windows.

I waved as the doorbell jingled.

"Juliet, how nice to see you." She set her shears on the concrete workstation. Bundles of wire framing for wreaths and garlands sat at the counter's edge.

"The shop looks so festive." I noted the balls of twinkle lights hanging from the ceiling and the romantic bunches of blushing pink roses in the case.

"Thanks. I always love to give it a refresher for the new year. Not that I have anything against red and green, but by the end of December, I'm ready for something new." She reached for an order form. "Speaking of that, what would you like for your January bouquets?"

We ordered weekly flowers from A Rose by Any Other Name for the tables, booths, espresso bar, and pastry case at Torte.

"Oooh, what about those pink roses?" I motioned to a bucket next to Janet's workstation, filled with roses so pale they reminded me of ballet slippers. "Those are so sweet."

"Those just came in, and I've been so eager to work with them." She took a quick note. "Is that why you're here?"

"No, actually, I'm worried about Richard." I glanced across the plaza toward the Merry Windsor.

"Oh no, what has he done now?" Janet snipped a six-inch piece of wire.

"Nothing. I'm worried about his health." I told her about his swollen face and breathlessness.

"He hasn't been in good health for years, and his stress level must be off the charts," Janet said with concern. "I'll finish this order and wander over there to check in with him. Thanks for letting me know."

"I tried to ask him if he was okay, but you know how he is with me."

Janet snipped thorns from the rose stems and wrapped them with the cut wire. "He's his own worst enemy."

"I feel better knowing that you're going to check on him. I would hate for anything to happen to him, especially given everything over the past few days."

"Thomas is upset too, understandably," Janet added the roses to a fluted ceramic vase. Then she walked to the other side of the workstation and gathered a bunch of white birch branches.

"Did you hear about the Hankwitz family?"

"You mean Kendall?"

"Yes, apparently the lodge is in financial trouble. She might have to close it before the season even really starts." She tucked the woody branches into the bouquet that was coming together before my eyes. Watching Janet create artistic arrangements was a sensory experience between the colors, textures, and floral aromas.

"No, I hadn't heard that," I told her honestly, although I wondered if that was why Kendall had insisted on wanting to speak with the Professor.

"Can you imagine winter in Ashland without skiing on Mount A? Closing the lodge would absolutely devastate the Rogue Valley."

"I can't imagine." Losing the lodge would have far-reaching impacts on the local business community, winter tourism, and outdoor adventure lovers.

"It's been such a struggle with the dwindling snowpack and late-season openings. I feel terrible for Kendall and her family. It has to be a very last resort to even consider closing now. It must mean that things are in bad shape." Janet turned the vase to study her design from every angle before adding more greenery.

"I wonder if there's anything we can do to help."

"Don't worry. I'll call your mom later, and we'll put our heads together. We've been through hard times before. If I know one thing about Ashland, it's that this community shows up to support friends in need."

"Very true."

We said our good-byes. Janet promised to swing by the Merry Windsor and keep me in the loop about plans to help save the lodge.

I headed home. It was almost time for our wine-tasting trip, but I couldn't stop thinking about Kendall and the lodge. Could her financial issues have any connection to Fitz's murder?

# Chapter Sixteen

I tried to take Mom's advice to heart as we piled into the car with Carlos, Luis, and Sophia. The sun accompanied us on our drive along the winding roads through wine country. Vineyards dormant for the winter dotted the hillsides. Grizzly Peak's snow-capped ridgeline glinted with another layer of fresh snow that had fallen overnight. I had arranged for three stops on our wine tour, each with its own unique slant. The first was at RoxyAnn vineyards. The orchard estate had been owned and operated by the same family since the early 1900s. Originally an apple and pear orchard, the winery was aptly named after the prominent peak in its backyard.

"This is lovely," Sophia commented as we approached the Honor Barn, a historic structure that now housed the tasting room.

Even though we were technically in Medford, the grounds had a bucolic country feel with the historic barn, outbuildings, grapevines, and views of RoxyAnn in the distance. Visitors could lounge in Adirondack chairs during the summer months or gather around outdoor fire pits.

"Just wait until you see the interior," I replied. "They've

renovated the inside with a bar, gift shops, and lots of cozy spots to linger and spend an afternoon tasting varietals."

"They must be producing a good volume of wine," Luis noted as we passed two large barns where the wine was barreled and bottled.

"Sí," Carlos replied. "They are just a bit bigger than our operation at Uva. Two hundred acres, and they produce over thirteen thousand cases each year."

Inside, the tasting room was warm and homey, with wood floors, barn signage, and wood-beamed ceilings painted bright white. The tasting room manager greeted us with small pours of their cabernet. "Welcome to Roxy-Ann; make yourselves at home."

"Salud," Sophia said in return as the tasting room manager showed us our table by the window. It offered a view of the sloping vineyards where a family of deer was curled up between the vines.

The tasting manager explained that she'd be walking us through a tasting flight starting with arguably the most popular wine in the valley—pinot noir.

One of the perks of owning Uva was that we had built friendships with other vintners in the region. The wine community was highly supportive. We partnered for special collaborations, sent tourists along the Rogue Valley wine map to taste the variety of world-class wines produced in the region, and even pitched in during harvest to ensure every vineyard was picked. Not a single grape went to waste.

Carlos and Luis fell into a conversation about soil and why the valley exclusively produced red grapes. Sophia scooted her chair closer to me.

"It has been wonderful to stay with you. I hope it hasn't

been too much of an inconvenience." Her face was soft and aglow from the sunlight filtering through the vast barn windows.

"Are you kidding? I love it. I just have felt bad not wanting to interfere with your time with Ramiro. We're so grateful that you're sharing him with us this year."

"He is thriving. It's strange being gone from him and seeing him turn into a young adult in front of my eyes." She ran her fingers along a hand-stitched throw pillow on her chair.

"Is it hard?" I leaned closer.

"Sí, and also lovely. That's life, yes?" She let out a shallow sigh. "Always a mix. A bittersweet mix."

I put my hand on my heart. "I can only imagine, but I will say that I have felt that with Ramiro. I was worried at first that he wouldn't feel comfortable or like our home was his, but fortunately that went away within a few days. I was so relieved and happy that he met friends and had things to do, but then all of a sudden, I realized we weren't going to see much of him."

Sophia chuckled, picking up her glass of pinot noir and swirling it with one hand. "This is parenting. They break open our hearts and then slowly keep breaking them. It is good, though. The alternative would be worse. That's why this trip has been important for me. I could tell from our calls and conversations that he was enjoying himself, but seeing him so happy makes my heart lighter."

"I'm glad." My body grew warmer with each sip of the earthy fruit-forward wine.

She stole a quick glance at Luis. "Can I give you some advice, woman to woman?"

"Sure, anything."

She paused when the tasting room manager came by our table with our next flight. The next wine was a deep red merlot. It was complex with herbal notes and a velvety mocha finish. At Uva, Carlos always recommended our merlot to anyone new to the wine scene, for its easy drinkability.

"Don't delay happiness." Sophia raised her glass to me after the tasting manager returned to the bar. "I did that for too long. It is one of my only regrets that I didn't allow Carlos to be a part of Ramiro's life earlier. I wish I could go back in time, but I was young and consumed by what my family thought was proper. If I could change it, I would."

"But it all worked out."

"Still, I can see how much you and Carlos love each other. You have that thing. The thing that we can never put words to. There's no explanation for it when you find that kind of love, you know."

"It seems true for you and Luis, too."

She couldn't contain a smile as she shifted her gaze in his direction for a second. "We met at the right time. I was ready for love."

"I think Carlos and I might have met too soon, initially. I had some growing up to do, and I'm so relieved that we came together again. If you had asked me a couple of years ago, I would have said that I didn't think this life was possible."

She massaged my hand. "This is what I'm saying about real love. It finds a way."

"We're both lucky." I raised my glass and clinked hers.

The men were still engrossed in conversation. Chatter in the barn picked up as a bachelorette party came in to celebrate. They gathered around two wooden wine barrels wrapped with fairy lights and clinked their glasses in a toast to the new bride.

"What about children for you?" Sophia asked pointedly.

"You mean not delaying my happiness?"

"You are still young."

"Not that young. My clock has certainly started to tick, but it comes down to being scared. I would love to have a family with Carlos, but what if it changes our dynamic?"

Sophia laughed out loud. "It will."

"Really?" Between the sun coming through the window and the wine, my cheeks were warm, and my body felt relaxed. This was exactly what I needed.

"That's not a bad thing. It could be for some people, but not you, Julieta."

I loved that she pronounced my name like Carlos did.

"You are a natural caregiver. You are empathetic and kind. You will make a great mother. You are already with Ramiro. I said that to Luis the other night. I never thought I would want to share my child with another woman, yet I'm so pleased he has you in his life."

Tears welled. I couldn't fight them back.

Sophia squeezed my hand again as her eyes misted.

Her words had a profound and unexpected effect on me. It was almost like I had been waiting for her blessing. Although I couldn't articulate why.

"If you decide you want children or a child, it will change your relationship and won't be without challenges, but I am sure it will only make you and Carlos stronger." She trailed her finger along the throw pillow.

I reached for a napkin to dab my eyes.

The tasting room manager appeared with our third

wine—a rich Malbec. I tried to regain control of my emotions. Sophia had released something that I had been holding deep in the recesses of my brain ever since I had found the letters from Ramiro on the ship. Knowing that we were tethered together in the best possible way because of Ramiro shifted that old anxiety, feelings of unworthiness, and grief.

I knew I didn't need permission from anyone other than myself, but hearing Sophia's heartfelt words of support and encouragement had shifted something.

Maybe I was ready.

Maybe I hadn't trusted myself.

Or maybe I had been harboring more than I had realized regarding my past. I had thought that I had let that go when Carlos and I decided to move forward and have him come to Ashland. It wasn't as if I hadn't spent the entire time we were apart dissecting our relationship and what had gone wrong.

I was proud of the self-reflection I'd done and the growth that resulted. Some of that came from being home and understanding my roots. Leaving Ashland had been necessary, but also a coping mechanism after Dad's death.

Everything had come full circle in the last year. My time with Sophia felt like the final piece of the pie I hadn't even known I was missing.

I wasn't sure what that would mean for my choice moving forward, but I was grateful for yet another opportunity to understand my journey to becoming the best version of myself.

# Chapter Seventeen

When I woke the next day, I couldn't believe that it was already New Year's Eve, and our time with the Torres family was coming to a close. Tonight was the party and fireworks celebration on Mount A, and tomorrow, Mom and the Professor would host their annual New Year's Day buffet. The next morning, we would take the Torreses to the airport and send them on to their next adventure. Ramiro would travel with them to explore the redwoods, ride the streetcar in San Francisco, and soak up the sun on the jagged Northern California coastline. Then they would continue south to take in the sights in Hollywood, Santa Monica pier, and a promised two-day stop at Disneyland for Marta. Not that Ramiro was putting up any resistance to spending a couple of thrill-seeking days at adventure parks.

The Torreses would fly home to Spain from Southern California, and Ramiro would be back with us for his last semester at Ashland High School. It felt like they had just arrived. I wasn't ready to say goodbye.

Torte would be open until four today and then closed on New Year's Day, so I opted to head in to bake the desserts for Mom's party while everyone slept in and enjoyed coffee and breakfast at home. I was used to walking to the bakeshop in the early morning hours, long before the sun made its rotation through the sky, but today, since I was getting a later start, a purple haze settled over the Siskiyou Mountains. I wondered if the violet-toned sky portended more snow. That would make for a wintery end to the year but could mean that getting up the mountain might be a bit tricky.

Andy and Sequoia were already slinging coffees when I arrived at Torte, and Rosa was managing the line of early birds out to pick up cakes dusted with edible glitter and topped with sparklers for their New Year's Eve celebrations.

"Happy New Year," Rosa said, greeting me by tipping her hot pink and silver party hat.

I had purchased a box of New Year's hats and noise makers for our team and enough to leave out on the pastry counter for any of our guests who might want to take one with their pastries.

"It looks so festive in here." I reached into the basket and picked out a shiny black plastic top hat wrapped with gold foil.

Andy had on a pair of iridescent flashing green fake glasses.

"How can you see with those?" I laughed.

He poured a shot into a mug. "You're looking at a coffee pro. This barista can pull shots in his sleep. I don't need to see."

I didn't doubt that. "I'm off to bake for the buffet tomorrow. Is there anything I can help with first?"

"We're good, boss." Andy winked through the blinking

glasses. "I heard a rumor that there might be cheesecake, so that's my priority. Get baking. Because cheesecake."

I gave him a salute. "I'm on it." I didn't bring up the lodge and what I had heard about Kendall's situation. No one in town wanted to see the lodge shut down, but Andy would be devastated. There was no reason for unnecessary worry. At this point, everything was speculation and rumor.

The kitchen was running like clockwork. Marty was brushing melted butter on top of loaves of our classic white bread while Sterling was sautéing veggies at the stove. Bethany and Steph had headphones in and concentrated on finishing the last of the New Year's custom orders.

Cheesecake needs to bake low and slow in a water bath and then be allowed ample time to cool and be fully chilled in the refrigerator. There wasn't enough time prior to closing early to bake whole cakes for the pastry case, but since I was already going to the effort to make the filling and crust, I could make a tray of mini cheesecakes that wouldn't take long to bake or chill.

I began with the crust for the cherry cheesecake by pulsing graham crackers and pecans in our food processor. Once they had pulverized, I added them to a large mixing bowl and poured melted butter over the mixture. I combined that with brown sugar and a touch of cinnamon. Then I pressed the crust into springform pans for Mom's party and miniature tart shells for the pastry case.

I slid them into the oven to bake while I repeated the process for my chocolate crust. Only this time, I used chocolate wafer cookies and hazelnuts and added white sugar and a splash of amaretto extract. The crusts would bake for five to ten minutes, just to firm up a bit before I filled them.

Soft cream cheese is a necessity for cheesecake. There's nothing worse than a lumpy cheesecake. To achieve a silky smooth texture, I cubed blocks of cream cheese and warmed them in the microwave at ten-second intervals. My preferred method of bringing cream cheese up to room temp was to simply set it out for about an hour before baking, but when in a crunch for time, the microwave was magic. However, if left in too long, it would turn into a puddle, which was no good.

With the cheese softened, I added it in small batches to the industrial mixer and set it low to begin to cream. The glistening soft cheese reminded me of snow, which turned my thoughts again to the lodge. I hoped that I would have a chance to see Kendall there tonight.

I wanted to know more about her financial situation and if there was anything Torte could do to support her family. I already had visions of a special Sunday Supper partnership at the lodge, where the proceeds of ticket sales could go directly to saving the lodge. Of course, there was also the issue of Fitz. I couldn't figure out how or why his death could be connected to the lodge's dwindling revenue, but maybe Kendall would be able to shed some light on their relationship.

Once the cheese was smooth and creamy, I added eggs, vanilla, and sugar and whipped it together. I scooped the filling into the par-baked crusts and set the pans in a water bath, known to professional pastry chefs as a bain-marie. The technique involved boiling water in a teakettle and placing the cheesecakes in large roasting pans, then carefully filling the space around the tins with the boiling water and covering the top with aluminum foil. This would ensure that the cakes baked with a luscious consistency and didn't turn gummy. A bain-marie prevented the cheesecakes from browning, cracking, or ending up rubbery—or worse—curdled.

There was no substitute. A water bath was necessary to achieve a satiny, smooth cheesecake. When I graduated from culinary school, I was surprised at how many new pastry chefs were intimidated by the mere mention of a bain-marie. I made it my mission to teach my team the proper way to bake cheesecakes to perfection every time.

After the first round of cakes were steaming in their bain-maries, I whipped more softened cream cheese with sugar, eggs, dark cocoa powder, and a touch of rum extract. Then I folded in chopped hazelnuts and mini semisweet chocolate chips. After that, the chocolate cheesecakes would get their own water baths.

"Hey, you don't happen to have a spare donut or two lying around?" Thomas poked his head into the kitchen as I slid the cheesecakes into the oven.

"Sadly, no donuts today, but can I interest you in a black sesame or coconut macaron? We're testing some new flavors for the new year." I directed him to a rack of the filled meringue cookies that Steph had designed in star shapes for the holiday.

"I guess if I have to." Thomas winked and helped himself to a macaron. He was the only person I knew who wore shorts in the dead of winter. Shorts, boots, and his police uniform were his standard attire whether there was a blizzard raging or a heat wave baking.

"What brings you to Torte?" I asked.

He closed his eyes briefly as he bit into the coconut

cream macaron. "Hold on; I'm going to need a minute because this is amazing."

I grinned. Nothing was quite as satisfying as watching a customer—or a friend—enjoy the fruits of our kitchen labors.

"Can we chat in the other room for a sec?" he asked after finishing the cookie in two bites.

"Sure." I wiped my hands on my apron and followed him to the couch next to the atomic fireplace. Fortunately, the basement was empty, aside from my staff, so we could talk openly.

He rested on the edge of the couch and devoured the black sesame macaron. "I hope both of these passed your test, because I'm going to dream about them tonight."

"I'm glad we have your seal of approval. I'll tell the team that we've got two winners, and if you're nice, I'll send you on your way with a box."

"Mission accepted." Thomas gave me a thumbs-up.

I sat across from him. "I'm guessing you aren't here just for our macarons."

"You guessed correctly. I'm here on official police business." He tapped the badge pinned to his chest and took out his iPad mini. "We're trying to establish a timeline of when January was seen last. I know you left the Professor a couple of messages yesterday that he could not return. Can you remember if she left right when you called him?"

I thought back to my conversation with her and Ruth. "Um, yeah. I mean fairly close to the time." I explained that Ruth had stayed for a few minutes before I had a chance to call the Professor a second time.

He made notes on his iPad. "Did she give you any indication where she was going?"

"Off the grid. Those were her exact words, but she didn't give me any specifics other than saying that she had spent time off the grid and could do it again." I wished I had more to share with him.

"And you haven't seen her since?"

I shook my head. "No, but we've been gone. Later that day, we went wine tasting."

"Got it." Thomas turned off his iPad.

"Does this mean that you're still looking for her?"

He craned his neck to one side and then to the other. "I can't comment on an active investigation, but I will say she is a person of interest, so if you or any of your staff see her or hear news about her, we would appreciate a call."

"Of course."

"I shouldn't keep you. I'm sure you're trying to get out of here early like everyone else in the plaza."

"Let me box you up some macarons. Are you and Kerry on duty tonight?"

He threw his head back. "Yes, don't remind me. I'm already anticipating the drunk and disorderly calls."

"Hopefully, these will help," I said, offering him an assortment of macarons. "Stay safe."

"You too, Jules." He lifted the lid of the box. "Do I have to share?"

"Have you met your wife?"

"Fair point. Fair point." He shut the box and gave me a wave. "Happy new year."

I watched him leave out the back entrance. Where had January gone? And why were the police homed in on finding her? Could it be that she was the prime suspect in Fitz's murder? It would explain why she'd vanished.

I tried to push the thought away as I refocused on my desserts.

With the cakes baking, I grabbed tart cherries from the walk-in and tossed them in a saucepan with butter. They would simmer in vanilla-infused sugar with a little cornstarch and water to thicken. The caramel sauce was a Torte favorite. We made it in large batches and sold it in mason jars during the holiday season.

For that, I melted butter with brown sugar and sea salt. The trick with caramel is keeping a close watch on it while stirring constantly. There's a brief flashpoint when the sugary base bubbles and transforms into a thick, dark golden sauce, but if you wait too long, it can easily burn and turn bitter.

As always, time in the kitchen was just what I needed. That sense of instant gratification that came with baking something with my own hands and seeing the rewards of my efforts in the form of silken cheesecakes and rich sauces.

By the time I needed to leave to get ready for the New Year's Eve bash on the mountain, the pastry case displayed my tiny cheesecakes, and tomorrow's desserts were resting in the fridge.

Back at home, everyone was bundling up for one last arctic night. Ramiro and Marta were going to ski, while the adults had opted to enjoy the new year's festivities indoors with cocktails and dancing.

"This is a far cry from our midnight buffets on the ship," Carlos said with a sexy grin as he tied his boots. "I'll never forget the moment I caught sight of you in that aqua blue cocktail dress with your hair aglow from the disco ball. I already knew I was in love with you, but that night, I knew you would forever hold my heart."

I kissed his head. "Snow boots and parkas have their own appeal." I had decided to wear a pair of thick black fleece leggings under a gold sequined skirt from my days on the ship, my boots, and a black turtleneck. I wanted a touch of sparkle but plenty of warmth and function.

"You could be wearing a coffee sack, and you would always be the most beautiful woman in the room, mi querida."

Carlos had never been afraid of professing his love. It was one of the reasons I had fallen for him—hard—in the early days of our time on the *Amour of the Seas*. Some of it was cultural. In Spain, it wasn't uncommon for men to express their love and admiration in ways that might put some American men out of their comfort zone. Carlos's ability to show vulnerability was one of my favorite qualities. His openness and ability to tell me how he was feeling had cracked something open in me.

I suppose that's what the best relationships do: highlight areas where there's an opportunity for growth. Not in a way that diminishes either partner but in a way that ignites a spark.

Carlos was my spark.

There was no denying that.

And sparks were going to fly tonight. Even with everything that had happened this past week with Fitz and the murder investigation, I was ready to put that aside and ring in the New Year with the people I loved.

# Chapter Eighteen

Later in the evening, once we'd made the harrowing drive up the ski road to the lodge, the buzz of energy on the glowing slope was contagious. A huge bonfire burned near the lodge, where people gathered around to warm their hands and drink something hot and sweet. A band played on the lodge's top deck under hundreds of paper lanterns. Kids were jammed up in line for the ski tube, and skiers and snowboarders zipped down the well-lit runs.

It was hard to believe that it had only been a couple of days ago that Fitz had been killed right here.

I tried not to stare at the spot as we made our way into the lodge, but I had trouble tearing my eyes away. This was the exact place where someone, maybe someone I knew, had intentionally cut the wire that sent the ski patrol dummy on a collision course with Fitz, who had carelessly entered the off-limits area at exactly the wrong time. I realized from this vantage point that the killer had a bird's-eye view of the landing area. It wouldn't have taken a genius to figure out the timing. The killer could have easily been waiting for just the right moment to snip the wire. They would have only needed to see Fitz enter the landing spot below, bend down, make a quick cut, and walk away. It would have taken seconds, and with the crowd's frenzy and the excitement of watching dummies launch into the air, they could have easily gone unnoticed. But there was still the issue of Fitz. What prompted him to wander into the restricted space?

Was it more likely that the killer spotted Fitz downslope and seized the opportunity to take him out?

If that was the case, what did it mean for my list of suspects?

Any one of the groups I had witnessed gathered in this space could be the killer. Hero, January, Kendall, Shawn, and Ruth had all been in the vicinity.

I kept returning to the question of whether the act had been planned or if the killer had made a spur-of-the-moment decision.

How did they cut the wire? Scissors would have been obvious. I mean, who shows up at downhill dummy with a pair of kitchen or garden shears in hand? And how strong would they need to be to sever the wire? Both Shawn and Hero likely had pocketknives as part of their emergency kits. What about Ruth and January? I tried to recall the image of them standing together, watching the competition. I didn't remember either of them having a purse or backpack. They were both in ski gear. But that didn't mean they hadn't hidden a box cutter or Swiss Army knife in a coat pocket.

And then there was Kendall. She had been passing around samples of hot chocolate. What if that was a smoke screen? On the one hand, it made sense that if the lodge was in danger of closing, she might have been trying to drum up extra business by handing out free cups of cocoa. But what if she had stashed a knife on the tray?

I didn't want to believe Kendall could be involved in Fitz's murder, but I couldn't take her off my list.

"Julieta, Julieta, are you coming?" Carlos was a few feet ahead of me.

"Yeah, sorry." I shook myself from my trance and caught up with him.

"You are thinking of the murder, sí?"

"I hadn't realized how much you could see from up this high. I mean, it makes sense obviously, but it also highlights that everyone who I've been considering a suspect could have done it."

Music blasted above us. People packed the side of the lodge near the entrance doors like a mosh pit, dancing to the beat of the thumping drums. Teens with neon glow stick bracelets and necklaces traveled in packs between the concession stand and the DJ dance party on the third floor. Metallic streamers and balloons hung from the archways and stairwells. Geometric stars and lanterns dangled from the pillars. Party attire ranged from ski suits to sequined dresses and everything in between. It was fun to watch people of all ages and interests gather to ring in the new year together.

Craft stations on the main floor were crammed with kids coloring paper hats and making noise makers with Popsicle sticks and fringed shimmery ribbons. Older groups sat near the fireplace, playing cards and board games. Couples swayed on the dance floor, waltzing beneath a ceiling of luminescent balloons.

Carlos cupped his hands around his mouth so I could

hear him over the band. "I will get us drinks. Luis and Sophia are heading to a table by the fireplace with Arlo."

"Okay. I'll meet you in a minute." I hadn't noticed Arlo
while I was studying the ski jump. That had to mean that
Lance was nearby. I glanced to my left and then to my
right. There was no sign of him. Maybe I had missed him,
too.

At that moment, I felt a tap on my shoulder.

"Looking for someone?"

I swiveled to see Lance standing behind me. His devilish grin told me he knew exactly who I'd been looking
for.

"Have you been standing behind me this entire time?"

"Wouldn't you like to know?" He linked his arm
through mine. "Now, listen, darling, we won't have much
time before our paramours steal us away for champagne
toasts and twirls around the dance floor."

"You look like you're ready for dancing. Where are
your boots?"

"Please." Lance tsked. "Boots are for commoners. It's
New Year's Eve. We might not be at a rooftop party in
Manhattan, but rest assured I dressed for the occasion."
He ran his arm from his shoulder down to his toes, posing like a model for me to take in his black velvet jacket,
skinny black jeans, and shiny black Oxfords with a
quarter-inch heel.

How he was managing not to get his expensive dress
shoes wet from the snow was beyond me. The slim-fit
jacket and crisp white shirt belonged at a swanky party,
not necessarily a ski lodge, but far be it from me to suggest as much.

"You look amazing," I said honestly.

"I know, darling. I know." He did a twirl so that I could get the full effect. "Do try to compose yourself, though. I realize it's difficult to be in the presence of style and greatness, but we have much to discuss."

"I'll try my best."

He swatted at my hand. "I don't like that tone. Sarcasm is my gig. You're the sugar to my saltiness."

I couldn't keep a straight face. "Okay, consider the tone gone."

"By the way, I'm loving gold sequins for you, darling." He swept his hand toward my skirt. "Chic meets comfort. Brilliant."

"That's what I was going for." I fluffed my skirt. "What do we need to discuss, though? Have you learned something?"

Lance took way too much pleasure in extending the drama of any moment. He strummed his fingers on his chin. "Perhaps."

"I thought you said we didn't have much time."

"Fine," he huffed. "Always the taskmaster."

"Tell me what you learned."

He checked our surroundings and dragged me downstairs and outside, away from the pulsing music and crowd noise. Four-foot icicles clung precariously to the eaves. I wouldn't have wanted to be standing under there in a windstorm. One strong gust could have freed them from their grasp and sent them hurling at us like icy daggers.

"I assume you've heard that the lodge is in financial ruin," Lance whispered.

"I mean, I heard that Kendall was struggling to keep the doors open due to the dwindling snowpack."

"It's much more than that." Lance brushed a snowflake

from his velvet jacket. "The lodge's demise has been years in the making, and it's all Kendall's doing."

"How so? She doesn't control the weather."

"No, but she does control the purse strings, and apparently, her purse has been anything but cinched tightly."

"I don't understand. I thought the ski resort was suffering because of weather changes."

"Oh, it is. Absolutely. There's no denying that. Does the lack of snow compound her financial troubles? Certainly, but according to my sources, so do her extravagant spending habits. It seems our little Rogue Valley mountaineer has a penchant for the finer things in life. Something I quite approve of, by the way. I'm not passing judgment. However, a judge might be soon. It seems she's leveraged the lodge, her family's acreage on the west slope of the mountain, and the vast majority of the equipment right down to the snowcats. The ski park is bleeding out cash, and from what I've heard, Kendall is on the brink of bankruptcy. Her claim that the lodge's money woes are due to Mother Nature is a convenient fabrication."

This was huge news and certainly gave Kendall a motive, that was if we could develop a financial connection between her and Fitz.

"I see those baby blues working overtime." Lance gave me a slow nod. "Money and murder, yes?"

"Yeah, but how was Fitz involved? Could he have learned about her financial situation and tried to blackmail her?"

"Oh no. It's even juicer than that." Lance smoothed his jacket. "Fitz worked for a lumber company that offered to buy her out. Her money problems would have been solved while the lodge and ski lifts were razed."

"But how would that give her a motive to kill him? Wouldn't she want him alive if he was negotiating a deal to sell the lodge?" I didn't get into how devastating it would be to lose the ski resort.

"Ah, this is where it gets interesting." He held up one finger in a Sherlock Holmes move. "Word on the mean streets of Ashland is that the day before the murder, Fitz reached out to his boss and recommended they pull out of the deal."

"Really?"

"My sources never lie."

Before I could respond, a cluster of icicles dislodged from the roofline and came sailing at our heads.

# Chapter Nineteen

Lance shoved me out of the way. We landed on the hard-packed snow with a thud as three icicles shattered next to us. I covered my head. Lance wrapped his arm around me like a hired bodyguard.

"Don't move." He kept his head tucked. "They could be launching more our way."

"Launching? Don't you mean falling?"

"No, I certainly don't mean falling." His tone was weary, like he was irritated that he had to spell it out for me, but also laced with worry. "Darling, that was no accident. Someone just hurled those straight at our heads. Someone just tried to kill us."

I glanced up in time to see a flash of movement above us. Was I imagining it, or was Lance right? It looked like someone was fleeing the scene.

The next thing I heard was the door to the third floor slam shut, and suddenly we were blanketed in snow falling from the roof.

We waited, frozen on the ground for a moment, before Lance released his brotherly grasp and stood up, reaching for my hand to pull me to my feet.

He brushed snow from his suit. "Lovely, the shoes are ruined."

I shook snow from my hair and burst into a fit of giggles. "That's what you're worried about? Your shoes and velvet suit jacket?"

Lance tried to look severe, but he started laughing with me. Neither of us could stop. My sides ached. My teeth hurt as they chattered together.

"I don't know why this is so funny," I said through gasps. I shook ice pellets from my skirt.

"Stress, darling. Stress." Lance clutched his stomach. "We nearly died."

"But that's not funny."

"Yet we came out unscathed, which means that our assailant is most definitely *not* laughing." He tried to brush more snow from his plush jacket but only managed to press the wet flakes into the material, creating long streaks. "You realize what this means, don't you?"

"What?" I wiped my wet palms as the cold began to settle in.

"The killer knows that we're onto them. This puts us in a very precarious situation."

"Do you think it's Kendall? Could she have overheard us?"

"I do." He reached for my hand. "She knows this lodge better than anyone. If she realized that we're aware of her nefarious actions, she easily could have hurried up to the third-floor deck, knocked off the icicles in hopes of slamming them into our precious noggins, and then made a quick retreat."

I glanced above us again. "Or it could have been anyone coming outside to get some fresh air, and the action of closing the heavy door dislodged the icicles and snow."

"Don't be practical at a moment like this. I know it. I feel it in my cold, cold bones. We're close to finding the killer, and they're spooked. This is equally good and bad. If we play our cards right, we may be the ones to bring Kendall to justice, but we have to watch our backs."

"How do you suggest bringing her to justice?"

"Simple, we get her to confess."

I laughed again. "Let's assume your theory is right and Kendall is the killer. If she thinks that *we think* she's the killer and she just tried to assault us with icicles, how do you suggest going about getting a confession from her without getting ourselves killed?"

Lance smashed damp snow into his jacket as he tried to rub his arm. "I'm working that out. But, for the moment, I suggest we go inside while we consider our options before we both turn into Popsicles."

I wasn't going to argue with that. The tips of my fingers had gone numb, and I was losing feeling in my toes. I was glad I had dressed for the weather instead of the occasion, but my leggings and hoodie weren't enough protection to stand outside in the elements for long.

"You know there's also the possibility that Kendall isn't the killer," I said, following him into the lodge. "And someone else was just eavesdropping on our conversation."

"More like dropping icicles from the eaves," Lance said under his breath and then stopped abruptly, as he came nose to nose with Kendall.

"Hey, you two look like you had a run-in with a snow-plow," Kendall said with an odd smile. "Do we need to find some new clothes for you? I'm sure we have some dry sweats in the lost and found."

"Oh, lord no. That won't be necessary. I would rather prance naked than rifle through the lost and found." Lance tugged off his jacket and folded it over his arm. "A few minutes by the fire, and she'll be good as new."

"What happened?" Kendall looked at me.

"We got caught under a snow drift falling from the roof." I hoped I sounded casual.

"Haven't you seen the signs?" Kendall's cheeks flamed, matching the color of her plaid shirt. "We have bright yellow signage posted all around the lodge and the perimeter warning people of the danger of falling snow and debris. I would have thought the two of you would be more cautious. You could have been seriously injured."

Was she concerned, or was that a veiled threat?

"What we could use is a stiff drink," Lance said. "Or a winter warmer, perhaps?"

Kendall hesitated. "Yes, of course. Come with me."

Lance flashed me a thumbs-up as we followed her to the bar.

Kendall scooted behind the bar and poured us hot toddies with cinnamon sticks and fresh lemon slices. I tried to stop the involuntary shivering as I watched skiers fly down the slopes outside.

"Would it be too much to ask if we might use your office momentarily to freshen up before we rejoin the revelry?" Lance asked with a smile so sweet it made my teeth ache.

Kendall's face looked like that was the last thing she wanted, but she forced a pained smile. "Sure, follow me."

Her office was on the third floor. A small sign reading

PRIVATE: AUTHORIZED STAFF ONLY hung on the nondescript door. She unlocked it and let us in.

Every inch of wall space was covered with ski posters dating back to the 1960s, when the lodge and first ski lift were constructed. Kendall's desk was carved from the same logs on the lodge's exterior and a smaller version of the iron chandelier from the main floor hung in the center of the room. Ski memorabilia and framed photos were propped between collections of books and paperwork on the bookcase on the far wall.

The room glowed a lush amber color, thanks to an antique wrought-iron light above Kendall's desk.

I tried to get Lance's attention when I noticed a second door with four-paned glass windows leading outside to the upper deck. If Kendall had been the person who had tried to launch icicles at us, she easily could have run out to the upper deck, freed the icy daggers, and returned through her side office door without ever being seen.

We had to be careful about how much we revealed. That was a tall order for Lance, who was prone to theatrics.

I caught his eye and nodded to the side door as Kendall cleared room on the edge of her desk for our drinks.

"I'm not sure I have much to offer you in the way of clothes, but I have an overstock of lost and found in that box." She pointed to a large cardboard box next to a bookcase stuffed with ski guides, maps, and brochures, along with more boxes of swag and Mount Ashland Lodge gear.

"Please don't go to any trouble." Lance sat on the tattered couch adjacent to Kendall's desk. He crossed one leg and leaned back in a show of comfort. "Honestly, Juliet and just I needed a moment to compose ourselves before we mingle after our little scare out there."

I sipped my hot toddy, grateful for something warm to soothe my throat.

"Maybe we need more signage." Kendall stared out her snowy window. "I don't know how you missed them. I've been worried about how long some of the icicles have gotten on the eaves and the snow pile on the roofline, but frankly, I'm in over my head with maintenance. We're struggling to keep the lifts running and the lights on. I guess that in the process, we've neglected basic necessities. I'll see if I can get them on it first thing tomorrow. I don't want to risk trying to clear snow tonight while there are so many people on the mountain."

I realized she had a view of the ski runs and the ski jump from this vantage point. Could that play into Fitz's murder? She might have been able to watch the first round of dummies to figure out the best time to strike.

"Don't give it a thought," Lance reassured her. "We're fine. It was our fault anyway, right, Juliet?"

"Yes, yes, exactly." I wasn't sure how to bring up the topic of the lodge's finances and still sound casual, but Kendall had given me an opening. "I'm glad we have a minute to talk. I heard that the lodge is struggling. Is there anything we can do? You know, Mom and I would gladly cohost a Torte Sunday Supper with all of the proceeds going to saving the lodge."

Kendall blinked twice and waved her hand in front of her face like she was about to cry. I couldn't tell if it was a sincere show of appreciation or a well-rehearsed act. "That's so kind of you, Jules. I appreciate it, really I do."

"The same goes for me." Lance raised his glass. "What do you need? Say the word. A winter performance? Dinner theater? I'll bring the crème de la crème of talent."

Kendall reached into the top drawer of her desk and pulled out a crumpled tissue. "Thank you. You both are the best. It's one of the things I'm going to miss most about this place. The community. I know you mean it and would do anything you could to save the lodge, but I'm afraid it's past the point of saving."

"Never." Lance nearly spilled his toddy as he reacted to Kendall's statement. "It's never too late. There's nothing like a big fat check or pot of cash from good old-fashioned fundraising to change your tune."

"Not in this case." She wadded up the tissue. "It's too late because I've already sold the lodge to Fitz's company."

Now it was my turn to almost end up with hot liquid on me. I steadied my cup. "You sold the lodge to Fitz?"

"Not Fitz. His company. He was scouting the area for a timber company—Redbud Timberland."

"Oh, I'm quite familiar with Redbud," Lance said with disdain. "They are well-known for their unethical business practices, but I didn't know that Fitz was involved."

Kendall pushed her chair back from her desk, stood, and started pacing in front of the window. "I realized that too late. I should have trusted my instincts, but I didn't know what else to do. I was out of options. The lodge has been bleeding money. I wasn't going to be able to pay my staff starting next week. I've been paying them from my personal bank account and not taking a salary myself for the last year, but the money has finally run out. The deal with Redbud will at least let me pay them through the end of the season. The company won't be able to start any harvesting on the west slope until the spring. They've agreed to let the lodge remain open until early April, and then demolition will begin."

I was shocked that Kendall had already gone through with the sale. Her story didn't align with what Lance had heard about her spending habits. If she was out of cash and near bankruptcy because she'd been paying her staff out of her personal funds, that changed the narrative. I had to keep an open mind, especially because I knew gossip spread faster than wildfire in some Ashland circles.

"I tried to back out last week," Kendall continued. "Fitz had promised me that he would build an out clause into the contract, but he didn't. He's such a weasel. He knew I was vulnerable and desperate, and took advantage of that. I've signed away everything. My family's legacy will be completely wiped out in a matter of months, but then I realized I couldn't afford not to take the deal. I'm out of other options, even though Fitz was the worst, what other choice did I have?"

It was impossible not to feel empathy for her situation. When I arrived in Ashland after leaving Carlos on the *Amour of the Seas*, Mom had been in similar circumstances. Richard Lord had tried to make a bid for Torte. Fortunately, we came up with a plan to save the bakeshop before he could get his hands on it. I couldn't imagine how devastating it would have been to see everything my parents had built slip away.

"How final is final?" Lance uncrossed his legs and sat up.

Kendall wiped her nose with the back of her hand. "Final. That's what Fitz told me."

"What about your legal team? You must have had lawyers involved." I plunged my cinnamon stick into my drink.

"I couldn't afford a lawyer. The prices for negotiating

the deal were way out of my budget. I had one guy who said he would take a cut of the final sale, but there's no room there either. I'm maxed out on my debt. I need every penny of the sale to cover costs to keep the lodge running through the season, keep staff employed, and pay off my debts. I used one of those legal sites online, and for two hundred bucks, a lawyer looked over the contract." She sniffled. "I know it's stupid, but I don't think you realize how dire the situation is."

Was it dire enough to kill Fitz? If Kendall had had second thoughts and wanted out of the deal, killing Fitz would have accomplished that. She was admitting her desperation. Could that desperation have led to murder? But then again, if she was locked into the sale, killing Fitz wouldn't change that.

# Chapter Twenty

"Let's back up for a moment." Lance was on his feet. He had abandoned his hot toddy and was in full PR crisis spin mode. "This sounds highly unethical and illegal. Not that I would expect less from Redbud. They are the textbook definition of the evil empire."

"I'm afraid it's not." Kendall hung her head. "The on-line legal consultant told me it wasn't a great deal, but like I said, this was *the* option. There weren't any other offers. Trust me, I've tried to garner interest, but no one wants to take on an aging lodge and small ski park in remote southern Oregon. There's no money in it. At least not to keep it as it is. Whoever buys the property is going to raze the lodge and build something modern and new."

She looked like she was on the brink of tears.

"As much as I pleaded my case to Fitz, he didn't care." Kendall tapped her forehead in distress. "He was in it for the money. He was getting his cut, which was the only thing he cared about."

"Is that why you were seen arguing with him?" I didn't even realize I was speaking until the words spilled out of my mouth.

"Where did you hear that? Oh, never mind. It doesn't even matter, because the truth is that he and I argued many times. But I didn't kill him. I wanted to. I'll admit that much. When I was having second thoughts about the deal at the last minute, he was actually the person who convinced me to stick to it."

Lance mumbled something unintelligible.

"It's true," Kendall insisted. "Without the money from Redbud Timberland, I was sunk. I was going to have to declare bankruptcy and then get nothing. At least with this deal, I can move on and not have mounds of debt."

"Fitz convinced you of this?" Lance sounded skeptical. I wondered if, like me, he was starting to wonder if the gossip about Kendall's finances was wrong.

"He did." Kendall nodded vigorously. "Look, I get it. I see why you might think I killed him, but I swear on my family name that I didn't. He was my only way out of this mess. Now that he's dead, I'm not sure what will happen."

Lance raised his index finger. "Hold up. Let's reevaluate. What are you suggesting? Now that Fitz is dead, it's possible the deal won't go through?"

"I don't know where the paperwork stands." She opened her desk drawer like she was looking at the paperwork. "I had signed the first round, but then the online lawyer gave me a few minor suggestions for changes, which Fitz agreed to."

"I bet he did," Lance interrupted.

"The problem is, I haven't signed the final document yet. If I don't get the first payment installment next week, I will not be able to pay any of my staff." Her eyes drifted to the crowded ski slope. "Payroll is due in five days. What am I going to do? How do you tell loyal staff that they aren't getting a paycheck? They've worked so hard over the holiday season to keep the runs groomed and the lifts moving, and I'm going to have to break the news that I can't pay them." Kendall buried her face in her hands.

Lance held up a finger. "I'd like to offer my services. Will you allow my legal team to intervene and at least look at the contract before you sign anything final?"

Kendall sighed. "Yeah, that would be very kind and generous of you, but what do I do in the meantime? All of these people have been so loyal to my family and me over the years—ski patrol, maintenance, and the food staff. I can't pay them." She sounded broken.

"We'll help with that," I said, an idea forming as I sipped my hot toddy. "You said it yourself. You know what Ashland is like when it comes to supporting our local community. I'll put my head together with Mom and Janet and Lance, and we'll come up with an idea. We might not make enough to get you through the end of the season, but I have no doubt that we can fundraise cash to pay your staff and keep the lights on through January."

My mind was already spinning with possibilities, like tomorrow night's dinner at Mom's. What if we swapped the Sunday Supper for a Ski Supper instead? It was short notice, but Mount A, the lodge, the ski slope, all of it, was beloved by our community and a huge asset for winter tourism. If we put the call out for help, I knew everyone would come.

"It's settled, then," Lance said, and added, "I'll review your paperwork with my legal team at no cost to you while Juliet commences Project Save the Slopes."

Kendall brushed a tear from her eye. "I can't thank you

enough. I've been hiding out up here wondering what in the world to do next."

"Speaking of that," Lance said, catching my eye for the briefest moment. "Were you on the deck before you bumped into us?"

"This deck?" Kendall pointed to the side door. "No. This deck is off-limits. The weight from the snow is too heavy right now. I was over by the dance floor. There was an issue with one of the balloon arches. It was sagging. Come to think of it, though; when I returned to my office for duct tape, I noticed Hero out there."

"Hero?" Lance and I asked in unison.

She nodded. "I told him he shouldn't be out there. I'm not sure the deck will hold under all of that snow. It's dangerous."

"Did he mention what he was doing?"

"He said that he got a call on the radio about something wrong with the lights in the upper bowl, and this was the best view." She trailed off as she focused her attention on the ski slopes. "Now that I think about it, it's weird. None of the lights are out, and I don't know why he would need to come up to the third-floor deck to see that. If the upper bowl was out of power, you could see that from the bunny hill."

Lance raised his eyebrows twice.

She glanced from the deck and then back to Lance. "You know, I haven't mentioned this to anyone other than the police, but I saw him and Fitz fighting right before Fitz was killed."

"You saw Fitz and Hero fighting?" I clarified, taking a final sip of my drink. The hot lemon and whiskey had done the trick. I was finally warm again.

Kendall pointed to the ski jump. "Right down there. I had come out with a tray of hot chocolate to try to encourage spectators to come inside for drinks and concessions after the event, not that even thousands of cups of hot chocolate would be enough to cover my debts. Still, in any event, I've been doing everything I could think of to bring in cash the last few months. The downhill dummy was great for getting people up here, but I needed to capitalize on their business, so I printed out coupons and poured tasting samples."

I tried not to let my lack of patience get to me. I wanted to hear more about Hero, but I could tell that Kendall was still trying to process losing the lodge.

"The samples were a hit," she continued. "I went through two tasting trays and had to go inside for a refill for another just as the dummy competition was winding down."

"Is that when you saw Hero and Fitz?" Lance paced in front of the windows.

I wondered if he was feeling the same as me.

"I saw them twice," Kendall said with certainty. "The first time was when I handed out samples near the bunny hill. Fitz pushed Hero, and Hero came after him."

"You mean physically?" Lance postured like he was playing the part of a defense lawyer.

"He tried to punch Fitz, but Fitz ducked away and took off." Kendall stood and pointed past the lifts to the ski patrol chalet. "Some of the patrol team saw it, too. They'll back me up."

This was news.

"Then, when I came out with the last round of samples, I saw them in the lobby. They were arguing so loud that

I almost considered intervening, but it was awkward because of the situation with Fitz. I needed him to finalize the contract. I didn't want to risk upsetting him and then having him go back to Redbud Timberland and tell them that the deal was off."

"Did you hear what they were arguing about?" I asked.

"No. I didn't stick around long enough to listen because I didn't want the drinks to get cold, and I knew that the dummy was almost over, and then hopefully, we would have a long line at concessions."

Could Hero have still been upset about the snowshoe tour? Or did he know what Fitz was really doing on the mountain? That would explain his reaction the night of our tour. Maybe he was well aware that Fitz was posing as a guide in order to ink out a contract for his employer. Hero wouldn't want the deal to go through either. His business would be ruined if the lodge closed and the mountain ended up clear-cut.

Come to think of it, anyone attached to the mountain who learned about Fitz's real intentions suddenly had a motive to kill him. My suspect list should have been shrinking at this point, but Kendall's revelation only made it bigger.

# Chapter Twenty-One

We finished our conversation with Kendall and agreed to be in touch first thing in the morning about hosting a spontaneous Sunday Ski Supper at the lodge as a fundraiser. I wasn't sure if we could pull off dinner tomorrow night, but if anyone could do it, Mom was the person for the job. We could commandeer Torte's kitchen to bake more meatloaves, and I knew my team would spring into action to bake extra desserts. Our New Year's Day staff party might need to be postponed, but I had a feeling that we wouldn't get any arguments. Everyone on the team loved the mountain. Andy would probably be so distraught to hear the news of the ski slope closing that he might never be able to roast another brew. We had to do everything we could to help Kendall and save the lodge.

That is, if she wasn't a killer. I believed her story. Her desperation was apparent, and if she had been using her own funds to pay her staff, that showed dedication. But there was still an outside possibility that her desperation could have led to murder.

She had been quick to point out that Hero was nearby

when Fitz was killed, but the truth was she was also in the vicinity, and her office had direct access to the deck. She could have been lying about Hero, trying to shift suspicion. I knew that as soon as I spoke with Mom about plans for a fundraising dinner, I wanted to talk to Hero and ask him a few questions.

When Lance and I returned to the party, Mom and the Professor were dancing under a blanket of gold and silver balloons with matching long ribbons. They looked happy and carefree, and I hated interrupting the moment, but there was a lot I needed to share. Lance took off to find Arlo while I made a beeline for the Professor.

"Juliet, happy new year." The Professor greeted me with a kiss. "As the Bard would say on an auspicious evening like tonight, 'Well, if I be served such another trick, I'll have my brains ta'en out and buttered, and give them to a dog for a new year's gift.'"

"Should we add that one to the chalkboard?" Mom asked me as she did a half twirl to show off her knee-length shimmery emerald green party skirt that she wore over a pair of snow pants and ski boots. "How's the look? We're twins, aren't we? Great minds think alike."

"Perfect and practical." I ran my fingers over my gold sequined skirt.

She fluffed the edges of her skirt. "My thoughts exactly. If I want to hit the slopes later. I'm ready."

"Listen, I hate to put a damper on your dancing, but is there a chance I can have a quick chat with you two? I have some news that really can't wait."

The Professor had to speak up to be heard over the five-piece jazz band playing "What Are You Doing New Year's Eve?"

"Downstairs." He motioned to the stairwell.

I weaved through streamers and deflated balloons on the ballroom floor and headed for the lobby. Skiers traipsed past, stomping their snow-coated boots on the mats outside and propping their skis on the racks. The doors blew in a steady, cold wind.

"Shall we grab our coats and step outside?" the Professor asked. "I believe we'll have a bit more privacy."

Standing underneath the dangerous icicles again made me slightly uneasy, but I was with the Professor this time. If the killer had tried to hurt Lance and me, they wouldn't risk doing it again, especially with Ashland's lead detective standing near my side.

At least, that's what I told myself as I stepped outside with them. This time I grabbed my parka and gloves.

"I'm assuming I'll want to take notes." The Professor had his notebook ready to go.

"It's a lot, and to be honest, I'm not sure how much of what I have to tell you is factual versus theories."

"Lance theories," Mom interjected, stuffing her hands in her ski jacket.

"Yeah." I tilted my head to the side as I nodded. Skiers zipped down the mountainside. "I guess what I'm saying is take this with a grain of salt. I figure it's better to tell you everything I've heard tonight, and then you can filter what is important from there."

"Interesting choice of idioms," the Professor said. "Did you know there's a theory that that particular sentiment is believed to have originated in ancient times from none other than Pliny the Elder?"

"No. I guess they didn't cover that in culinary school."

"A fellow Shakespearean scholar friend believes that

Pliny the Elder used the phrase when translating an antidote for poison—to take it with a grain of salt. Quite fitting for this circumstance, don't you think?"

"I think I need more than a grain." I smiled as tiny skiers made their way to the bunny hill in puffy snowsuits.

He rubbed his hands together. "Apologies, I digress; please share anything you can."

I told him about Lance's and my near miss with the icicles, what we had learned about Kendall and the lodge's financial situation, Fitz's real motive for being on Mount A, and Kendall's theory that Hero could have been involved in his death.

When I finished, he drew in a long breath and looked at Mom. She sighed, releasing a puff of cold air. "Oh, honey, what a night. This was supposed to be a celebration."

"I'm afraid I owe you another apology." The Professor sounded concerned. "It wasn't fair of me to ask you to be another witness. Your mother is right. I'm on duty tonight, but neither of you should have your New Year's Eve occupied by this."

"It's fine. You don't need to apologize. Mom knows I couldn't let it go. Neither could Lance."

"I understand. This has been most helpful, but please go enjoy yourselves. Dance. Drink champagne. Ring in the new year." He tucked his notebook in his pocket and zipped his jacket.

"What about you, Doug?" Mom asked.

"I'll join you shortly. I have two loose ends that need some tying up." He didn't elaborate.

"What about January?" I asked. "Have you been able to track her down? And any news on whether or not she's actually connected to the UEP?"

"As for tracking her down, not as of yet, but my team is following a few leads, including her employment history." He kissed Mom and promised to find her before midnight.

"I'm so sorry to ruin your night," I said to Mom, who was already moving inside.

"This is the nature of detective work. I knew that part of Doug's motivation to come this evening was to observe. It's not your fault, honey, but he's right. It's also not your responsibility. Let's go find the others." She shrugged off her coat.

"One more thing." I told her about Kendall. "Do you think we could pull off a fundraiser tomorrow night? I know it's super short notice, but she needs cash to pay her staff. Otherwise, no one will get paychecks next week."

"You are speaking my language." She pointed to herself. "Meatloaf for a crowd is my specialty. The team will pitch in. I'll call Janet, Wendy, and Marcia. We'll have a fundraising dinner ready to go."

She tugged at one of the many dangly streamers as we walked up the stairwell. "We won't even need to decorate much. We'll pull all the tables to the dance floor and set out fresh linens and flowers, but I think it would be beautiful with these balloons and festive decorations. Some votive candles, a fire, and delicious food. No problem."

I leaned into her shoulder. "That's why I love you." There was never a shred of doubt that Mom and her friends could pull off any miracle, but I appreciated that she didn't even hesitate.

With that settled, I went to find Carlos. He was at a table by himself, sipping from a champagne flute. "Mi querida, I thought I was going to have to dance alone at midnight."

"Sorry. I wasn't intending on being gone for so long, but . . ." I trailed off.

"Sí, I heard from Arlo." He nodded toward the stairway.

I glanced around us. The dance floor was packed with people. "Where is everyone?"

"Dancing. Luis and Sophia are upstairs with Arlo and Lance. They wanted to observe the mosh pit."

I laughed. The upstairs dance floor had a DJ and strobe lights, attracting a younger crowd, whereas the main ballroom had the jazz band and people of all ages waltzing to the sultry sounds of the saxophone.

"Where do you want to go?"

He patted the seat next to him. "I want you to sit for a minute."

"That sounds great." Relief flooded my body.

Carlos offered me a glass of champagne. "Have a drink. Are you hungry?"

"I'm famished." I took the glass from him, not realizing that I'd been running on nothing but adrenaline since our near miss with the icicles. "I should go get something at the buffet."

"You sit. I will make you a plate," Carlos insisted. His narrow eyes told me there was no debating. That was fine by me. Knowing that the Professor was informed and I was no longer in imminent danger brought a sense of relief. I hadn't realized how stressed I'd been. Suddenly I felt exhausted, shaky, and queasy.

I set the champagne to the side. "Would you mind getting me a cup of tea too?"

"Sí. Tea and food. You sit; I'll return in a flash." He snapped and disappeared into the sea of dancers.

My stomach rumbled like a jet revving its engines for

takeoff. I wasn't exaggerating when I told Carlos I was famished. I felt like I could eat the entire buffet table, yet I couldn't silence the worry. I was too involved. I was making myself sick by trying to insert myself into the murder investigation. This wasn't healthy. It was time to listen to everyone's advice and enjoy the night.

# Chapter Twenty-Two

Food helped calm my nerves. I scarfed down antipasto, puffed pastry sausage rolls, bacon-wrapped dates, salted custard tarts, and blood orange custard. I couldn't touch the champagne, though. Carlos and I danced and counted down to midnight. It was easy to get lost in his arms and the music. The ambiance of the crackling fireplace and the dreamy vibe of a rustic mountain lodge on a snowy New Year's Eve transported me out of my head and into my body.

We chanted the countdown to midnight with the crowd and shared a long kiss as "Auld Lang Syne" played. Then we tugged on our coats and hats and shuffled outside to watch fireworks burst in the starry sky. It was impossible not to get caught up in the magic of the moment.

Once the show was over, I was more than ready for my bed. Tomorrow was going to be a busy day of baking that I hadn't anticipated. That was fine. I was eager to do my part to help save the lodge, but I needed some sleep.

The next morning Sophia and Luis were focused on laundry and packing for the rest of their trip. Carlos came with me to the bakeshop. He had offered to make sides to accompany the meatloaf, and if we were going to attempt to feed half of Ashland tonight, having all hands on deck, as we used to say on the ship, was necessary.

Carlos and Sterling teamed up to start on mashed potatoes, Brussels sprouts, and salads. Marty took over bread production. Steph and Bethany baked brownies and cookies. They weren't as fancy as cheesecakes, but they would do the job. Sometimes the simplest, most unassuming desserts make the best statement. For the brownies, Bethany cut out paper snowflakes. After the brownies were cooled and cut into squares, she placed snowflake patterns on the top and dusted them with powdered sugar. Once the paper was removed, beautiful snowy designs rested on each delectable chocolate brownie.

Steph played on the same theme by baking spiced gingerbread snowflake cutout cookies and embossing them with white royal icing to give them the texture of snow. She put out the word on social media, and we were bombarded by responses within an hour. Seats sold out before I had finished my second cup of coffee.

Two cheesecakes weren't enough for the crowd we expected, so I improvised. It was a skill I had honed on the ship. During my years at sea, we were at the mercy of whatever deliveries we could get at each port of call. That meant that sometimes when I had planned to serve mango flan, mangoes were out of stock, and I had to switch paths and bake blueberry bread pudding instead. Since I already had two cheesecakes ready to go, I decided we would slice them into bite-size squares and serve them on paper doilies cut to match Bethany and Steph's snowflakes.

I also wanted to bake something we could serve warm. There wasn't much extra kitchen space at the lodge, so

I decided on mocha pudding cakes. We could assemble them at Torte, bake them in their ramekin containers, and then reheat them at the lodge.

That would give guests a cold cheesecake bite, molten mocha pudding, gingerbread cookies, and brownies. I felt good about the new dessert lineup and began preparing the batter for the mocha pudding by whisking melted butter, sugar, and hot milk together. Then I added eggs, vanilla, cocoa powder, and flour. I coated dozens of ramekins with nonstick spray and used an ice cream scoop to ensure each portion of batter was even. For the cakes to have a pudding-like constituency, I combined coffee, cocoa powder, brown sugar, and hot water and poured a little into each of the ramekins.

They would bake for fifteen to twenty minutes. Then, once we transported them to the lodge, we could give them a bonus two or three minutes in the oven to warm them and then top them with house-made chocolate whipping cream.

"This is like being on the *Amour* again, Julieta," Carlos said as he chopped enough romaine lettuce to feed the Roman army.

"We have a small but mighty kitchen," I agreed. One common misconception for those unfamiliar with the culinary world was that most professional kitchens were large and expansive. The opposite was usually true. Some of the world's best kitchens were half the size of Torte's. On the cruise ship, the galley kitchens that Carlos and I operated were well organized but not large by any measure. The difference with a professional kitchen is embracing mise en place. Everything and everyone who entered our kitchen had its place.

My background running a pastry kitchen on the boutique cruise ship was much like Lance's when he staged a play. It might appear seamless to the audience, but hours of work and organization went on behind the scenes. I couldn't count how many times a guest would ask for a tour of the ship's kitchen only to be left speechless when they saw how little space it took to create three-tiered cakes and tray upon tray of glossy pastries.

It was always fun to see the shock on their faces when they realized that only a small handful of us made their breakfast croissants and tropical custards.

With the desserts done, I packed my baking tool kit, coordinated arrival times, and checked in with the rest of the team. Mom and I planned to meet at the lodge with Janet, Marcia, and Wendy to decorate before guests began arriving. Carlos would come later with the rest of the family.

Everything was going according to plan, and the team was fine, except for Andy. When I went upstairs with my supplies, Bethany was leaning over the edge of the espresso counter, whispering in low tones like she was trying to console him. I put my things on an empty table and went to see what was wrong. I wasn't sure why she was whispering, since the bakeshop was closed for the holiday. There was no one around to overhear their conversation. Andy had shown up to help with prep and offered to make coffees for the team.

"Hey, sorry to interrupt, but is there a problem?"

Andy threw his arms up. "Yeah, there's a huge problem. The lodge. What if tonight doesn't work? What if it closes for good? What am I going to do without the mountain? It's my happy place."

"I thought this was your happy place," I teased, trying to lighten his mood.

"Exactly," Bethany chimed in, shooting me a look of gratitude. "I've been telling him the same thing for an hour. And the lodge isn't going to close. We're going to save it. I'm sure of it. You have to think positively."

I appreciated her enthusiasm. I was confident we could raise enough tonight to keep things running for a month or so. The fact that the event had sold out within an hour of announcing it online told me that we weren't alone in our efforts to keep the lifts running. Everyone would answer the call to save our beloved ski resort. But when it came to the long-term future of the lodge, that was another story. Keeping the ski slope afloat would take more capital than a Torte dinner could solve.

"Tonight is a good start," I said, backing up Bethany. "And it's just one night. There's a lot more we can do. Don't lose faith."

Andy reached for a canister of beans. "I was just saying to Bethany that maybe I should get to work on a Mount A blend. I could donate the proceeds to the lodge."

"That's a great idea. I'm sure Kendall is going to be eager to brainstorm lots of ideas in the days ahead. But, for now, let's focus on tonight and see how much we raise, and then we can start thinking of plan B."

Andy blew out a breath and patted the canister. "Okay, I'll start putting together a flavor profile of my favorite slope."

"That's the spirit." Bethany squeezed his hand.

I had a bus to catch, so I didn't stick around, but it was impossible to miss the fact that Andy and Bethany's connection was growing. Ah, young love. Who knew? Maybe

Torte would have another wedding to celebrate in the years ahead.

*You're getting way ahead of yourself, Jules.*

I chuckled at myself as I grabbed a seat on the ski bus. The steamy window and humidity inside the bus immediately brought back memories of my middle and high school years when Thomas and I, along with groups of friends, would cram onto the bus with money in our pockets for snacks at the lodge and extra layers of gear. Of course, we didn't have cell phones back then. A few of my friends had flip phones, but for the most part, we said goodbye to our parents after breakfast, boarded the bus, spent the day on the mountain, and then returned home after dark. In hindsight, it was such a freeing time to come of age. We had the slopes to ourselves and the freedom to explore trails or congregate for hours on the third-floor couches of the lodge drinking copious amounts of hot chocolate.

I smiled at the memory as the bus picked up speed, entering the freeway.

Sugar pines, Douglas firs, and cedars flashed in my side view. The snowplows had come through earlier, packing the snow so deep on both sides of the highway that it felt like we were driving through a dusty white cave.

The lodge and ski lifts couldn't close permanently. Mount A was a winter treasure.

Tonight's dinner was a start, but I knew Kendall would need to raise more capital and find additional funding sources to keep the resort running. I wondered if Lance would be able to assist Kendall in securing investors. He was connected with OSF donors who had deep pockets. We just needed to put a call out to snow lovers who might want to bequeath their legacy to the lodge.

The drive up the mountain didn't take long. I was one of only a handful of people on the bus. The die-hard New Year's Day skiers were already on the slopes, whereas bigger crowds wouldn't show up until much later in the afternoon. I had a feeling that those who had taken part in last night's fireworks display and torch parade were likely still snug in their beds.

The ski shop rental area confirmed my suspicions. There were only a handful of youngsters being fitted for boots and no one in line for concessions. The second and third levels were roped off with signage that the lodge was closed for a private event.

I ducked under the sign and headed upstairs.

A faint hint of woodsmoke lingered in the air. Most of the balloons still clung to the ceiling. Unfortunately, a few had drifted to the floor. I would deal with those later.

I was surprised that there wasn't a cleaning crew already working, but then again, maybe Kendall couldn't afford the extra help. Discarded party hats, noise makers, cups, napkins, and champagne glasses were scattered on the ballroom tables.

I looked around for garbage cans, but the only ones I found were already overflowing. It was a good thing I had opted to arrive early; we were going to have our work cut out for us to get the space sparkling again.

We also needed large folding tables and extra chairs. The round high-top bar tables had been fine for last night's party. But our goal was to feed as many people as possible, which meant that the dance floor was going to need to become a dining area. I had no idea where to find tables and chairs, and there were no staff onsite to ask, so I decided to go up to the third floor to see if Kendall was in her office.

A strange feeling came over me as the stairs creaked beneath my feet. Was someone watching me?

"Hello? Is anyone up here?" I called.

An eerie silence greeted me.

"Kendall, it's Jules; I'm here to set up for dinner," I said louder, hoping my tone held a confidence I didn't feel.

I crested the stairs.

The upper alcove to my right was where the DJ station had been set up last night. More balloons, streamers, and party favors littered the small dance floor. The shades had been drawn, making it nearly impossible to see in the cavernous room. Despite its twenty-foot ceilings, it felt like the space was closing in on me.

"Kendall, are you around?" I kept my voice light as I blinked to adjust to the darkness.

Her office was down the narrow hallway to my left, which was also plunged into blackness. I fumbled along the wall, trying to find a light switch.

Maybe I was the first one to arrive.

Otherwise, why would the whole upper level be completely dark?

Was this a bad idea?

What if the killer was hiding out, waiting to attack me?

*You're being ridiculous, Jules.*

What were the odds that the killer knew I was here, let alone that they had staked out higher ground in hopes that I would wander upstairs and they could strike?

I chuckled out loud.

*You've been spending too much time with Lance.*

I continued down the dimly lit hallway until I found Kendall's door. I knocked on it twice.

No one answered, so I tried the handle.

Surprisingly it turned with ease.

I twisted it slowly as I announced myself again. I didn't want to spook Kendall if she was on a call. "Kendall, it's Jules. I'm looking for garbage cans and tables," I said as I stepped into the pitch-black room.

At the same moment, Kendall's side door that led out to the deck swung open. A flash of light briefly illuminated her office.

"Kendall?"

Whoever had opened the door slammed it behind them. The room went dark again.

I froze. Should I follow after them? Technically speaking, I was trespassing in Kendall's private space, but then again, I had a dinner to put on. There was no logical reason for Kendall to run away from me.

Unless she wasn't.

What if Kendall wasn't running from me?

What if she was in danger and trying to get away from the killer?

Or what if that wasn't Kendall after all?

# Chapter Twenty-Three

My heartbeat thudded in my neck. A rushing sound reverberated in my ears. I stood paralyzed in Kendall's office door frame.

What should I do? Had I seen Kendall or someone else?

Who had been in her office, and why had they raced off when I came inside?

I felt the wall next to the door for a light switch. This time I found one. The instant the lights went on, I knew why the person had taken off.

Kendall's desk drawers had been overturned. Their contents were dumped on the floor like the New Year's Eve confetti in the ballroom. Her chair had been knocked over. Books had been tossed on the floor near her bookcase.

This was no coincidence.

Someone had rummaged through her things and now was trying to get away.

I raced to the side door. Adrenaline shot through my system. It felt like I had just slugged straight shots of espresso.

The knob wouldn't budge.

Whoever was outside must have been clutching it so I couldn't open it.

I yanked harder.

No luck.

My pulse throbbed in my neck. I couldn't stop now. I had to know who was out there.

Suddenly a new thought came to me. There was another way to catch whoever had torn apart Kendall's office. I could go around to the main doors that led from the alcove to the deck.

However, I didn't want to alert them to my move, so I slowly released my grasp on the handle, locked it, and tiptoed away from the door. I made a careful exit from the main office door.

For the moment, I had the upper hand and wanted to keep it that way.

As long as the culprit was unaware of my plan, I could lock the lodge doors from the inside and trap them on the deck. Then there would be nowhere for them to go. The deck was at least sixty feet from the ground. Their only option would be to try and jump, and they wouldn't survive the fall.

I was glad for the dimly lit hallways on this floor as I inched along the timbered walls toward the glass sliders. It smelled musty from years of wet boots and melted snow.

As I got closer to the doors, light from outside trickled in, casting shadows on the carpet and reflecting off the silver balloons. An abandoned neon green jacket hung on the snowboard coatrack. Oversized beanbag chairs had been pushed against the bookcases, and more party hats and noise makers were scattered on the couches and the old mining cart coffee table.

The antler chandeliers were off, so my only light was the gray sky filtering through the sliding doors that opened onto the deck. Three-foot-high snow berms encompassed the deck. A path had been shoveled from Kendall's office door to the far railing.

The whooshing sound in my ears grew stronger as I entered the alcove. My heartbeat pulsed faster. It wasn't particularly warm, but sweat beaded on my forehead. This was dangerous. There was no denying it. I was intentionally putting myself in harm's way. But what other choice did I have?

I was mere feet away from catching the person who most likely killed Fitz. I had to take the risk. There was no turning back now.

I peeked about an inch forward, careful to keep most of my body out of the door frame. The person was dressed in black ski gear. Their back was turned to me, so I couldn't tell who it was.

They still had one hand on Kendall's door.

I moved forward with cautious intention. I couldn't let them see me. At least not until I got these doors locked.

I twisted the lock on the first slider. Gray clouds rolling in over the summit shrouded the weather station.

*One down, three to go. You can do this, Jules.*

My eyes remained focused on the skier in black as I locked the second slider. But as I stepped closer to the last set of doors, they jiggled Kendall's office door handle.

The pounding in my chest grew more vigorous.

I ran to the next slider, not caring if they saw me now. It locked with ease.

The person pounded on the office door. Realization must have started to sink in.

I reached for the fourth and final lock.

It stuck.

It wouldn't turn.

The person swiveled their head in my direction.

I panicked.

The lock slipped through my fingers.

Why wouldn't it lock?

The person abandoned the side door and stomped toward me.

I didn't get a good look at them because I was using my entire body weight to shove the slider in its track.

*Lock, please lock.*

Footsteps thudded on the deck.

Snow dumped from the roofline.

The lock still wouldn't turn.

I was out of luck.

I searched around for anything I could wedge in the base of the track. There was a stack of firewood about five feet away. If I could reach it in time, I could shove a piece of wood in the bottom of the door.

I didn't allow myself time to consider an alternative.

It was now or never.

I raced to the wood stack, grabbed the smallest piece I could find, and jammed it in the door just as the figure reached for the handle.

"Let me in!"

I looked up to see Hero on the other side of the glass.

"What are you doing?"

He yanked on the handle. "Let me in."

"Not until you tell me what you were doing in Kendall's office."

He tugged harder.

I wasn't sure the stick of kindling was going to hold. Hero was a big guy, and I could tell from the deep lines etched around his eyes that he was using all his might to get the door open.

"You have no idea what you're doing. You have to let me in." His eyes were wild.

"Why were you in her office?" I repeated, shaking my head and folding my arms across my chest. I hoped it made me look resolved to stand my ground. In actuality, I was trying to figure out if a better idea was to sprint downstairs. I had been a runner in high school. It would probably take Hero a minute or two to break the kindling. That would buy me enough time to get to help first.

"Look, you don't get it. You have to let me in now!" His voice elevated in a panicked pitch.

"I'm not going to let you in so you can hurt me."

"Hurt you? I'm trying to save you," he yelled through the thin glass.

"Save me?"

"We are *both* in danger right now. Let me in." His voice sounded like he was scared.

Was it an act to get me to open the door?

Hero's eyes bulged. "Please, I'm not going to hurt you. We have to get out of here now. There isn't time."

I wanted to believe him.

Unless he had been taking private acting classes with Lance, the fear on his face made my stomach sink.

"Now, open it—now," he commanded, looking with horror from Kendall's office to me and then back again.

I gnawed on the inside of my cheek as I bent over and yanked the piece of wood from the track. Hero slid the door open in one lightning-fast, fluid move, grabbed my hand, and dragged me down the stairs.

"What are you doing?"

"We have to evacuate the building now!"

"You're acting like there's a bomb or something."

He didn't waiver in his response as he took the stairs two at a time. "There is."

# Chapter Twenty-Four

What was Hero talking about? A bomb at the lodge?

Hero barreled down the stairwell, tossing streamers out of his face and skipping the last step. He flailed his arms as he shouted, "Get out! Everyone outside!"

Skiers in line at concessions looked at us with amusement and disbelief, like they thought Hero was playing a practical joke.

"You need to evacuate the lodge—now!" He used both arms to push everyone forward.

His urgency shifted the tone.

One woman dropped her popcorn. Another scooped up her toddler and started for the door. People began to scream and run for the exits. The small staff behind the walk-up counter abandoned their posts and raced for the stairs with us.

Fortunately, the lodge wasn't very crowded. Although there were probably twenty or thirty of us at most, a backup formed at the stairs even with our small numbers. Hero shoved his way forward and flung open the doors.

"Outside—get as far away from the lodge as possible."

He propped the door open with his body and reached for a walkie-talkie in his pocket. His emergency training had obviously kicked in, because he was entirely in command of the situation.

"Hit the fire alarm. It's right over there," he said to me while trying to get a signal on the walkie.

I did as he instructed. If this was an elaborate ruse, the authorities could deal with Hero. On the other hand, if there was even a tiny chance that he was right about a bomb threat, I wasn't going to risk anyone's life, including my own.

I pulled the fire alarm, setting off an ear-piercing repeated blare.

People scattered on the mountainside as the lifts came to a screeching halt. Ski patrol zoomed toward the lodge while everyone else raced away in the opposite direction. Shawn was at the front of the pack.

"What's going on, man?" he asked Hero. Given that he was in uniform and responding to the emergency, I assumed he must still be employed.

Every muscle in Hero's neck strained as he widened his stance to block Shawn or any of his colleagues from coming any closer. "There could be an explosion."

I vacated the entryway and ran toward them, thankful for my runs through Lithia Park and morning walks to the bakeshop. My legs moved like they were being controlled by someone else.

"I don't know if the building is clear." Hero stood frozen, maintaining a physical barricade between us and the lodge.

"We can do a sweep." Shawn pushed his UV sunglasses onto the top of his head and took a step forward.

Hero thrust his arm out to stop him. "It's not worth it, dude. We need to move farther away."

The ski patrol team agreed with Hero. "We're not trained for fire or explosives," one of them said to Shawn. "We have to wait for the fire department to arrive. This is way outside the scope of our training."

Shawn scanned the three-story lodge as if expecting to see someone waving to be rescued from one of the upper windows. "Okay, yeah, I guess so."

Given his close friendship with Andy, I had been fairly convinced that Shawn wasn't a killer since day one. The fact that he wanted to run into a building that might explode at any minute strengthened my conviction. Shawn was acting like a true hero.

"Come on, man, let's move away," Hero said, scanning the mountainside like he was trying to count every person on the slope.

I followed along with them. Once we were about fifty feet away from the lodge, we stopped.

"What's the deal? Why do you think there could be an explosive inside?" Shawn asked Hero. He unbuckled his vest and took out his satellite phone. "I have to call this in. It's the official procedure, but they're going to want more details."

Pulling the fire alarm sent an automatic signal to the fire and police departments. I wondered how long it would take for them to arrive.

"There's an explosive device in Kendall's office on the third floor." Hero clenched his eyes shut and then did the same with his hands, balling them into tight fists.

"What kind of device?" Shawn studied him with a calm that I didn't feel.

"It's a pipe bomb, I think."

"You think?" Shawn spoke with newfound authority. "Listen, I know this is stressful, man, but we're going to need more than that to go on."

I agreed.

I was glad that Shawn was asking the same questions I was thinking. How did Hero know there was a pipe bomb? Had he planted it there right before I had caught him in Kendall's office?

Hero flicked the zipper on his ski jacket. "It's complicated."

"Nah, bro. That's not good enough." Shawn angled the satellite phone toward Hero and stood ready to make the call. "We're going to need details, and we're going to need them now."

I was impressed that he was holding firm.

"I got intel that someone had planted a bomb in Kendall's office," Hero said with resignation. He slanted his gaze to the ground, staring at his ski boots. "I went up there to try and find it and get it out of the lodge."

I wanted to interrupt and ask him exactly how he had intended to defuse a bomb.

"I couldn't find it, and then she saw me digging through the office." He looked up and motioned to me. "I freaked and ran outside, and then she locked me out."

Everyone turned to stare at me as Hero pointed in my direction.

I shrugged. "I was looking for Kendall and found her office completely ransacked." I wasn't sure that Hero's story was adding up. "If you were worried about a destructive device in her office, why did you run outside instead of warning me?"

Shawn bobbed his head in agreement. "Yeah, man, this is sounding pretty wild."

"I was trying to help someone, okay?" Hero stole a glance toward the chair lifts.

I followed his gaze, trying to see who he was looking at, but the crowd was packed together like sardines.

"How much time do we have?" I interjected. "Is the bomb going to go off at any minute? Are we far enough away?"

Hero shook his head. "I don't know. I couldn't find it. I'm not sure if it's even there. It could have been removed before I got up there. Or it could be a dud."

"You're going have to give us more," Shawn said with a frustrated shake of his head. He tapped the phone. "I've got to call this in. What kind of bomb are we talking about, and who put it there?"

Hero swallowed hard, like he was forcing himself to work up the courage to speak. "January. It was January."

"January put a bomb in Kendall's office?" I blurted out.

Hero glanced around like he was looking for help. "I think so. She might have had second thoughts, though. I tried to talk her out of it."

"What? Why?" Shawn scrunched his forehead.

"She learned that Kendall was going to sell the west slope and allow it to be clear-cut. She works for an environmental group that has a history of some guerilla-like tactics."

"You mean like planting bombs?" I asked, not bothering to control the incredulous tone in my voice. The wind had kicked up as more ominous clouds blocked the sun. Thankfully I hadn't taken my parka off when looking for

Kendall. I rubbed my hands together and wiggled my toes to try and keep warm.

"She wasn't going to hurt anyone." Hero sounded defensive. "It was supposed to go off last night after everyone left. She was going to put it in Kendall's office after the party. No one stays at the lodge overnight. The goal was to destroy the paperwork and make sure the sale couldn't go through."

"Isn't most paperwork digital these days?" I asked.

"Yeah, but it was also to send a message," Hero said, tugging his earlobe.

"Where's January now, and how do you know this?" Shawn made eye contact with another member of ski patrol who moved to Hero's left.

"I don't know." Hero craned his neck toward the crowd gathered under the lift. "I can't find her. She told me about it last night, and I begged her not to do it. She said she had to. It's her life's purpose to save the planet."

"And potentially kill or injure innocent people in the process?" I added, trying to squash the trembling feeling in my legs. I felt like my knees were going to give out at any second. January had planted a bomb, and Hero had let her go through with it. I had been up in Kendall's office moments ago; if the device had gone off then . . . I couldn't finish the thought.

*Stop, Jules.*

*Don't go there.*

"No, really." Hero's face sagged. "That's the thing. You don't understand. She would never hurt anyone intentionally. She's trying to protect the planet. She's trying to save all of our futures. The plan was to trigger the explosion when the lodge was vacant. It wasn't to hurt anyone."

I thought back to my conversation with January. She admitted that she had been arrested in the past for her involvement with the environmental group. I wondered how honest she had been. Could she have caused more than minor property damage? And if she was willing to plant a homemade bomb in Kendall's office, what else was she capable of? The other looming question was, where was she? When I last saw her, she talked about escaping and going off the grid. What if that was because she had already planted the bomb? January could very well be the killer. And she might be plotting to kill again.

# Chapter Twenty-Five

Shawn continued to pummel Hero with questions that he struggled to answer.

"How did she make the bomb? When did she plant it? What kind of materials did she use?" As he interrogated his friend, the rest of the ski patrol team fanned out to encircle Hero.

Hero kept forcing himself to swallow as he tried to answer Shawn's questions. It was like he couldn't stomach having to tell the truth.

Were he and January in it together?

Maybe they had killed Fitz and now were trying to get rid of the evidence. Or they were both extremists who would go to any length to stop the destruction of the wild forest lands. Where was she? I needed a timeline of when she had last been seen.

Hero tipped his head back and stared at the ski lifts. "Like I said, I tried to stop her last night. She watched a video demonstration on how to build a pipe bomb. I told her it was too dangerous. She might kill herself in the process, but she wouldn't listen. She was determined."

"When did you see her last?" I asked, wondering if Hero was watching the lifts for January.

"I was supposed to see her here this morning." He scanned the ski slope again before turning to me. "She wanted to meet when the lifts opened to see the damage before staff and ski patrol arrived. I got here first and couldn't find her. It was obvious that the bomb hadn't gone off, so I panicked. I didn't know what to do. Had she had a change of heart? Was she up in Kendall's office trying to detonate it by hand? I searched everywhere for her. I've called her cell like a million times. It goes straight to voicemail, so she must have shut it off, or . . ."

"Or what?" Shawn asked.

"I don't know." Hero gave him a halfhearted shrug. "Maybe something happened to her. Maybe the killer got to her."

The killer? He still believed that January was innocent.

Or, again, I couldn't help but wonder if they had teamed up. There was a chance that Hero knew exactly where January was right now.

"I'm not kidding. I've searched every square inch of the mountain." He swept his hands toward the lifts and then to the cross-country ski trails. "I went out to the warming hut, checked the ski patrol bunk rooms, and searched all around the lifts. She's nowhere. Then staff and skiers started showing up. I had to do something. I checked the lodge. The kitchen, the ballroom, everywhere, and still couldn't find her, so the only thing left was to try and find the bomb."

"You didn't find it?" Shawn asked.

"No. I tore Kendall's office apart. I don't think it's there, but that doesn't mean that it might not be somewhere else in the lodge. What if January put it in another room? The lodge is huge. It could be anywhere."

"How big is the bomb?"

"I'm not sure. I didn't see it. She just told me about it."

"Why didn't you alert the police last night?" I asked. My stomach knotted like I had eaten an entire batch of cookies. I didn't trust what Hero was telling us. If he had been concerned about public safety, he would have gone to the police immediately.

Hero exhaled. "I should have. I know it. I regret it. January and I have gotten pretty close the last couple of months, and I thought she wouldn't go through with it. She's a good person. She cares deeply about the planet, you know?"

"That doesn't justify her actions," I said. "You can also be named an accessory to her crimes. If you had knowledge about an explosive device and didn't share that with the authorities, you could be arrested, too."

"I know. That's why I tried to do the right thing." Hero stared at the upper deck.

Had he been the person who had launched icicles at Lance and me last night? What if he and January had been trying to plant the bomb? They might have gotten nervous that we had heard their conversation and decided to scare us off.

It was odd that the icicles had come from the third-floor deck.

He took a tube of ChapStick out of his safety vest and ran it over his lips. "I'm hoping she had a change of heart, but I had to sound the alarm and evacuate the lodge in case she didn't."

Shawn had heard enough. He called the police.

Half of the ski patrol crew were holding skiers and boarders away from the action, while the other half kept a close eye on Hero. Empty chair lifts swung in the wind.

I could hear the wail of sirens in the distance. Hopefully, the fire department would arrive soon. Although I wondered if they could enter the building. They might have to call in reinforcements from Medford. Come to think of it, did the Rogue Valley even have a bomb squad?

Hero yanked off his ski hat and ran his hands through his hair. "Look, I'm sorry about this. You all know me. You know I'm a good guy. I care about safety. I care about my clients." He looked at me to confirm his point. "I know I should have called the police right away when January told me her plans, but I really thought I could talk her out of it. Maybe I did. It has to be a good sign that I didn't find anything in Kendall's office, right?"

He sounded sincere in his regret, but I still wasn't sure I entirely trusted his story. The timing of his sudden change of heart seemed too coincidental. And I was confused about how he had planned to get rid of the bomb if he had found it. There were too many things that didn't line up.

First and foremost, I thought about the timing. January had vanished, and as far as I had heard, no one had seen her in over forty-eight hours. Hero claimed she was at the lodge last night and that they were supposed to meet this morning. The Professor hadn't gone into specifics, but based on our conversation, he had certainly seemed to imply that they were still looking for her.

Hero was, in theory, the only person who had seen her since she'd said she was going off the grid.

The other piece that was impossible to ignore was this

mysterious bomb. Was there really a bomb, or was it simply a smokescreen? A tactic to distract us all?

I didn't buy his sudden heroism, his name notwithstanding. If he had known that January intended to blow up Kendall's office, why hadn't he immediately contacted the police? Why hadn't he called them this morning? Why had he waited so long to get inside? And, finally, did he have any intention of trying to find the bomb?

That felt like another lie.

What was he really doing in Kendall's office?

I blew on my hands to keep my fingers warm as another icy thought invaded.

What if Hero knew exactly where January was because he had killed her too?

I didn't have time to dwell on the thought, because two fire engines and three police cars roared into view with their lights flashing and sirens wailing.

The Professor took charge of the scene after Shawn gave him a brief report. He moved Hero away from us and told the fire department to hold off entering the building for a moment. They spread across the slope, moving bystanders farther away from the lodge.

I felt relieved to know that the authorities were on-site, but I couldn't get warm. The stress of the morning, of finding Hero, and then the potential of the bomb had finally caught up with me. My knees felt weak, like they might give out at any moment. My teeth ached from the cold. I hadn't come prepared for the elements. I had thought I would be sweaty inside, running up and down the stairs, setting up tables, and prepping for the dinner.

Speaking of the dinner, it was also odd that Kendall

hadn't shown up yet. She had been so excited and grateful about hosting the fundraiser last night.

My mind raced with more possibilities. What if Hero had attacked her and then dug through her office to either find something he had left behind or create this elaborate fabrication of a bomb threat? The more I thought about it, the more guilty his actions appeared.

The Professor had finished questioning Hero and had gathered the team of first responders. It looked like they were planning their next move, probably escalating the situation and calling in the bomb squad.

Before they finished their huddle, a figure appeared on the third-floor deck. "I'm here," the woman called from above.

We all turned to see January holding both arms over her head in a show of surrender.

# Chapter Twenty-Six

The Professor used a megaphone to address her. "Are you safe?"

In the movies, situations like the one unfolding in front of me were dramatized with special task forces and trained hostage negotiators. However, the reality of life in a small town in southern Oregon meant that the Professor had to wear many hats. In this case, it appeared that it was up to him to determine whether January was a threat.

She kept her arms raised as she answered. "I'm fine. There's no bomb."

"Can you elaborate?" he said into the megaphone.

"There's no bomb," she yelled louder. "I didn't go through with it." She stayed put, not moving a single muscle as she shouted to him.

I wouldn't have wanted to be in his position. I knew that he was astute when it came to reading people and body language, but how could he be one hundred percent sure that January wasn't bluffing and couldn't detonate an explosive device at any minute?

"Why don't you come down, and we'll talk about it?"

The Professor's velvety tone put me at ease. I hoped it was doing the same for January.

"You're going to arrest me. I'm not coming down. If you want to talk, come up here." January's voice was pitchy and hoarse.

Was it a trap?

Was she trying to get him and the other first responders in the building only to detonate the bomb?

The Professor didn't react, at least not outwardly. Instead, he gave her a slight nod. "Give me a moment to confer with my colleagues."

"January, don't do this," Hero pleaded.

She shook her head, her arms still rigid. "I'm in too deep."

What did that mean?

Every fiber of my body made me want to throw my arms around the Professor and stop him from going into the lodge. The crowd had grown in the last hour. People smashed together behind me watching the scene unfold like we were at an outdoor performance of an impromptu OSF show.

Only it wasn't fiction. The Professor was my family.

What if January was unhinged?

What if this was her ultimate plan?

It could be a setup to get the police and firefighters inside to do the most damage.

I thought I might actually be sick when, after a brief discussion with his fellow police and fire squads, the Professor addressed her on the bullhorn. "We will come inside to chat with you, but we need you to meet us halfway."

"What's halfway?" January yelled as her voice broke.

"The ballroom," the Professor answered, pointing to the second-floor windows.

January thought for a minute and then nodded. "Okay, the ballroom."

Teams of uniformed officers, firefighters, and ski patrol spread in every direction. Their blue, black, and red jackets stood out starkly against the white snow.

I didn't have a chance to warn the Professor. Instead, I held my breath and watched with trepidation as they mounted the stairs and disappeared into the lodge.

Shawn came up next to me. "You look pretty freaked. Don't worry. They train for this."

"But what if she has a bomb?" I couldn't shake the sense that something could go terribly wrong.

"That's probably why they're getting her to the second floor." He placed a hand on my shoulder in a show of solidarity. "They have procedures for this, I swear. I'd be in there myself, but technically I'm on probation at the moment. But I swear, not a single first responder would go into that building if they thought they were in danger. We've simulated events like this in my training for ski patrol. They're not going to put themselves at risk."

"I hope you're right." I watched apprehensively for any sign of movement on the second floor.

I couldn't concentrate as we waited for anyone to re-emerge from the lodge. It took what felt like three hours, but in reality, it was closer to twenty minutes. January came out first, her arms handcuffed behind her back and the Professor at her side. None of the firefighters exited. I wondered if that meant they were combing the lodge for any evidence of explosives.

The Professor escorted January to a waiting squad car, chatted briefly with two officers, and then joined us. I threw my arms around him. "I'm so glad you're okay. I was so worried."

"I appreciate the concern but I do not believe we were at risk." He squeezed me tight. "And I can assure you that the threat has been resolved. We will be taking extra precautions before we allow anyone to return inside. I understand that preparations for tonight's event are due to begin. However, I must ask that you wait until we receive the final all-clear."

"Of course." I had no interest in setting up for dinner before it was safe. "Did January have an explosive device?"

"In parts, yes. That's why we're bringing her in to the station. She will likely need a mental health evaluation and some support."

"Do you mean literally in parts?" I asked.

"Indeed I do. She confessed to her intent to cause property damage. It sounds as if she wrestled with her conscience. Thankfully it won out, and she did not assemble the device."

I couldn't believe she had planned to do it or that she had confessed.

"The fire crew will be removing the materials she brought along. Again, another extreme precaution. The fire chief is not concerned that any of the chemicals or materials independent of one another are in danger of causing an explosion. They are taking the utmost caution in removing them, but January's efforts appeared to be quite rudimentary. The chief doesn't believe she had the right combination of chemicals." He motioned to another officer nearby. "One moment."

I tried to make sense of this new information while he conferred with the police officer. Had January solely wanted to cause property damage, or had her mission been more sinister? It was a considerable risk to set off an explosive inside the lodge. There was no possible way she could have known without a shred of doubt that the building was completely empty. Surely if she had wanted to sabotage the deal or destroy the contract Fitz had drawn up, there would have been another way.

The Professor returned shortly. "I can't say much more. I'm needed in multiple places at the moment."

"I don't want to keep you. But do you think proceeding with the dinner tonight is safe?"

He glanced at the lodge. "Once the fire crew completes their search and gives us the green light, I can't think of any reason why not. In fact, I can think of several reasons why you should go ahead with it."

"You mean so that we can raise enough money for Kendall to pay staff?"

"Yes." He tapped his finger to his chin. "I would also appreciate an opportunity to observe our suspects up close and personal this evening, as long as this turn of events hasn't been too unsettling for you."

"Not at all. As Lance would say, I'm happy to have the show go on."

"Excellent." He twisted the cashmere scarf tighter around his neck. "As the Bard says, 'Suspicion always haunts the guilty mind,' and I believe we are closing in on the guilty party."

"Do you think it was January?"

"January has her own challenges and demons to face, but I wouldn't say that murder is one of them. Her passion for the planet is commendable. Her actions, on the other hand, could use some channeling for good."

"You don't think she was trying to hurt anyone?"

"At this point, it's too soon to eliminate her completely, but I'm inclined to believe that her commitment to saving the forest overrode her rational thought process. Was her intent to do damage? Yes. Injure or harm? Doubtful."

"What about Hero?" I knew the Professor had work to do, but I also didn't want to be stuck in the lodge with Hero if he had any involvement in the bomb scheme or Fitz's death.

The Professor's eyes narrowed. "He will also be taking a ride to the station. I'm not at liberty to divulge more, but I certainly have additional questions that will need answering before I feel comfortable."

"Okay, thanks for the update. I feel better knowing that. Once I hear from the fire chief, we'll resume setup, and I'll see you later."

"Wonderful. As always, thank you for your assistance, and be watchful."

I took his words seriously.

He left to escort Hero to the waiting squad car. There wasn't much for me to do other than try to stay warm by dancing back and forth and constantly wiggling my fingers and toes. By the time the fire chief announced that lodge and ski operations could resume, the tips of my fingers were purple, my nose was drippy, and my cheeks stung.

I was eager to get inside to start warming my extremities and concentrate on decorating the ballroom for dinner. I needed to do something to keep my head from spinning. The problem was that I was completely clueless, even though the Professor sounded like he had a solid sense of who could have killed Fitz.

January didn't seem like a viable suspect any longer. Neither did Hero. I had a feeling the Professor wanted to question him more about the bomb. Shawn had truly been heroic during the evacuation process. There were still Kendall and Ruth, and I hadn't come up with a reason to clear either of them from my list of potential suspects. But the fact that it was down to two made me nervous that I was overlooking something critical.

# Chapter Twenty-Seven

I didn't have time to dwell on any of it. The bomb scare had put us behind schedule. I spent the next three hours racing up and down the stairs, taking loads of garbage and recycling out to the bins, bringing in folding tables, and rearranging the ballroom. When Mom and Janet showed up with boxes of flowers and candles for the centerpieces, I left them to put together the final touches of décor and went to check on space in the kitchen.

Kendall was waiting for me in front of the snack bar. "Oh, thank goodness you're here. I've been looking everywhere for you." She tugged on the strings of her Mount Ashland lodge hoodie.

"For me? I've been looking for you. Did you hear what happened earlier?"

"You mean about Hero and January?" She sounded nonchalant, like someone had accidentally spilled hot chocolate on the counter, not attempted to blow up her office. "The police informed me, but we really need to focus on tonight. I've let my staff know that they can serve concessions for twenty more minutes. Then we'll go through our cleaning protocols and hand the kitchen over to you. What else do you need from my end?"

Was she serious? How was she glossing over an attempted attack—on her?

"I'm fine. I don't think we'll need anything else, but are you sure you're okay? Have you seen your office?" I motioned above us.

"Yes, yes, the police did a walk-through with me." She ran her hands over her hoodie and sweats. "I haven't even had a chance to get dressed. They woke me up from such a peaceful sleep for this ridiculousness. January was trying to get attention. I'm sure she thought she'd make front-page news. That's her goal—she's a sensationalist. The police activity inside is nothing more than a formality. I'm not concerned that it will impact tonight's fundraiser, which is my only focus now. It should be yours as well, Jules. You are up for catering, right?"

Kendall had gone through a dramatic shift. It was like she was a completely different person.

"I'm not trying to be rude. I appreciate everything you're doing for me, my family, and the lodge, but I cannot be bothered with these silly distractions from January right now. We have well over one hundred people arriving within the next hour. I absolutely cannot disappoint. Your mom and Janet suggested a live auction, and if we can impress them with the food, the ambiance, the entire vibe, then I just might have a shot at saving the resort." Kendall motioned to one of her staff. "I'll be with you in a moment." Then she finished her speech to me. "I've asked Shawn to speak about ski patrol's role in public safety here on the mountain. I'm preparing a slide show, and Lance will be the MC of the event and is offering a New Year's

Day pantomime. It's a far cry from where I was a day or so ago. I thought I was out of hope. You've changed that. I cannot thank you enough, and I refuse to let January's attempt to scare me sway us from our mission tonight."

She excused herself to speak with her staff member.

Her intensity mirrored her sentiment. I understood her drive to save the resort and lodge, but I also couldn't imagine being so cavalier if I had learned that Torte had been threatened.

What if there was another explanation for her behavior? Could she have been aware of January's intentions? Could she have been in on it with January and Hero?

I considered the possibility. They shared a common goal. Kendall wanted to preserve the lodge and her family's legacy, and January wanted to preserve the forest. What if it had all been an elaborate ruse?

I still wondered where Kendall had been this entire time. She had magically appeared as if nothing had happened. Could she have rummaged through her office herself?

She and January could have hidden out together and let Hero take the fall.

Maybe the three of them had masterminded the entire setup.

"Juliet, hello, hello." The sound of my name shook me out of my head.

I turned to see Lance and Arlo cresting the stairs, carrying boxes of props.

"Do you need a hand?" I offered.

"Not at all. Don't move a finger, darling." Lance lifted his box with one arm. "It's as light as a feather. Tricks of the trade, you know."

"What are the props for?"

"Our interactive performance." Lance raised his eyebrows twice and gave me an impish smile that immediately struck fear in my heart.

"Interactive?"

"Don't ask," Arlo warned, giving me a playful grimace. "Not knowing will be much better; trust me on this."

"Gladly." I patted his arm in thanks.

"The place is coming together." Lance peered into the dining area. "Do be a dear, and run these upstairs, won't you? I need a moment with Juliet." He thrust his box into Arlo's arms and shooed him away.

Arlo whispered, "Good luck" to me.

Lance didn't waste one second. "A bomb, darling? A bomb. And you didn't think to call yours truly?" He tugged me out of earshot of the concessions counter over to the corner of the top of the entryway stairs.

"The next time you have to evacuate because of a bomb threat, you tell me if your first thought is to call anyone other than the police."

"Trivial details, darling. I need you to spill the tea." He circled his hands to indicate that I should get to the point.

"There's not much tea to spill." I told him about Hero, January, and my latest conversation with Kendall.

"The plot thickens." He was pensive for a minute. "Although."

"Although what?"

"It's something I saw that now has me wondering." Lance was being intentionally vague.

"But you're not going to share because you're mad that I didn't call you instead of the authorities during a bomb scare."

"I wouldn't use the term mad—it's so pedestrian. Miffed, perhaps." He thrust his bottom lip out in a pout.

"Lance."

"It's not so much what I saw," he said. "It's *where*."

I knew he would drag this on as long as he had me as a captive audience. "I need to finish dessert prep."

"Fine." He sighed and ran his hands over his navy pea coat. "You never let me have any fun."

"Because we have an event soon." I tapped my wrist.

"Right. Well, in that case, I'll cut to the chase. What I saw was January and Ruth at the ATM."

"Where?"

"Right over there." He spun his index finger like a magic wand until it landed in the hallway to the rental shop. An ATM was installed a few years ago. The rental shop lent skis, snowboards, snowshoes, and gear and sold tours and ski school classes. Having an ATM on-site made for quicker transactions for guests.

"Is that important?" I squinted in the hallway as if Lance was showing me physical evidence.

"I didn't register it at the time, but now I suspect it might be."

"Were they just in line to get cash out?"

"*Just* emphasize that word." He rubbed his thumb and index finger together.

"I don't understand what you're hinting at." Lance loved to speak in riddles and code that only he could decipher.

"They were in line, but not by happenstance. I got the impression that January was under some level of duress."

Realization of what he was hinting at began to dawn on me. "You mean that Ruth was forcing her to take cash out?"

"In retrospect, yes."

"Why would she need cash from January?"

A slow smile built. "That is the question, isn't it, darling?"

"Is it a question you have an answer for?"

"In one word, yes."

I waited for him to reveal the word.

He sucked his cheeks in and gave me a devilish smile. "Blackmail, of course."

# Chapter Twenty-Eight

A group of snowboarders traipsed by, their heavy boots echoing with every step. Cold air and a howling wind followed them in. I scooted closer to the corner to make room for them to pass and waited until they were gone to respond. The snow was starting to dump outside. I hoped it wouldn't make the drive home too treacherous.

"Blackmail? Do you think that Ruth was blackmailing January? Why? Because she knew that January was secretly working for the environmental group?"

"It's not so far-fetched."

"Maybe." I wasn't sure I agreed. "Ruth doesn't strike me as the blackmailing type. If she is, she picked the wrong target. January doesn't have any money. She couch surfs and does odd gigs when she can. I don't think she makes anything for her work with the UEP."

"Have money? Uh, yes. I beg to differ." He jutted his chin and rolled up his shirtsleeves. Then he tilted his wrist to show off his gold bracelets. "She's dripping in money like this. She could buy the entire Rogue Valley with her trust fund."

"What?" I deliberately blinked. "January has a trust fund?"

"You didn't know?"

I shook my head.

"Her family trust dwarfs mine. She could write one check and buy us all out." He flicked his hand in the air as if signing away his fortune.

"Then why wouldn't she? That logic doesn't add up. She could have purchased the lodge and resort on her own if she had personal funds to save the timberland."

He paused for a moment, and half bowed to a family who traipsed past us carrying red sleds and bags of home-made trail mix. Once they were far enough away, Lance continued, "I concede that is the piece of this mystery I have yet to figure out. But, rest assured, my superior brain cells are working overtime right now, and I have not a shred of doubt that an aha moment is merely minutes away."

"Wait, how do you know about January's trust fund?" A dull headache was starting to form. I wasn't sure if it was from the stress of the bomb scare or from trying to make sense of this new revelation.

"It takes a trust fund to know one." Lance stretched his lanky arms and cracked his knuckles.

"You're not exactly forthcoming about your family's fortune." It had taken years for him to be honest with me about his past, and despite his tendency to want to be in the spotlight, in reality, he was one of the most generous and humble people I knew when it came to distributing his funds. He anonymously partnered with and sponsored too many nonprofits and charities throughout the community to begin to count.

"True. This is a different scenario. January might play

the role of climate activist beautifully with her cheap secondhand-store attire and last year's snow boots. Still, her reality is vastly different from the façade she's created. Did you know that she flew here in her father's private jet? Or that she's been staying at a vineyard outside of Jacksonville?"

"No, really?" Activity in the lodge had started picking up as the afternoon wore on. The heavy front doors swung open again, sending an icy blast of wind in our direction.

"Oh yes, she's absolutely dripping with money that apparently she has no issue spending when it comes to her personal pampering. Her solid dedication to protecting this third rock from the sun quickly crumbles into sand when met with anything that might hinder her own need for pampering and luxury. Didn't she tell you that she could go off the grid?"

I nodded.

"Off grid for January likely means hiding out at the vineyard cottage complete with a soaking tub, sauna, personal chef, and masseuse."

"I'm shocked by this. I honestly am speechless." I rubbed my shoulders.

"Right?" Lance's pitch shifted to match my surprise. "Get her on the stage, that's what I say. She might not be destined for living off the land, but the woman can certainly act."

"What does it mean in connection with Fitz's murder and her connection with Ruth?"

Lance clapped twice. "This is what we need to unearth. Oh, look at me with my puns. I'm too good; they just slip out."

"Okay, puns aside. Let's think this through. Could there be a chance that January is posing as an activist?"

"No, no. I wouldn't say posing. I believe that she is intent on and committed to imparting change. I also believe that she's accustomed to a certain lifestyle that she might find challenging to let go."

"In that case, if we assume that January has been misguided in her intentions and maybe got wrapped up in the wrong kind of activism, then she and Hero could be telling the truth. She might have had second thoughts about damaging the lodge and ending up with another arrest on her record, but why wouldn't she buy the resort, and how does that explain what you witnessed?"

"That's the conundrum, isn't it?" Lance exhaled. "I'm convinced Ruth was in charge when I happened past them at the ATM. It was clear from January's body language that she was uncomfortable. I should have thought of it sooner. It's a missed detail on my part, and I take full responsibility for that."

"We've both had a lot on our mind." I smiled. "So if Ruth was blackmailing January, you think it's because of her family money, not her work with the UEP?"

He put up a finger to stop me. "I didn't say that."

"It's possible, though, don't you think? If Ruth found out, maybe that first night that I met them on the snowshoe tour, that January was living a lie—advocating for environmental protections while flying around the world in her dad's private jet—it stands to reason that she could have used that information to blackmail January. But again, I'm stuck with Fitz. So what's the tie-in?"

"What if she was working with him?" Lance whispered as another group of snowboarders lugged their boards past us.

"January?" I mouthed.

"No, Ruth." Lance waved one hand like he was trying to get me to catch up.

"Ruth and Fitz working together," I said out loud. It felt like we were so close to piecing everything together. And yet something still didn't fit.

"Working against January," Lance suggested.

"Yeah, okay, that could be right. What if January tried to use her family's money to buy the lodge from being demolished and clear-cutting the forest? If Ruth and Fitz were partners, that could explain the cash. Maybe January was getting out enough cash for a down payment." Even as I said it, it sounded like a stretch.

"I can see from those fine frown lines around your eyes that you realize that math doesn't work."

"No, I'm guessing the ATM daily limit probably isn't anywhere near what January would have to put down on an offer like this, but it could have been a good-faith installment to show that she was serious. That makes more sense than blackmail."

"You obviously haven't read enough Shakespeare, darling."

I shook my head and chuckled. "Shakespeare aside, did you see them at the ATM before or after Fitz died?"

"It was that morning."

I inhaled, catching a hint of pine and woodsmoke. Mom and Janet must have lit a fire in the ballroom. I needed to plate the desserts, but I didn't want to end this conversation. It was like everything I had learned was about to unlock a vault in my head.

"Wait, I might have it." I froze, not wanting to lose momentum. "What if the three of them—January, Ruth, and Fitz—were working together, and something happened on the night of the snowshoe? Something that broke up their partnership. Maybe Ruth and January decided to partner together—just the two of them—and take Fitz completely out of the equation."

"You mean by *murdering* him." Lance emphasized the word *murder* a bit too loudly.

"Shhhh, we don't want anyone to hear us."

"Too late." Lance's eyes grew wide as he stared behind me. "Act normal. Don't turn around. Ruth is coming our way."

# Chapter Twenty-Nine

"Composure, composure, darling," Lance shushed.

"Did I hear my name?" Ruth asked as she approached us. She had her clipboard under one arm and a pencil tucked behind her ear. "Why are you standing here? It's freezing."

"We were just discussing this absolutely shocking turn of events with January and pondering whether you might have been in any danger," Lance lied, without the slightest hint of hesitation. "I'm so relieved to see you here."

If Ruth saw through his act, she didn't give any indication. "Thank you. I'm fine."

"Are you coming to the fundraiser?" I asked.

"I wasn't aware there was a fundraiser." She glanced at her clipboard as if she had missed something on her notes. "What are you raising money for?"

"The lodge." I pointed above us to the second-story stairwell where Mom and Janet had wrapped the banisters in garland adorned with glittery gold and silver stars. "We're trying to raise enough to allow Kendall to keep the lodge running through the end of the season."

"That's a lofty goal," Ruth scoffed.

"How so?" Lance asked with a casual air.

"The lodge is in debt for millions. It would take more than a quaint dinner to put a dent into the money Kendall would need to come up with." She removed her pencil from her ear and tapped it on her clipboard.

"I wasn't aware you were in the loop on the lodge's financial standing." Lance kicked me, and not very subtly, to indicate that I needed to be careful.

I flinched and tried to recover by following up with another question. "Did you say millions? I thought Kendall's issues were more about cash flow, having funds to cover salaries while waiting for the first ski season revenue to come through."

"No, you're mistaken." Ruth furrowed her brow. "I'm not sure where you got that information, but the lodge is long past saving. This isn't breaking news. It's well known."

"Is that why you're here?" I asked without thinking.

She took a step backward as if I had offended her. Then she underlined a note on her clipboard. "No, as I've already told you. I'm here to provide a detailed assessment of the lodge, ski park, and every asset associated with both."

"So the sale can go through?" Lance added.

"I didn't say that. That isn't at all what I said. You're putting words in my . . . Well . . ." She fumbled over what she was trying to say.

It was apparent that she was flustered. Why?

"Listen, I don't have time for this. I have a report to deliver that's not finished because there's been so much chaos around here. I need to be on my way."

"Your report is due on New Year's Day?" Lance asked.

She shook her body like she was trying to free herself

from the conversation. "I don't need to explain myself to you."

With that, she tucked her pencil behind her ear again and headed toward the second floor.

"Did she reveal that she knows much more about the lodge than she's been letting anyone believe?" I watched her race up the stairs and then turn toward Kendall's office.

"My sentiments exactly." Lance followed my gaze.

"How would she know the exact dollar amount?"

"And why would Kendall underplay her extensive debt if she needed our help?"

"Last question—why is Ruth here?"

"If you ask me, it's a mystery. Ooh, I rhythmed, didn't I?" Lance offered me his arm. "Shall we take a stroll and see what we can spy with our little eyes?"

"You want to follow her now?"

"What better time? We must seize the moment." He grabbed my wrist and dragged me toward the stairs.

"I do have work to do. Dinner starts in less than an hour."

"Exactly. We must close the case so we can partake in the festivities. Ruth was skittish at best. She's up to something nefarious. I can feel it. Now is our chance to catch her in the act. Don't dally."

Lance's lanky legs made short work of the stairs. We breezed past Mom, Janet, and Kendall, along with a handful of staff setting out plates and silverware on the main floor. The dining room looked as if setup was complete. Long tables had been draped with white tablecloths and decorated with dozens of tea lights, votive candles, and Janet's sweet pink rose bouquets.

Arlo was hanging a backdrop for Lance's performance at the far end of the room, and lodge staff members tended to the fire and set out additional chairs.

"Hi, you two," Mom said, lighting a votive candle. "It's taking shape, don't you think? Not bad for a one-night turnaround."

"It's perfect," I replied, slowing my pace.

"No time to stop. Quick errand. We'll be back in a flash." Lance gave a parade-style wave as we passed through the ballroom and yanked me toward the stairs.

The hallway leading to Kendall's office and the alcove was dark.

"Lance, I don't think this is such a good idea," I protested.

"Darling, we've come this far. There's no turning back now." He took the stairs two at a time.

"What if Ruth is involved?"

"That's what we're trying to determine, yes?"

"I know, but what if she realizes her mistake? We could be walking into danger." I froze at the top of the stairwell.

"Fair point." He paused. "Hold that thought. I have a brilliant idea. Stay here. Watch the hallway so she can't make an escape. I shall return momentarily."

He didn't give me a chance to argue.

The hallway was empty and silent except for the internal sound of my breathing, which was getting faster and shallower with each minute. Memories from the morning flooded my mind. I knew that the Professor and first responders had assured us that there was never a threat of a bomb, but I couldn't stop replaying seeing Kendall's office in shambles. If there had been a bomb, I would have been there when it went off.

My throat tightened.

Maybe this was a bad idea from an emotional perspective. Yes, I wanted to know who killed Fitz and put his murder behind me, but I wasn't sure I was prepared for another confrontation.

*There are people right below you, Jules.*

My rational brain tried to take over.

I could hear the activity echoing from the ballroom, plates and silverware clinking, music, and the chatter of everyone talking as they finished setting up for the fundraiser. But the pervasive silence on this side of the lodge made me wonder if I should follow Lance or abandon the entire idea and go slice cheesecakes in the kitchen.

What were we going to do if we confronted Ruth? We had no authority, nor did we have anything solid to go on other than her odd reaction and admission that she was well aware of the lodge's financial standing.

Before I had a chance to reconsider and leave the sleuthing to the professionals, Lance returned with something in his right hand. It was hard to make out what the object was in the dim lighting.

"Ready and armed." He held it out.

I squinted, hoping my eyes were playing tricks on me, because whatever Lance had in his hand looked suspiciously like a gun. "Uh, Lance, what is that?"

"A gun, darling." He flipped it in his fingers like he was in an old Western movie. "Obviously, a gun. If we're about to take down a killer, we need a weapon, don't we?"

"You have a gun?" I gasped.

He let out an exasperated sigh. "It's not a real gun. It's a prop for my performance later."

"What are we going to do with a prop gun?"

"Ruth doesn't know that it's a prop, which is all that matters." He held the gun like part of a SWAT team readying to go into battle. "This way."

Against my better judgment, I followed him.

We checked Kendall's office first. This time the door was locked.

That didn't mean that Ruth wasn't barricaded inside, but Lance whispered to keep going. "Let's check the alcove first; then we can circle back."

I nodded.

My hands went cold. It wasn't freezing in the lodge. If anything, I should be sweating. Instead, the heat from the massive fireplaces had settled on the third floor like a heavy fog.

"Are you freaked out?" I said with a hush.

"Every cell in my body is on high alert," he whispered. "It's a sign that we are about to close the case. I can feel it. Don't lose your resolve, Juliet. We are about to become heroes."

Heroes? That was a stretch.

"Who's there?" a woman's voice called from the edge of the alcove. "Don't come any closer, or I'll shoot."

"So will we, dearest, so will we." Lance pointed the fake gun at the far wall and flipped on his flashlight app on his phone with the other.

A spotlight haloed Ruth's head. Her back was pressed against the bookshelves as she used both hands to steady a shotgun.

# Chapter Thirty

This was bad.

Lance and Ruth were in a standoff, and one of them had a prop gun.

How long until Ruth realized that or until she decided to shoot regardless?

"It's over. Put your smoking gun down," Lance commanded in a tone he usually reserved for dealing with actors with inflated egos.

"I'm not going anywhere. You put your gun down, and this can end without anyone else getting hurt, but I promise you, I will not back down." Her nostrils flared as she spoke.

"Lance—" I started.

"I've got this, Juliet."

He didn't.

We were in way over our heads.

I considered my options. I could try to sneak away and get help or scream for help. The ballroom was directly beneath us. Someone would probably hear, especially if I pounded on the floor with my snow boots. But there was one looming problem—either of those choices could lead to Ruth pulling the trigger.

She reminded me of a deer in headlights with her wide eyes illuminated by Lance's phone.

Was she scared, unstable, or both?

"I'm serious; I will shoot." She lifted the barrel of the gun higher.

The best plan was probably to keep her talking. Mom, Janet, Kendall, everyone had seen us pass by them. Lance had said we would be right back. If we gave it enough time, surely someone would come looking for us.

Of course, that could put them in danger, too.

I went with my gut, asking her questions and trying to distract her from escalating the situation for as long as possible.

"No one wants that. There's no reason for more violence," I said to Ruth. "If you can tell us what happened, we can help. The Professor is my family. I'm sure we can work out a deal."

"My deal is already done. This property is mine, and I'm taking what is rightfully and legally meant to belong to me."

"What do you mean, rightfully and legally?" It was good that she was talking, but now I had to figure out my exit strategy without any guns being fired.

Ruth let out a hollow laugh. "She didn't tell you?"

"Who?" I scanned the bookshelves for anything that might serve as another form of protection or distraction. Hardcover books and collections of vintage ski posters probably weren't much of a match for Ruth's shotgun. It didn't look as if anyone had come to clean up the alcove.

Party hats and noise makers were still scattered on the couches and coffee table.

"Kendall."

Jazz hummed below us. Someone must have turned the volume up. If I could subtly start tapping my feet, would anyone downstairs notice over the sound of bass and trumpets?

"What would Kendall have told us?" Lance voiced what I was thinking.

"Like you don't know." Ruth repositioned the shotgun. It looked like an antique. Was she bluffing too?

Could the gun be a decoration from bygone eras on the mountain? The lodge had retro ski decorations—wooden skis, ice skates, sleds, and axes. What if she had found it mounted to a wall or stuffed in the back of a closet?

It wasn't worth the risk, but the way she was using her left hand to help prop up her right hand made me wonder if she even knew how to use the shotgun.

"We don't know," I said truthfully. "Honestly, Ruth."

"Like Kendall didn't tell you."

"Tell us what?" Lance didn't move a muscle as he spoke.

"About her attempt to cut me out of what was rightfully mine?" Ruth scoffed.

Lance remained rigid, frozen in position. It was likely due to his years of training and acting on the stage. I felt restless and more confused than ever.

"I don't understand. What's your connection to Kendall?" I tried to catch his eye. This was a moment when our years of friendship came into play. Surely we could communicate a plan with facial gestures, but he was locked in on Ruth and Ruth alone.

"My connection is that I am the rightful owner of this land and this property, and I'm taking what's mine." The biting tone of her words mirrored her jerky head movements and made me wonder if she was about to snap.

Was she delusional?

"I thought you were here in an official capacity to complete an assessment of the lodge?" I inched my toe forward. Maybe if I could make micromovements toward her, that would give Lance a chance to overtake her while she was distracted.

"No. That was a story I had to fabricate in order to get in. I needed access to the lodge to find proof of ownership. Fortunately, Kendall had no idea who I was—at least at first."

This was good. I had to keep her talking.

If Lance noticed my minute progress forward, he gave no indication.

"Now Kendall knows who you are?" I asked, while trying to figure out whether I could dive into the grouping of beanbags if Ruth realized that I was moving toward her and tried to shoot.

Ruth positioned the shotgun again. "She wishes she didn't. She should have made the right choice at the beginning. If she had, she wouldn't be in the predicament she's in now. But that's her problem. Not mine."

"Can you start at the beginning? I'm confused. If you had ownership of the lodge, how did Kendall not know that? And how do you have ownership? The Hankwitz family has owned and operated the lodge and ski park for as long as I can remember." I froze again as my boot almost came in contact with a party favor on the floor. The last thing I needed was to squash a noise maker and alert Ruth to the fact that I was trying to get closer to her.

"Because my family had the original deed," Ruth said, clearing her throat. "Kendall and the Hankwitz family have illegally possessed this property for nearly five decades. My grandfather hid it here on the property, and I had to find it before she destroyed the evidence. That's why she paid January to blow up her office, you know."

I gasped. "Kendall intentionally tried to sabotage her office?"

"Yes. The deed is hidden in there somewhere. She hired Hero and January to find it. I don't know how much she was paying them, probably not a lot, since she's broke. What I think they were really after was having free reign of the lodge. When they couldn't find the deed, she paid them to make it look like someone had broken in and gone through her things." Was I imagining things, or had Ruth's grasp on the shotgun relaxed slightly?

"Wait, so was there ever a real bomb?" I took another tiny step closer.

"I don't think so, but I don't know. That woman is nuts. Maybe she was going to blow the whole place up for the insurance money."

None of this was making any sense.

I was impressed that Lance was still maintaining his statuesque position.

"You believe that you have ownership of the lodge?"

"I don't believe it. I *know* it. Kendall's family illegally took possession of the property in the 1970s after my grandfather died. My family has been searching for the original deed ever since. I found my grandfather's journal last summer, and he stated clearly that he hid the deed for safekeeping here at the lodge. It's been a race between Kendall and me to see who can find it first. It has to be me. Otherwise, she'll destroy the only remaining evidence that I am the sole and rightful owner of the resort."

I was stunned by her revelation, but I still wasn't sure I believed her. And I had no idea how we were getting out of this. Music and happy laughter wafted from downstairs. Guests would be arriving for dinner soon. How long had we been talking?

Having a gun pointed at my face made my sense of time fuzzy.

Shouldn't Mom or Arlo have come looking for us by now?

"How is this connected with Fitz's murder?" I asked.

"Isn't it obvious?"

In a voice barely audible, Lance remained stoic but whispered, "She killed him."

"I don't know her motive, but I'm convinced she killed Fitz." Ruth took her left hand off the gun. "The only thing I can figure out is that he discovered the truth. I'm guessing he found the deed, and she killed him."

"Then why are you holding us at gunpoint, dearest?" Lance's voice was louder this time.

"Because you're holding one at me," Ruth retorted. "I wouldn't have needed to defend myself if I had known it was you two. I thought you were Kendall."

"Can we all put the guns down?" I suggested, holding my arms out in a sign that we were ready to call a truce.

Ruth lowered the shotgun. "I don't think this is real. I pulled it off the wall."

"Mine's a prop." Lance flipped the gun like he was playing with a toy.

"What a relief." Ruth placed the shotgun on the floor.

"So, is Kendall aware that you're searching for the deed?" I asked.

"Yeah. That's the problem. I have to find it now. If she finds it first . . ." She trailed off.

I felt a presence behind me and turned in slow motion to see Kendall standing in the door frame.

She took a second to register what was happening and then broke out in a sprint as Ruth yelled, "Stop her!"

# Chapter Thirty-One

Lance raced after Kendall. So did Ruth. I followed them to the ballroom, where Mom and Janet stood looking as confused and bewildered as I felt.

"It's Kendall," I said, pointing to the stairwell. "She's getting away."

"She won't get far," Mom said with a knowing smile.

"But she's the killer."

"Don't worry, honey. Doug is right there."

I looked down to see Kendall smack into the Professor's chest as she tried to flee the lodge. After that, the next few minutes were a blur. But Mom was right, there was no need to worry.

We watched it all unfold from a few feet away. The Professor halted Kendall's progress and deftly handcuffed her in a matter of seconds. Kendall didn't resist arrest. She hung her head and refused to look at anyone as two uniformed officers escorted her outside. The Professor called Ruth over to speak with him.

Lance leaned close and whispered, "Such a shame. That was too easy. I had high hopes for Hamlet versus Laertes.

Is it too much to ask for a Shakespearean battle to cap off this night? I was ready to step in with my firearm." He winked as he stuffed the prop gun inside his navy pea coat.

There wasn't anything else we could do about Kendall, so we kept busy with prep as guests began to queue outside the lodge. I headed to the kitchen to plate desserts. Mom came with me under the guise of helping, but I knew she was worried about me, and after this day, I wasn't about to turn down any moral support, especially from her.

"Put me to work, honey." She washed her hands and tied on an apron.

I removed the cheesecakes from the fridge. "Can you slice these into bite-sized pieces? The knives are behind the sink." I directed her to the magnetic strip attached to the wall. "Do you think the Professor will have the fundraiser go as planned? What will happen to the lodge now? Will Ruth take control?"

"Good questions." She ran a flat-edge blade knife under hot water. Warming a knife before cutting a cheesecake helps melt the mixture and create a clean slice. "Guests have paid for dinner and a show, so I don't anticipate him having any objections to proceeding with the meal. As for the paddle raising and asking for further donations, we'll wait and see if Doug can give us any guidance."

"I can't believe that Kendall's family doesn't own the lodge." I placed the second cheesecake on the narrow counter, which seriously lacked space. The kitchen was designed for quick meals, with a fry station for burgers and onion rings, and there was minimal workspace.

Mom wiped her knife to remove the extra cheesecake

mixture before dipping it in hot water again and cutting the next piece. "It's a lot to take in."

"Now Ruth's behavior makes much more sense. There was never an assessment. She's been trying to find the original deed and proof of ownership this entire time." I removed a tub of extra cherry compote and added spoonfuls to the top of the squares. "There are so many lingering questions, like why Hero and January agreed to ransack Kendall's office and where the deed is. If Fitz found it, I wonder if it will be recovered. Could that put the lodge in danger of closing? I mean, if there's a legal battle, that could shut down operations indefinitely."

Mom tucked a strand of hair behind her ear. "All valid concerns, but we won't know more until Doug completes his investigation."

"You're right." I inhaled slowly, firming my feet to the distressed wood floor. "I should concentrate on the fact that he has Kendall in custody."

"And that we have a dinner to host." Mom lifted a tray of cheesecake bites.

She was right.

We took baskets of bread to the dining room. Carlos, Andy, Bethany, and the rest of the team arrived. Everyone fell into a familiar pre-party routine. Sterling, Marty, and Carlos took over the kitchen to prep the appetizers.

The ballroom looked spectacular. White linen tablecloths and matching white plates were balanced with winter bouquets, sparklers, and bottles of Uva wines. Baskets of fresh-baked bread and herb-infused butter awaited guests. As amber flames popped and crackled in the fireplace, jazz played in the background.

"At least the ambiance is wonderful, and we know the

food will be good," I said to Mom as Carlos and Marty brought up the first round of appetizer platters.

I wasn't sure if the guests would be hungry by the time we served the main course. Carlos hadn't skimped on starters. There were crispy cauliflower cheese balls, mushroom tarts, cranberry Brie puffs, lemon feta dip, and tomato basil bruschetta.

Andy, Sterling, Steph, and Bethany had agreed to be runners. We would serve the appetizers family style, followed by a salad, soup, the main course, and then dessert.

"Jules, I just wanted to take a sec to say thanks." Bethany's bouncy curls caught the light from the iridescent balloons and streamers as she set a water pitcher on the table. She pressed her hands together in a prayer pose. "Andy has been wigging out about Shawn, Hero, and the future fate of the mountain, and I know that talking to you helped him chill."

"You're welcome, but honestly, I'm not sure I did much. I've been anxious and as concerned as him."

"What?" Bethany's entire face scrunched like a squirrel with its cheeks stuffed with nuts. "You're like our bakeshop mom. You always know the right thing to say."

"That's nice of you. I guess I learned from the best." I chuckled, thinking of my conversation minutes ago with Mom. I still might have more work to do on finding my inner balance, but at least I was absorbing some of her wisdom and passing it on to my young team. "How are things going with you two?"

"Good. I think." Red splotches bloomed on her neck and cheeks. "It's weird to go from being friends to maybe something more, but he's a super good guy, and his coffee, well, it's the bomb. Did you know that he made me my own personal roast? How romantic is that?"

"Your own personal coffee roast is worthy of a rom-com," I said with a grin.

"Exactly. As they say, 'love is in the air, and it smells like coffee.'" She batted her eyes. "I should get back to filling waters, but seriously, thanks again, Jules."

I was happy to hear that she and Andy were continuing to build a connection. Who knew where it would take them, but in my experience, love and coffee always aligned.

The Professor arrived in the ballroom as Sterling and Andy began plating salads at each place setting. He was followed closely behind by Lance and Ruth.

"Could you join me over by the fire for a moment?" he asked Mom and me as he brushed snow from his olive parka.

"Is everything settled?" Mom asked, reaching for his hand.

The Professor gave her a half nod. "Kendall is being escorted to the station by one of my officers. I'll need to duck out briefly but will try to return in time for the dessert course." He shook off his parka.

Lance made space for Ruth to stand next to the flames. He toasted his hands like marshmallows on a stick.

"Did she confess?" I asked.

Lance responded first. "No, but she didn't need to."

The Professor caught his eye and cleared his throat.

Lance bowed formally. "Apologies, please do tell."

"Thank you." The Professor's eyes twinkled as he acknowledged Lance. "We were already en route to bring her into custody. Hero and January confessed to their roles and had the receipts to prove it, quite literally. January had the foresight to document payments from Kendall, which were made from the lodge's business account. It appears that she was trying to funnel those funds to other climate action groups. We were also able to examine the contents of the so-called bomb and determine that there was no danger of an explosion. The materials she had amassed would have created a child's baking soda and vinegar volcano and nothing more."

"That's a relief." I exhaled deeply. "So, did Kendall kill Fitz?"

"A jury will have to decide on her innocence or guilt." The Professor toasted his hands, too. "The answer is clear in my book, and I believe the evidence will lead to a conviction. The coroner found the original deed to the resort and lodge hidden in Fitz's snow boot."

I gasped.

"It's just like I said," Ruth interjected. Her lips had a slight tinge of blue from being out in the cold for too long. "He must have been trying to blackmail her, so she killed him. I never trusted him. He was always hanging around in places he shouldn't have been. However, I do wonder about him. That night that January and I were stranded with him, I swear he was trying to get rid of us. That could have been because he knew January was working for a climate action group, and I just happened to tag along and end up in the wrong place at the wrong time. Still, he didn't deserve to die."

"But she must not have realized that he had the deed on him," I added.

"Exactly." The Professor nodded. "According to the

handful of employees left on staff and surveillance cameras, Kendall has been searching every nook and cranny in the lodge since his death. We suspect that he lied about the deed's whereabouts intentionally to blackmail her into moving forward with the sale of the lodge and ski park."

"Smart. Evil but smart," Lance said with appreciation.

"Except that it ultimately got him killed," Ruth replied.

"Touché." Lance twirled his wrist and stretched out his palm to Ruth. "Although I do have a question. Why was January handing you cash at the ATM?"

"You saw that?" Ruth shot him a puzzled look. "That was nothing. She owed me for gear rentals. I covered the cost of our rental equipment the night we went out with Fitz. She kept meaning to pay me back and since the ATM was right there, she grabbed cash while we were talking."

"What happens now?" I asked the Professor.

"Paperwork. Miles and miles of paperwork. No one claimed that the life of a detective is glamourous." The Professor smiled. "On that note, I must make my departure. Enjoy the dinner. And do save me a slice of your secret meatloaf, Helen."

"We'll save you an entire plate," Mom promised.

After he left, I turned to Ruth. "What do you want to do about the fundraiser?"

"If it's all right with you, I'd love to have it continue as planned. Doug believes that the deed will be enough to prove my case, but I'm looking at hefty legal bills, and it sounds like Kendall wasn't lying about the resort's finances. I understand if you want to cancel. I should never have threatened either of you. I panicked."

"Ah, water under the bridge. If it hadn't been for our

standoff, we never would have found the smoking gun, or should I say bun?" Lance replied with his cat-like grin.

Mom groaned.

I punched him before responding to Ruth. "Terrible puns aside, we would love to host the dinner as long as you can answer one looming question."

"Sure, anything."

"Are you going to bulldoze the lodge and harvest the west slope?"

"Never. I wasn't lying about taking notes and photos. I mean, I was trying to find the deed the entire time, but I was really also trying to get a feel for the structural integrity and what can be done to expand our services. I have big visions for Mount A, and none of those visions include bulldozing the lodge. I want to make it even better, and I would love your support in that."

"I believe this calls for a toast." Lance went to the table and poured us glasses of sparkling wine. He passed around drinks. "To a murderess behind bars and to the future of Mount A."

We clinked our glasses.

I took a sip and breathed in deeply. I wasn't sure I could toast to both of his sentiments. I felt sad for Kendall. Not that her actions were justified, but I'd known her for decades and I understood the deep attachment that came with owning a family business. Kendall clearly loved the lodge and Mount A. She had taken drastic measures to preserve her family's legacy, including trying to implicate nearly everyone else for the murder she had committed. I thought back to the day Fitz was killed, Kendall had immediately accused Shawn and later Hero when all along it had been her.

"Why the glum face?" Lance asked.

"Kendall. I wish it could have been someone else or that she could have found a different way to try and preserve her connection with the lodge."

Ruth's face softened. "I agree. If she had been up front with me, maybe there's a way we could have worked something out. It didn't need to come to murder."

"At least no one else is in danger and the lodge is in good hands," Lance acknowledged Ruth with another lift of his glass.

He was right about that. Fitz's killer had been caught, and the lodge would live to see another day. Now it was time to serve dinner and raise funds to save our beloved mountain.

# Chapter Thirty-Two

The rest of the evening went much more smoothly than it had started. Our rustic lodge dinner was a hit with the guests and with my team. Mom's meatloaf didn't disappoint. It was rich and savory, with a trio of herbs and a thick barbecue tomato sauce. Paired with our smashed garlic rosemary potatoes, salads, balsamic Brussels sprouts, and Marty's fresh bread, it was the ultimate feast to ring in the new year.

Lance and Arlo were seated next to us, along with Janet and the Torres family.

"Helen, you absolutely must reveal the secret to this sauce and tender meatloaf," Lance demanded, wielding his fork like a weapon. "It's absolutely divine, and I must confess I've never been able to stomach a greasy loaf of meat. This is nothing of the sort."

Mom's eyes glowed with mischief. "I'll tell you on one condition."

"Anything. Your wish is my command, and my lips will be forever sealed." Lance pretended to zip his lips and toss away the key.

Mom huddled everyone close. "Here's the secret."

"Wait, do we need a drumroll?" Carlos asked, and then proceeded to strum the table.

"I knew there was a reason, aside from your dashingly good looks, to adore you. Well done." Lance clapped twice.

Arlo trilled along with Carlos's drumming while Mom pressed both hands to her cheeks. "The secret is there is no meat in my meatloaf."

In a show of dramatics, Lance nearly fell off his chair. "Meatless meatloaf! Impossible."

"It is impossible," Mom agreed. "Impossible meat. No grease. Packed with flavor. And healthy."

"Consider me a meatloaf convert," Lance said, sitting back in his chair. "Your secret is safe with me."

They drifted off into a separate conversation about non-meat alternatives. Janet scooted her chair closer to me. "I wanted to follow up about Richard Lord. I was able to have a chat with him the other day after you stopped by the shop."

"I nearly forgot about that." I buttered a slice of bread and waited for her to continue.

"Getting information out of Richard is worse than dethorning roses." She motioned to the dainty bouquet in the center of the table. "It took some digging, but I did manage to learn that he's not suffering from heart issues."

"That's good news," I replied truthfully. As irritating as Richard was, I didn't wish him harm.

"This news will be out tomorrow, so I'm not breaking any confidence by sharing this with you." Janet smoothed her napkin. "Richard has been selected to be on a reality TV show."

"What?" I was glad I hadn't taken a bite of bread. "What show?"

"You're not going to believe this." Janet tapped her forehead and shook her head. "*Make a Millionaire Match*. It's a dating show for the wealthy."

I clasped my hand over my mouth. "That's really rich—pun intended—because there's no way Richard is a millionaire."

"He'd like us all to think that, wouldn't he?" Janet hunched over as she resisted the urge to laugh.

"But his health is fine?"

"Oh, yes, that's the other piece of gossip, this one I would appreciate if you don't repeat. Apparently, the producers of the show recommended that Richard get a touch-up done before filming begins. So he had Botox and lip filler. He said he's getting headshots next week, and then the producers will start seeing who he matches with.

"I won't say a word, but thank you for this nugget. I'll treasure it." I placed my hand over my heart. "Can you imagine the poor women he gets set up with?"

Janet scowled. "No, but then again, if you sign up for a show called *Make a Millionaire Match*, you probably have more in common with Richard than us."

"Good point." I chuckled. "Watch party when the first episode drops?"

Janet reached for her wineglass. "Please, I'll bring wine."

The conversation shifted as Lance and his small group of actors prepared for their one-act show.

Gathering familiar faces, friends, and family around the long dining tables was also the antidote we all needed.

Everyone turned their chairs to face the makeshift stage Arlo had erected at the far end of the ballroom.

In a fitting nod to himself, Lance had selected a scene from the second act of *Two Gentlemen of Verona* featuring none other than Proteus's servant Lance, who is forced to travel to Milan and manages to sneak his beloved dog, Crab, along on his adventure.

He stole the show with his performance, pulling audience members into the action by dancing between the tables with silly props and his quick-witted ability to riff on the spot. No one was safe. Lance managed to rope everyone in. The laughter was raucous, and the applause when he took his final bow was thunderous. Lance knew how to entertain and hold an audience captive, but the whoops and cheers and five-minute standing ovation when he finished were a testament to how important it was to put the last week in the past and focus on the year ahead.

Carlos offered Mom and me a toast and asked Ramiro, Sophia, Marta, and Luis to stand. "I would like to thank you, my Ashland family, for making my family so welcome. It has been a gift to have you here. Spain will be lucky to get you back, but know that you always have a place in the Rogue Valley. Salud."

"Salud." Everyone raised their glasses and clapped.

I couldn't believe they were leaving tomorrow. Their visit felt so fast, and yet as Carlos said in his toast, it had been so seamless to have them with us that it also felt like they had been in Ashland for years.

Before I knew it, Ramiro would be finishing his studies and returning home, too. I made a promise to myself to savor the time we had left with him. I glanced at the far end of the next table where Lance and Arlo had pushed their chairs together and were sharing a private toast. I wondered what was next for them.

I had the same question about my staff. Sterling and Steph's relationship continued to flourish, and Bethany and Andy appeared to be getting more serious, too. Soon I was going to need to start mapping out plans and schedules for the busy spring season and the reopening of Scoops. Carlos would be busy preparing the vines at Uva and expanding the tasting room outdoor space with large decks and more seating.

Mom and the Professor had discussed taking a road trip to visit national parks and having Thomas and Kerry take the lead at police headquarters.

Things were changing.

I could feel it in every cell of my body.

It wasn't a bad thing.

I used to resist change. Now I welcomed it.

I wasn't sure what this new year would bring. I suspected that there might be some surprises ahead. However, being in the warm and cheerful room surrounded by so many people I loved reassured me that I could handle whatever changes were to come.

Would Lance stay with OSF? Were Sterling and Steph going to venture out on their own? What about Mom? Would she finally retire for real and take the vacation she deserved? What was next for Torte? Was it time to settle in and be contented with the little empire we had built in Ashland, or was I still hungry for something new?

Questions and future visions swirled in my head.

The biggest question was about our family. I felt a rumble in my stomach and placed my hand on my belly to silence it. The quivering didn't stop.

Carlos caught my eye from the far edge of the table. The passion in his dark eyes sent another round of flutters through my abdomen.

Were we ready to expand our family?

How do you know when you're ready?

Or is it even possible to ever really be ready?

Is it more about taking the plunge, like we did on that fateful day in Marseilles many years ago?

Love was worth the risk.

Wasn't it?

I gulped down my anxiety as I returned his gaze.

He whispered, "I love you."

I mouthed it back and grinned.

How could I have ever imagined that we would end up here? It was like an ongoing dream—a dream I never wanted to be woken from.

Having a baby might change that.

It would change that.

But maybe what I was coming to understand was that my capacity to love had grown exponentially in the time I'd been in Ashland. This room was proof of that.

I didn't want to go back to making my circle small.

I wanted to embrace the goodness, even if that sometimes was shadowed by sadness, like Fitz's death. Life, death, the past, and the future were my ruminations for the first day of a dawning year. I had 365 days ahead to figure out what this new beginning would bring, and I was content to let that unfold, surrounded by my family and friends.

# Recipes

## Persimmon Bread

**Ingredients:**
½ cup (1 stick) unsalted butter
1 cup granulated sugar
2 large eggs
1 teaspoon ground cinnamon
½ teaspoon ground nutmeg
½ teaspoon ground cloves
1 teaspoon rum extract
2 tablespoons honey
1 cup persimmon pulp
½ cup buttermilk
2 cups flour
½ teaspoon salt
½ teaspoon baking soda
2-3 ripe persimmons, thinly sliced (for topping)

**Directions:**

Preheat your oven to 350°F (175°C). Start by scooping out the pulp from ripe persimmons and mashing it until you have a cup of persimmon pulp. Set it aside. In a large mixing bowl or electric mixer, cream together the butter and granulated sugar until the mixture is light and fluffy. Beat in the eggs one at a time. Mix in the ground cinnamon, nutmeg, cloves, rum extract, and honey to the batter. Gently fold in the persimmon pulp until evenly distributed.

In a separate bowl, whisk together the flour, salt, and baking soda. Gradually add the dry ingredients to the batter, alternating with buttermilk, beginning and ending with the dry ingredients. Mix until just combined. Do not overmix. Grease and flour a 9x5-inch loaf pan. Pour the batter into the prepared pan. Thinly slice the additional persimmons and arrange the slices on top of the batter in a decorative pattern. Bake the bread for 45-55 minutes or until a toothpick inserted into the center comes out clean. Allow the persimmon bread to cool in the pans for about 10 minutes, then transfer it to a wire rack to cool completely.

## Chai Spice Cookies

**Ingredients:**
**For the cookies:**
1 cup unsalted butter
½ cup white sugar
½ cup brown sugar
2 teaspoons ground cardamom
½ teaspoon ground cloves

1 teaspoon ground cinnamon
½ teaspoon ground nutmeg
½ teaspoon ground ginger
¼ teaspoon ground black pepper
2 large eggs
1 teaspoon vanilla extract
2½ cups flour
1 teaspoon baking soda
½ teaspoon salt
Additional cinnamon for dusting

**For the Eggnog Glaze:**
½ cup eggnog
2 cups powdered sugar
½ teaspoon vanilla extract

**Directions:**
Preheat your oven to 350°F (175°C) and line baking sheets with parchment paper. In a mixing bowl or electric mixer, cream together the butter and sugars until the mixture is smooth and creamy. Mix in the ground cardamom, cloves, cinnamon, nutmeg, ginger, and black pepper until well combined. Add the eggs and vanilla extract to the mixture, then add the flour, baking soda, and salt and mix until a thick batter forms. Scoop the dough into two-inch balls and place them on the prepared baking sheets. Dust the cookies with a pinch of ground cinnamon for extra flavor. Bake in the preheated oven for about 10–12 minutes or until the edges are lightly golden.

**Prepare the Glaze:**
In a separate bowl, combine the eggnog, powdered sugar, and vanilla extract. Whisk the mixture until it is smooth and almost translucent. Once the cookies are completely cooled, drizzle or spread the eggnog glaze over the top of each cookie. Allow the glaze to set for about 15–20 minutes until it becomes slightly firm.

## Chicken and Chickpea Buns

**Ingredients:**
**For the Filling:**
1 tablespoon vegetable oil
1 cup finely chopped onions
½ cup finely chopped carrots
½ cup finely chopped celery
1 large bunch chopped cilantro (stalks and leaves)
3 cloves of chopped garlic
1 pound ground chicken (or substitute canned chickpeas for a vegetarian option)
2 tablespoons tomato paste
1 teaspoon turmeric powder
1 teaspoon smoked paprika
1½ teaspoons chili powder
1 teaspoon ginger paste or finely grated ginger
1 teaspoon ground coriander
1 tablespoon balsamic vinegar
Salt and pepper
Prepared bread dough (you can use Torte's bun recipe or store-bought dough)

Black sesame seeds
1 egg, beaten (for egg wash)

**Directions:**
Preheat your oven to the temperature recommended for your dough (usually around 350-375°F or 180-190°C). Heat the vegetable oil in a large skillet or pan over medium heat. Add the chopped onions, carrots, celery, cilantro, and garlic. Sauté until they soften and the onions turn translucent, about 10 minutes. If using ground chicken, add it to the pan with the sautéed vegetables. Cook, breaking it apart with a spatula, until it's no longer pink and cooked through. If using chickpeas, add them to the pan and cook for a few minutes until heated through. Stir in the tomato paste, turmeric, smoked paprika, chili powder, ginger, ground coriander, balsamic vinegar, salt, and pepper. Cook for a few minutes to allow the flavors to meld together. Remove from heat and let the filling cool.

While the mixture is cooling, roll out your dough on a floured surface to about ¼-inch thickness. Cut the dough into circles using a round cutter or the mouth of a glass.

Place a spoonful (about 2-3 tablespoons) of the chicken and chickpea mixture in the center of each dough circle. Fold the dough over to create a half-moon shape and pinch the edges to seal the bun. Place the filled buns upside down on a parchment-lined baking tray. Brush the tops of the buns with the beaten egg for a shiny finish. Sprinkle each bun with black sesame seeds for added flavor and texture.

Bake the buns in the preheated oven for about 15-20 minutes or until they are golden brown and cooked through.

## Torte Buns

**Ingredients:**
1½ cups all-purpose flour
½ cup milk
¾ tablespoon active dry yeast
1 tablespoon sugar
Salt, to taste
3 tablespoons extra virgin olive oil
1 teaspoon black sesame seeds (for topping)
1 teaspoon sesame seeds (for topping)

**Directions:**
Preheat your oven to 375°F (190°C). Warm the milk slightly. It should be just warm to the touch, not hot. In a small bowl, combine the warm milk, sugar, and active dry yeast. Stir gently and let it sit for about 5-10 minutes until the yeast activates and becomes frothy. In a large mixing bowl, combine the all-purpose flour and a pinch of salt. Gradually pour the activated yeast mixture into the flour. Add 2 tablespoons of extra virgin olive oil. Mix the ingredients until a dough forms. Transfer the dough to a floured surface and knead it for about 8-10 minutes until it becomes smooth and elastic. You may need to add a little more flour if the dough is too sticky.

Place the dough in a greased bowl and cover it with a cloth. Let it rise in a warm place for about 45 minutes or until it has doubled in size. Once the dough has risen, punch it down to release the air. Divide the dough into equal portions to make the desired number of buns (recipes makes 4 large buns or 8 smaller ones). Shape each portion into a smooth, round ball and place them on a baking tray lined with parchment paper. Cover the buns with a clean kitchen towel and allow them to rise again for about 30 minutes, or until they puff up.

In a small bowl, mix the remaining 1 tablespoon of olive oil with the black and regular sesame seeds. Brush the tops of the buns with this mixture, ensuring they are well-coated. Bake for 15-20 minutes until they turn golden brown. Large buns may need to bake for 20-25 minutes.

## Cheesecake

**Ingredients:**
**For the Crust:**
1½ cups graham cracker crumbs
½ cup finely chopped pecans
¼ cup melted butter
2 tablespoons brown sugar
¼ teaspoon ground cinnamon

**For the Cheesecake Filling:**
2 8-ounce packages of cream cheese, softened
⅔ cup granulated sugar
2 large eggs
1 teaspoon vanilla extract

## Directions:

### For the Crust:

Preheat your oven to 325°F (160°C). In a food processor, pulse the graham crackers and pecans until they are finely ground. Transfer the graham cracker and pecan mixture to a large mixing bowl. Pour the melted butter over the crumbs and stir to combine. Add the brown sugar and ground cinnamon and mix until the mixture resembles coarse, wet sand. Grease mini springform pans (or a regular-sized if preferred). Divide the crust mixture evenly among the pans. Use the back of a spoon or the bottom of a glass to press the mixture firmly into the bottoms of the pans to create an even crust layer. Place the crust-filled pans in the preheated oven and bake for about 10 minutes. Remove from the oven and allow them to cool while you prepare the cheesecake filling.

### For the Cheesecake Filling:

In a large mixing bowl, beat the softened cream cheese until it is smooth and creamy. Gradually add the granulated sugar and continue to beat until well combined. Add the eggs, one at a time, mixing well after each addition. Stir in the vanilla extract. Scoop the cream cheese filling into the par-baked crusts, dividing it evenly among the pans. Create a water bath (bain-marie) by placing the mini cheesecake pans in a larger roasting pan. Carefully pour the boiling water into the larger roasting pan to create a water bath around the mini cheesecakes. Be sure not to get water into the cheesecakes. Cover the top of the roasting pan with aluminum foil. Bake the mini cheesecakes for about 25-30 minutes, or until the edges are set but the centers still have a slight jiggle. Remove the cheesecakes from the water bath and let them cool to room temperature. Once cool, refrigerate the cheesecakes for at least 4 hours or overnight to set. Before serving, you can top the mini cheesecakes like Jules with cherry compote, chocolate chips and hazelnuts, a caramel drizzle, or whatever you prefer.

## Mom's Meatloaf

**Ingredients:**
**For the Meatloaf:**
1 pound (16 ounces) Impossible meat (plant-based meat substitute)
½ cup breadcrumbs (plain or seasoned)
½ cup finely chopped onion
2 cloves garlic, minced
1¼ cup chopped fresh parsley
1 teaspoon dried thyme
1 teaspoon dried oregano
1 teaspoon dried basil
Salt and black pepper to taste
¼ cup milk (plant-based or dairy)
¼ cup barbecue sauce (plus extra for topping)

**For the Sauce:**
½ cup barbecue sauce
¼ cup ketchup
2 tablespoons brown sugar
1 tablespoon Worcestershire sauce
Salt and black pepper to taste

**Directions:**
Preheat your oven to 350°F (175°C). In a large mixing bowl, combine the Impossible meat, breadcrumbs, chopped onion, minced garlic, fresh parsley, dried thyme, dried oregano, dried basil, salt, and black pepper. Pour in the milk and ¼ cup of barbecue sauce into the mixture. These ingredients help bind the meatloaf together and add moisture and flavor. Use your hands or a wooden spoon to thoroughly mix all the ingredients until well combined. Make sure not to overmix, as this can make the meatloaf tough. Shape the meat mixture into a loaf shape and place it in a greased or parchment-lined baking dish.

In a small bowl, mix together ½ cup barbecue sauce, ketchup, brown sugar, Worcestershire sauce, salt, and black pepper. Spread a generous amount of the sauce over the top of the meatloaf, reserving some for serving. Place the meatloaf in the preheated oven and bake for approximately 45-55 minutes. Remove the meatloaf from the oven and let it rest for a few minutes before slicing. Serve the slices with extra sauce on the side.

## Winter Warmer Latte

Andy's winter warmer is the perfect après ski drink, whether you spent a day braving the slopes or curled up in front of the fireplace.

**Ingredients:**
2 shots of spiced winter roast coffee (or any dark roast coffee of your choice)

½ cup milk (oat milk, almond milk, or your preferred milk)
2 tablespoons white chocolate chips
1 tablespoon orange syrup
1 tablespoon raspberry syrup
1 tablespoon cranberry syrup
1 large marshmallow

In a small saucepan, combine the orange syrup, raspberry syrup, and cranberry syrup. Heat over low heat, stirring, until the syrups are well-mixed and warmed through. Set aside. In another saucepan, heat the milk over medium heat until it's hot but not boiling. Add the white chocolate chips to the hot milk and whisk until the chocolate is fully melted and the mixture is smooth. In a latte glass or mug, pour in the brewed espresso shots. Then add the prepared orange, raspberry, and cranberry syrups and stir gently. Add the warmed milk and white chocolate mixture to the coffee and stir to combine. Serve hot with a large marshmallow.

**READ ON FOR AN EXCERPT FROM**
*STICKS AND SCONES*—
**THE NEXT BAKESHOP MYSTERY,**
**COMING SOON FROM ELLIE ALEXANDER**
**AND ST. MARTIN'S PAPERBACKS!**

They say that you have to let go of the past to step into your future. My future was now. Here, in my hometown of Ashland, Oregon, where organic pear orchards were bursting with fragrant white blossoms, gangly wild turkeys and spotted baby deer stumbled on wobbly new legs in Lithia Park, and the Oregon Shakespeare Festival was back in the swing of entertaining audiences with dozens of performances each week. Our remote location, nestled in the Siskiyou Mountains, blocked any light pollution, which meant that outdoor evening productions at the Elizabethan Theater made it feel like you were being blanketed by thousands of dazzling stars—both real and celestial. One of the things that made living in Ashland unique was bumping into actors while shopping at the co-op or sipping an iced latte at my family bakeshop, Torte.

Of course, I was biased, but spring in the Rogue Valley had a special touch of magic.

This morning, I was doing my best to make some magic in Torte's kitchen in the form of rising loaves of cinnamon raisin bread and chocolate hazelnut muffins. Soon there would be a palpable buzz of energy in the basement in our open-concept kitchen once the rest of the team arrived. For the moment, I was glad for a reprieve because I was doing everything I could to stay upright. Lately, I'd been plagued with dizzy spells. It reminded me of being back on the *Amour of the Seas*, the boutique cruise ship where I'd spent the early part of my culinary career. My years at sea taught me resiliency and how to stay upright in the middle of a storm. The resiliency was a gift I carried with me, but struggling to find my land legs after being permanently cemented to Ashland was an unexpected challenge.

"Are you okay, boss?" Andy, our head barista, asked with a look of concern as I grabbed the counter to steady myself.

I hadn't heard him come in, and I didn't want to worry him or any of my other staff. "Fine," I lied, plastering on a smile and securing a death grip on the countertop. "Too much coffee, that's all."

Andy shrugged off his thin jacket and gasped. His huge youthful eyes widened with disbelief. "Honestly, I didn't think I would ever hear Jules Capshaw utter those words. Too much coffee? I would have sworn that you were immune to the effects of caffeine." He joined me at the island, setting down a canister of coffee beans. "I guess it's good to see that you're human."

"It's probably because I haven't eaten breakfast." I motioned to the trays of rising bread and the muffin tins. That was true. I had gotten an early start at Torte, my family's artisan bakeshop. There was something innately calming about the whir of the mixer whipping creamy butter and the aroma of applewood burning in the pizza oven. Mornings were my favorite time in the kitchen before the team arrived when I could linger over a strong cup (or five) of coffee and map out a plan for the day. As Torte continued to expand our offerings, carving out a few moments to set the tone and make sure schedules, orders, and deliveries were in alignment had become critical. In addition to keeping our main pastry cases stocked, we were preparing to reopen Scoops, our summer pop-up ice cream shop for the season and Uva, our winery, was in high demand for wine-tasting parties, weddings, and now a new endeavor—live theater.

My best friend, Lance, the artistic director at the Oregon Shakespeare Festival, had his own project blooming—his Fair Verona Players. Never one to pass up an opportunity to entertain, Lance was launching his own spin-off production company. The Fair Verona Players would be staging their first performance in Uva's vineyard in a few short days. Lance had served as Artistic Director for the Oregon Shakespeare Festival (or OSF if you were a local) for nearly a decade. His innovation and creativity when it came to staging a mix of gender-bending modern productions with Shakespearean classics had made OSF one of the most esteemed repertoire theaters in the county. Lately though he had confessed that he needed a new challenge— something smaller, more personal that would allow him the freedom to leave his inedible mark on a new generation of actors and patrons. In Lance's words, the concept of hosting intimate productions amongst the vines where patrons and actors could engage and interact in a gorgeous, lush outdoor setting provided a space for raw expression.

"There's nothing that can compare with the vulnerability of putting on a stripped-down show," he explained to me when he first pitched the idea of partnering. "This isn't going to be Shakespeare with sequins and glittery lighting, no, no, darling. We're taking plays with a small yet mighty cast, bringing the audience on a journey with us that will leave them forever changed. In the process I'm going to change too. Creativity does not thrive if we stay stagnant."

Lance had an unmatched gift for embellishing, but I didn't put up a fight. I loved the concept. Watching a show on a warm spring evening amongst the vines while sipping on an earthy glass of our Malbec sounded like a dream, and I could appreciate his need to stretch himself. I felt the same way about Torte. It was one of the reasons I had been so intent on expanding our offerings and partnerships at the bakeshop.

The question was, Had I been too ambitious? I tended to take a lot on—it was a blessing and a curse. Until recently, I thought I was managing our varied projects well, but now I was starting to second-guess myself.

"Jules, are you sure you're good?" Andy asked, waving a hand in front of my face to get my attention. His face was tanned from spring skiing on Mount A. There was a touch of auburn stubble on his chin and cheeks. When I had first returned home, Andy was a college student at Southern Oregon University. He had opted to drop out in favor of pursuing his passion—coffee roasting. Mom and I had agreed to support him and do whatever we could to help him grow his roasting operation.

He never called me Jules. Usually Andy was all about the coffee banter, but he stared at me with such an intense gaze that I wondered if I looked worse than I felt.

"No, I promise, I'm fine." I lifted one hand off the counter as proof and pointed to the empty coffee carafe. "I polished off the entire pot before you got here. I just need to eat something." I couldn't tell if I was trying to convince him or me.

"Okay," he hesitated and scrunched his wide forehead like he was trying to assess whether I was in danger of passing out. "I guess you probably don't want to sample my latest roast?"

"Of course I do." I peeled my other hand free and kept my eyes focused on the built-in brick oven at the far end of the kitchen. As long as I didn't look down or to the side, I should be all right. That could be problematic with the day of baking we had ahead of us, but I didn't want to freak him out. "My egg bake and chocolate muffins will be done soon. I'll fuel myself and be ready to savor your next masterpiece."

"I'll fire up the espresso machine and be back soon." Andy took off for upstairs.

As soon as he was out of sight, I inched along the wall to steady myself. The dizziness came in waves with no predictable pattern. It had been happening on and off for a few weeks. Eating sometimes helped but if it continued like this, I was going to have to make a doctor's appointment.

My egg bread bowls were ready, so I carefully removed them and rested them on cooling racks. They bubbled with steam and smelled heavenly. The bake was simple. I had halved and hollowed-out crusty leftover buns. Then I cracked eggs in each half and topped them off with a splash of heavy cream, fresh herbs, and salt and pepper. The eggs would bake in the bread, creating a soft creamy center and a perfect vessel for breakfast on the go.

While I waited for the egg bread to cool, I turned my attention to the next item on my to-do list—opening night party pastries. Lance had requested spring pastries and small bites for the first show. We had landed on lemon curd cupcakes, mini coconut cream pies, grapefruit tartlets, and chocolate dipped almond Tuiles for sweet options. Additionally, we would serve crostini with arugula pesto, naan and falafels with roasted red pepper hummus, feta and chicken skewered meatballs, and edible Parmesan cups filled with spring vegetables.

I wanted to start on the cupcakes before the kitchen was buzzing with activity, so I took a few timid steps toward the pantry and walk-in fridge to gather ingredients. To begin, I creamed butter and sugar together, then I added vanilla, lemon rind, and fresh lemon juice. Once those were incorporated, I shifted in flour, baking soda, and salt, and alternated adding in buttermilk until a smooth batter had formed. I filled silicone cupcake trays with an ice cream scoop to ensure that each cupcake would be consistent, and then I slid them into the oven to bake.

The egg bowls had cooled enough, so I pulled up a stool and took a seat. The dizziness seemed to be subsiding, and eating could only help. One of our mantras in the bakeshop was "we eat with our eyes first," and my eyes were more than pleased to cut into the flaky layered egg dish. It had a touch of an herbaceous aroma from the fresh sprinkling of parsley and thyme and a perfectly cooked soft-boiled egg that oozed as I stabbed it with my fork.

"Good morning, honey." Mom breezed in through the back stairwell. She tugged off a lightweight jacket and hung it on the coat rack before coming into the kitchen. Fine lines were etched on either side of her walnut eyes, a sign of her years of wisdom.

"You're here early," I said, with a smile, digging my

fork into the eggy mixture. "I'm taking a breakfast break; want to join me?"

"These smell as good as they look." She leaned over the tray to examine the egg bowls. "I already ate, but I'm tempted to be a hobbit and have a second breakfast. Now, if there's coffee, I wouldn't turn down a second cup."

"There was, but I drank it all," I admitted. "That's why I'm eating. I got really dizzy for a couple of minutes. I think I might have to cut back on my caffeine intake."

"This is the third time in a week that you've been dizzy." Mom's eager eyes narrowed. She glanced upstairs, then lowered her voice, her entire face lighting up with excitement. "Could there be another reason you might be dizzy? You know, when I was pregnant with you, that was my first clue."

I shook my head and took another bite of the gooey egg, using the runny yolk to soak up the buttery pastry. "No, it's not that. I did a test." I had taken twelve tests, but I didn't want to share that with her or anyone else yet. When Carlos and I decided to start trying for a baby I figured I would be pregnant quickly, but thus far that hadn't been the case.

The briefest flash of disappointment crossed her face. She patted my shoulder and tied on a fire-engine red Torte apron with a silhouette of a single layer torte embroidered in teal blue. When my parents had first opened the bakeshop, they decided to pay homage to the Bard by decorating the space in royal colors and adding touches of Shakespeare like the rotating quote on the chalkboard menu upstairs. "Don't worry; it will happen."

I nodded but didn't say more. I wished that my dizzy spells were connected to happy news. But they weren't.

I wasn't prone to worry, and I didn't want to upset Mom, but I couldn't shake the feeling that there might be something wrong.

Steph and Sterling arrived together, followed closely by Marty and Bethany, which saved me from having to go any deeper into the subject.

Sterling, our sous chef, had an uncanny ability to read people, especially me. I think it stemmed from our shared grief. We had both lost parents young, leaving an indelible mark on our tender souls. His steel blue eyes caught mine ever so briefly as he passed me on his way to the sink to wash his hands.

No words were exchanged, just a subtle nod of acknowledgment that told me he must have heard the tail end of my conversation with Mom.

I swallowed back my emotions and gave him a grateful smile.

Bethany removed the specialty order forms from the whiteboard as everyone gathered around the island. She tied up her bouncy curls and reviewed the list of specialty cakes for the day. Her pink T-shirt had an illustration of chocolate chip cookie dough and read: SERIOUSLY, DOUGH.

"Nice one." Andy came downstairs, balancing a tray of sample coffees, and nodded in approval at Bethany's punny shirt.

Rosa and Sequoia, the final two members of our team, joined us for our morning meeting. Rosa managed the dining room and Sequoia was a barista, although she had recently started classes at massage school, so I wasn't sure how long we'd be lucky enough to have her on staff.

I liked to gather everyone to run through the rotation, schedules, and sample our daily specials. Steph helped me cut slices of the egg bake, muffins, and raisin bread.

"Okay, everyone, I want your honest input as always," Andy said, passing out the samples. "I paired my latest espresso roast with house-made vanilla syrup, cherry blossom water, brown sugar, and oat milk."

"It smells like I'm walking through Tokyo in the spring," Marty noted, rolling up the sleeves of his button-down shirt. Marty was in his sixties with white hair and a jovial, warm face that reminded me (and all of the kids who traipsed into the bakeshop) of Santa Claus. "This transports me back to a trip my wife and I took many years ago to experience the cherry blossoms." He paused for a moment to breathe in Andy's creation before taking a long, slow sip. A nostalgic smile spread across his face. "Yes, this is why we do what we do. There's nothing that can capture a memory like food."

Andy's cheeks tinged pink with pride. "Thanks, man. I'm glad to hear that."

Steph sipped her coffee in contemplation. She reached for a sketch pad and began drawing the outline of a cherry tree. "This gives me inspiration. What if we do cherry blossom cakes with light cherry buttercream and fresh preserves? We can pipe something like this." She held her sketch out for everyone to see.

"I love it." Bethany bobbed her fluffy curls in agreement. "I'm starting on our delivery boxes this week, and I think mini cakes and chocolate cherry brownies would be such a great pairing. Maybe we even do a cherry theme. We could hand paint sugar cookies with cherry blossoms and make cherry bark."

"What about a cherry and arugula pizza with goat cheese?" Sterling asked, looking to Marty for his input.

"Count me in. We could do a cherry bacon jam, too," Marty replied.

Mom raised her coffee in a toast to Andy. "Look at this wonderful collaboration, all from your drink."

Andy shrugged, trying to downplay her praise. "Aww, Mrs. The Professor, stop."

She winked and took another sip of his latte, keeping her proud gaze on him.

The creamy latte with a touch of sweetness from the cherry blossom water and brown sugar was the perfect antidote for my nausea. It settled my stomach as we went through the plan for the day. Rosa would swap out Torte's window display to mirror our cherry-baking theme and advertise our partnership with The Fair Verona Players. Sequoia and Andy would manage the espresso bar, while Sterling and Marty focused on savory items and lunch specials. Mom, Bethany, Steph, and I would oversee stocking Torte's pastry case with cakes, cookies, croissants, and crumpets.

Everyone disseminated to their workstations. I turned my attention to the lemon curd for my cupcakes. I squeezed fresh lemons from the farmer's market into a saucepan and added butter and cornstarch. I whisked the mixture over low heat until it began to thicken. I made a mental note to swing by the theater later and check in with Lance. I had a feeling that he might want to add some additional items to the menu for opening weekend. The cherry blossom cakes and chocolate cherry brownies seemed like a perfect fit, but I didn't want to alter his menu without touching base. Plus, I never turned down an excuse to walk to the "bricks" as we affectionally called the OSF campus, to see Lance.

The morning breezed by in an aromatic symphony of baking bread, simmering soups, and the waft of coffee coming from overhead. By the time we opened the doors to our first customers, the kitchen was a sea of activity, and the pastry case was a feast for the eyes. It never got old to see Torte humming with happy customers. A group of preschoolers camped out near the chalkboard doodling on the bottom half, which we reserved exclusively for our youngest guests. The corrugated metal wainscotting, red and teal accents, and dainty bouquets of yellow tulips made me forget about my dizziness.

This week's quote read: "April hath put a spirit of youth in everything." Shakespeare's words felt fitting for the vibe.

A little before noon, I went upstairs to restock cherry hand pies and discovered Lance in line for coffee. He stood out in his tapered jeans, tailored checkered shirt, and skinny tie.

"Darling, there you are. I was going to come to find you, but it's already been a morning, so coffee is my first priority." Lance greeted me with a kiss on both cheeks before pulling away with his eyebrows arched in concern. "Oh, dear. You're looking a bit peckish today. Are you feeling all right?"

"Fine." I motioned to the counter where Andy had set Lance's flat white. "Too much coffee. Not enough sleep."

"Story of my life." Lance reached for his drink and then pointed to a window booth. "Can you chat for a minute?"

"Yes, in fact, I was going to come see you later."

"How fortuitous." He waggled his brows and waited for me, making a grand sweeping gesture in front of him. "Beauty before beauty."

I rolled my eyes and headed for a booth. Rosa was stringing cherry blossom branches from A Rose by Any Other Name next door from the window frame. She had already sprinkled petals across the base of the display, making it look like the window was coated in pale pink snow. I couldn't wait to see the finished product. Thanks to Rosa and Steph's creativity, our window displays had become a talking point for tourists and locals alike.

Lance slid into the booth across from me. His angular cheekbones and dark hair caught the light, casting a halo over him. He wore his dark hair shorter than normal and had shaved off any trace of facial hair.

"You look like you're backlit for the stage," I said.

He posed with one hand on the side of his cheek. "The light knows where to find me, darling. Always."

I grinned.

"Speaking of the stage. How are things coming along with the menu for opening?" He dipped his pinkie into the foam on his flat white.

"Great. That's one of the reasons I wanted to talk to you, though. We're doing a cherry theme here, as you can see." I motioned to Rosa. "And I wondered if you want us to add a few cherry options to the mix?"

"If it's anything like that, then yes." Lance pointed to one of Steph's tiered cherry blossom cakes on display at the pastry counter.

"Exactly. Although smaller versions for the dessert bar."

"Brilliant. Love it. Love it all." He strummed his fingers together. Then he leaned closer. "Let me tell you what I don't love."

"What?"

"The flack I'm getting for staging *Taming of the Shrew.*"

*Taming of the Shrew* was the inaugural production for the Fair Verona Players. "To be honest, I'm kind of surprised, too. Isn't that play a little outdated?"

"Aren't the gender roles a bit, shall we say, problematic?" Lance nodded emphatically. "Yes, obviously, but let me tell you, we've put our own little spin on it. This is not your grandmother's Shakespeare, okay? This is Will Shakes, Ashland style. We've got Katherine as a fierce and independent woman who doesn't take any nonsense from Petruchio and Petruchio as a hapless buffoon who is constantly tripping over his own words. It's a diverse cast, and it's going to be outrageously fun. We need something whimsical and over the top to draw in a new audience. I'm confident that this production and the talent I've pulled together for the Fair Verona Players is going to leave the audience speechless, gasping for breath and begging for more."

"I love your humility," I teased.

"When you're sitting with greatness," Lance sighed dramatically, "what can you do?"

I shook my head. "You're too much, even for you."

His eyes twinkled, but then he cleared his throat and lowered his voice, his tone turning serious. "Here's the thing. I'm a bit concerned that nefarious things are afoot. I have the sense that someone is trying to sabotage my Fair Verona Players before we break legs. Things have gone missing—costumes, props. Two days ago, we had a little incident where the set collapsed during a fight scene.

Thankfully, no one was injured. And then, mysteriously, a prop gun misfired during a scene. I have no idea how the prop gun even made it onto set. Then yesterday, one of our actors took a tumble during a particularly acrobatic dance sequence. We've added a few extra crash mats to the stage, just in case. I'm beginning to wonder if we're cursed. I mean, it's not uncommon for theater gremlins to be up to their antics before opening, but I have a bad feeling about this."

Lance, like most theater directors, was quite superstitious, but I could tell from his fidgety body language and the way that he ran his finger along the rim of his coffee mug that he was worried.

"Who would want to sabotage the show?" I asked.

"That's the question, isn't it?" He blew out a long breath and clutched his coffee. "The problem is that my suspect list is growing, and we open in two days. If these supposed accidents continue to happen on set, I'm concerned that one of my fair actors could end up in serious danger, or worse . . ." he trailed off.

Was Lance merely caught up in theatrics—or was his latest venture teetering on the edge of disaster?